GENUINE GOLD

What Reviewers Say About Ann Aptaker's Work

Criminal Gold

"A brilliant crime novel set in New York City in 1949 featuring Cantor Gold, dapper dyke-about-town, smuggler of fine art and saviour of damsels in distress."—*Curve Magazine*

"An author can make a time and place come alive and this was certainly true of Ann Aptaker's book *Criminal Gold.* We're plunged into the heart of 1940s criminal New York with a thrilling tale of murder and deception. ...Aptaker has set herself up for a cracking series not only because of the character of Cantor Gold but for choosing a period of time that is fascinating to read about."—*Crimepieces.com*

"Cantor Gold is a woman ahead of her time. [She] insists on living openly; she is a free woman because she has taken her freedom and this is much unlike those of us who had to fight to live openly as we do. ...This is author Aptaker's first novel and if this is an indication of what she can do, we need to welcome her to the canon of gay literature."—*Reviews by Amos Lassen*

Tarnished Gold

"Ann Aptaker delivers again in a great noir set in the world of 1950s art smuggling. ...Be prepared for another noir where Cantor navigates through society, both high and low. This is another point in favor of the Cantor series: It shows the entire gamut of society—the rich collector as well as the nighttime smuggler—all of who might be involved in the smuggling of art."—*Curve Magazine*

"This is the magnificent follow-up novel to *Criminal Gold*, and it is delightfully even more engaging than the opening book. Once again, Cantor Gold is astounding as the primary lead within this splendid story. ...Cantor Gold is an inimitable and larger than life tour de force. This is a triumphant second book in a series that is likely to be nonpareil! Provocatively formidable!"—*Rainbow Book Reviews*

Visit us at www.boldstrokesbooks.com

By the Author

Criminal Gold

Tarnished Gold

Genuine Gold

GENUINE GOLD

by

Ann Aptaker

2017

GENUINE GOLD
© 2017 BY ANN APTAKER. ALL RIGHTS RESERVED.

ISBN 13: 978-1-62639-730-9

THIS TRADE PAPERBACK ORIGINAL IS PUBLISHED BY
BOLD STROKES BOOKS, INC.
P.O. BOX 249
VALLEY FALLS, NY 12185

FIRST EDITION: JANUARY 2017

___

CREDITS
EDITOR: RUTH STERNGLANTZ
PRODUCTION DESIGN: SUSAN RAMUNDO
COVER DESIGN BY PHILOMENA MARANO (WWW.PHILOMENAMARANO.COM)

Acknowledgments

This book would not have been possible without the willingness of Coney Island's veterans and boosters to share their memories, the generosity of others willing to share their expertise, and friends and family who made sure I could keep going.

Stanley Fox, for sharing his memories of growing up in his family's amusements and arcades in the 1950s.

Dick Zigun, "Mayor of Coney Island," Founder of Coney Island USA and the Coney Island Circus Sideshow, for his stories of—and introductions to—Coney's notable characters.

Richard Eagan, for sharing his memories of life as a Coney Island performer and games operator.

Amanda Deutch, Coney Island poet and member of the Coney Island History Project.

Alfie Cruz, for sharing his Coney Island fortune telling lore.

Clare Toohey and Lisa Shiroff for sharing their Tarot card expertise.

Paulo Tonn, for his technical graphics expertise.

And…Stan Coplan, Jan Schleiger, Karen Lauria Saillant, Jacquie Hawley, Allan Neuwirth, and my wonderful sister Yren Berry, for their love and support.

Dedication

This book is dedicated to everyone who carries
the magic of Coney Island in their soul.

CHAPTER ONE

Early January 1952
Piraeus, Port of Athens, Greece
Two a.m. ...or so

Someday, the people of Greece will demand their treasures back, treasures ripped from their ancient ground or pulled from their ruined temples by centuries of invaders and thieves. The invaders, at least, have been honest in their larceny, taking what they want as a right of conquest. The thieves are another story. A lot of them still kid themselves into believing that as archeologists they're rescuing Greek antiquity by shipping it off, piece by uprooted piece, to museums or collectors in London, Paris, or New York. And sometimes even the thieves get robbed: maybe a statue, a carved panel, or an urn is destined for one museum or collector but another museum or collector wants it, and suddenly, under cover of night—*whoosh!*—the treasure's journey changes course.

Someday, the Greeks of Athens and Delphi, Corinth and Thessaloniki, and all the islands in Homer's wine-dark sea will demand the return of their patrimony from the famous museums and private collectors who hire me to smuggle these treasures into their laps.

But not today. Today a small piece of Greek antiquity is thickly wrapped in a canvas satchel slung over my shoulder while I sit and drink, and kiss a pretty woman at a corner table in a shadowy taverna in Piraeus. The taverna is a suitable stop on this little treasure's illicit journey; the clientele here practice my kind of love, women with women, and the twenty-four-hundred-year-old treasure in my satchel, a small Classical period clay jar called a pyxis that I lifted from an archeological dig at the ancient town of Eleusis—dressed as a digger and with the cooperation of an American graduate student who needed cash—mimics that passion with steamy scenes of naked women dancing. It's a rare intact piece of pottery by an unknown artist who seemed to specialize in such scenes, and who archeologists and art historians call the Dancing Goddess Painter.

This taverna, like all the dives in Athens that cater to a preference for women, even the classier joints, is hidden in a dark street to keep it safe from mischief by local thugs or raids by police. The ancient Greeks and their pantheon of gods and goddesses might've winked at Sapphic love from time to time—Greek men of antiquity certainly did more than wink at other men—but the old crowd of frisky deities has been replaced by a stern church, frowning above its beard. The patrons of modern Athens's fancier woman-love places have a little easier time of it, their well-connected families paying bribes to protect the clans' reputations. I've been to some of those places on previous adventures in Greece, had a swell time of it, too. Perfumed skin has its pleasures. But I'm shipping out of Athens tonight and need to stay dockside in Piraeus, ready to move at a moment's notice.

Meantime, the taverna, with its whispering crowd of savvy sweeties who recognize an American butch ripe for the picking, provides a satisfying end to a dangerous week of slipping my Dancing Goddess pot past cops and the Greek underworld. Both gangs would want to sell or smuggle it themselves.

I've been lounging here nearly two hours, enjoying shots of pine-tasting ouzo and the hospitality of a dark-haired, dark-eyed, well-endowed local beauty whose name I don't know but who gives off an intoxicating scent of ouzo and saltwater. She speaks no English and I speak just enough Greek to buy liquor and cigarettes and whatever else I need to buy around town, including the time and talents of this local beauty. My shots of ouzo are a restorative from the hour I spent partaking of the lady's talents in a dingy room upstairs. The tender way she fondled my Smith & Wesson .38 revolver in my shoulder rig before she hung the rig on the chair where I put my satchel, the careful way she folded my khaki pants and rough sweater and placed them over the chair, and the sweetly sexy way she ran her fingers through my short but untamable tangle of hair—like a brown broom, some have said—were the last gentle things she did in that dingy room. The rest of her activity was a testament to the woman's imaginative vigor.

But down here in the saloon, she's gentle now, kissing the scars on my face between downing slugs of ouzo. She uses the tip of her tongue to trace the curved scar above my right eye, travels down to the jagged scar on my left cheek, licks the straight-line scar on my chin, and works her way up to kiss the little knife-shaped number above my lip. Her lips are soft, her tongue is warm, knowledgeable, and tempting me to take her upstairs again. I consider it, or rather the tingle between my legs considers it, but a gruff, deep-throated call of "Cantor?" from the doorway intrudes on the erotic mood.

"Cantor Gold," the rough voice calls again. "It's time you go now. It's time."

The voice belongs to a short, beefy guy named Stavros. Stavros is a Piraeus dockworker with arms as thick as trees, legs solid as capstans, and a head lumpy as a boulder but filled with more gutter-smarts than a high IQ sewer rat back home in New York. Stavros always arranges my passage out of Piraeus, slipping me past customs officials and looking out for thieves who watch the docks, guys who hide in the shadows and pounce for a smuggler's treasure, which they'll sell fast and cheap to the local antique shops that cater to tourists. Sell enough of them, and a dock thug can earn himself a hundred bucks American in a couple of days, a fortune in these parts.

The appetizing lady at my side earns one last kiss, well worth the money I slip into her cleavage, then I close my pea coat, adjust the satchel across my shoulder, and follow Stavros out the door.

The middle-of-the-night air is cold and damp. Not as cold as an icy New York winter, but chilly enough for the seaside air to seep right through me and bite my innards along the way as Stavros leads me through cobblestoned alleys. Low whitewashed buildings, only partly revealed by the moonlight, are tucked deep in the alleys. They hide secrets as ancient and seductive as Athens itself.

We finally reach an out-of-the-way corner of Piraeus, where a fishing trawler waits dockside, her gangplank extended. But no light shines from the trawler because the boat's business isn't strictly fishing. It's a stealth ship, her captain and crew making spare cash ferrying people out of the Port of Athens, people like fugitives on the lam, revolutionaries on the run, and smugglers like me. The trawler's been hired to catch up to a New York-bound freighter that sailed out of port minutes ago. I'll board the freighter on the open sea, beyond Greek jurisdiction.

Stavros shakes my hand, says, "*Kaló taxídi*, Cantor," wishing me safe travels.

"Thank you, my friend," I say, and hand him an envelope of cash. He's worth every drachma of it.

With a nod from me and a wave from Stavros, I start up the gangplank, but halfway up I see the glare of a car's headlights rake the trawler, then hear a harsh, strangled grunt behind me. I turn around and see a beat-up, prewar roadster, one of those small jobs Europeans specialize in, its door open, its fender-mounted headlamps silhouetting a thug running toward me. Stavros is sprawled on the ground. I don't know if he's dead or alive. The thug's cap is pulled low, his face hidden in the shadow of the brim. He waves a knife; it glints in the light of the car's headlamps. I go for my gun but the guy's too fast, already on me before I can grab the gun from its rig.

His knife keeps coming at me, missing me by slivers as I bob and weave away from the blade. He uses his free hand to try to wrestle the satchel from me. I don't dare let go—it's worth twenty grand to me!—and I don't dare let it drop and break what's inside, but the guy's tough and relentless, jabbing at me, pulling the satchel, and bending away just enough to keep me from kneeing him.

I'm losing this battle. I can't hold this guy off much longer, can't get a good grip on the satchel. But I can't give up, because even if I let go, the guy might kill me anyway, knife me and toss me into the harbor. So I keep twisting my head away from the blade that comes ever closer as I get more tangled in the battle.

I'll be a goner any minute. I know it, because even through the stinging sweat dripping into my eyes, blurring my vision, I see the gleam of the blade heading right for my throat.

The guy's eyes open wide.

He goes down. Stavros, pale and bleeding behind him, pulls his own knife out of the guy's back.

❖

New York City, a week later
Eight p.m.

The backseat of Rosie Bliss's big Checker Cab is a lot more comfortable than the rusty cabin on the freighter that brought me home from Athens. By the time the Brooklyn beaches came in sight, my bones were so damp they sloshed. I was damn glad to jump ship and onto Red Drogan's tugboat at the entrance to New York Harbor; it's how I avoid the harbor police and US Customs. Red and I have danced that dance before. He's a master at catching me dangling from ships' rope ladders and ferrying me past the Law. I pay him well for those skills. He'll get his cut of tonight's job in the morning.

After a quick trip to a rendezvous spot on an abandoned pier in an out-of-the-way arm of the river, where Rosie met me with her cab and drove me to my apartment to shower and change into a fresh suit—a double-breasted navy blue number, silk, like all my suits, and custom tailored to camouflage the gun in my shoulder rig—we're tootling down upper Fifth Avenue on a cold winter's night. My gray wool overcoat and gray cap, the brim pulled low, keep me warm. The satchel with the Dancing Goddess pyxis at my side reminds me to keep alert.

Not that I expect any thuggery in this part of town. Even at night, upper Fifth Avenue is a golden street, glittery with high-hat apartment buildings on one side, Central Park on the other, and not a lot of pedestrians to dirty up the place. The shiny dimes who live along here have their chauffeurs drive them across the street into the park, where Victorian-era lamps throw a genteel glow across snaking paths. Out on Fifth Avenue, streetlights throw a patina on the late-model Lincolns, Cadillacs, Imperials, and other fat, pampered cars parked along the curb, their chrome glistening with the luster of money.

At Sixty-Fourth Street, Rosie pulls up in front of a doozy of a building: fourteen stories of pale limestone, the lower floors shimmering in Fifth Avenue's street lamps, the upper floors ascending into the moonlight. The entrance, with its carved Italianate molding around the door and its glass and wrought iron awning stretching to the curb, announces that only the city's most highfalutin ladies and gents can live here. Money alone won't get you an apartment in this joint. The right lineage has to ride along on the dollar. The longer the lineage, the higher the floor.

Light from street lamps and the lobby of the apartment building seeps into the cab, touches Rosie's pale blond hair, turns it into a froth of mist under her cabbie's cap. It's one of the delicious things I like about Rosie. I also like her blue eyes in a peaches-and-cream complexion, and the way every curve and mound of her luscious body accepts mine when we're in my bed. I like her voice, mellow as warm, buttered brandy. I like her fondness for the scar above my lip. And I'm crazy about her skill behind the wheel. Even in thick New York traffic, Rosie can lose a cop car, or any other unwanted tail, with moves deft as a shell-game hustle. If I was smart I'd fall in love with her, but I can't fall in love with Rosie or with anyone else. I'm still in love with someone who was taken from me, kidnapped more than three years ago and forced onto a flesh boat sailing God knows where and still not found, though I'm working on it. Meantime, I hold tight to my heart, protect its battered remnants.

Rosie puts the engine in neutral and turns around to face me. The light drifting into the cab casts an alluring glow on one side of her face, leaving an equally alluring shadow on the other. I lean close to her, gently lift her chin. "I won't be long," I say. "How about we go for a drink, maybe spin around the dance floor at the Green Door Club when I come back?"

She gives me a sultry smile. "Sorry, can't tonight, Cantor."

My surprise must be all over my face, because when Rosie strokes my cheek it's as if she's trying to rub my bafflement away. Softly, sweetly, her voice wrapping me in its warmth, she says, "Listen, one of my regular fares needs me to ferry her around tonight, paying me good money, and I don't want to lose the business."

After my rough exit from Piraeus and a cold week on a damp ship, I don't want to lose Rosie tonight, so I lean in even closer, brush my lips on hers. "Okay, later, then," I say. "Meet me at my place after you drop your fare and I'll open a bottle of Chivas. We'll relax awhile, let the scotch smooth us out, and then I'll open…something else."

Rosie's breathy, purring, "Mmmm," is so seductive I want to climb over the seat and take her right now, even if it's in full view of the doorman who's coming our way. "Tempting," she says. "But I don't know how late I'll be. Better not wait up."

That sure throws ice water on me. I need a deep breath to get clear of my oafish disappointment. "Sure," I say, "don't worry about it," and mean every word of it, even though I've just been shoved to the side of the road. I have no right to Rosie. She deserves the love I can't give her. And if she finds it in someone else's arms, like maybe the arms of this regular fare, she's entitled to it.

The doorman opens the cab door. I grab the satchel, get out of the cab, and watch Rosie drive away, the cab's red taillights absorbed into the sea of other red taillights in Fifth Avenue traffic, hiding Rosie's journey to I don't know where.

The washout of losing Rosie for the evening is soothed a bit by the anticipation of twenty-thousand in cash crossing my palm when I deliver the pyxis to the client in the penthouse. Money can soothe the pain of almost anything.

Almost anything.

But not everything. Not the loss of my beloved Sophie. Sophie de la Luna y Sol, my Sophie of the Moon and the Sun, stolen from me, grabbed off the street, sold to a flesh boat heading to parts unknown. Nothing—not all the money I make, not all the booze I drink, not all the women I bed to satisfy my rutting urges—is able to heal that wound.

The doorman's, "Are you expected?" jolts me out of my memories. The way he looks me over, like he's just swallowed something sour that's giving him gas, I'm afraid he'll pop the shiny brass buttons on his fancy brown uniform.

"Yeah, I'm expected," I say. "Tell Mrs. van Zell that Cantor Gold is here."

"Wait here," he says, and goes to the intercom beside the entry door. While he's dialing upstairs, I brush my coat, position my cap, and make myself presentable to meet with one of the highest of New York's high society darlings, Mrs. Miranda van Zell, widow of Rupert van Zell. Yeah, *those* van Zells, real Knickerbockers, descendants of the folks who came over with Peter Stuyvesant when the Dutch sent him to govern their New Amsterdam colony. As far as I know, Rupert had little or no interest in art. I'd never met the man before he died a couple of years ago. A freak accident, the papers said. Choked on a cherry pit at a dinner party. Maybe it's true. His widow, though, is crazy about art, especially ancient Greek stuff. She sits on the board of the fanciest museum in town and throws a lot of the van Zell money toward stocking the museum's Greek collections. Which is where I come in. This isn't my first waltz with Miranda van Z.

All spiffed up and ready to go, I head for the entrance. I can almost feel that twenty grand tickling my palm. Instead, I feel a rough tug on my shoulder spinning me around, and I see a brawny guy in a dark fedora and overcoat, see his jowly face, hard, hooded eyes, and bulby red nose just before he throws his thick fist into my cheekbone, setting it on fire. It's followed by a hard pull on the satchel, ripping it from my hand. I'm reeling from the jab to my face, the pain burning right through cartilage and bone, but I make a grab to get the satchel back, yanking the strap like an angry animal. I can't shake it loose; the guy has a grip on the satchel tight as a steel coil. The doorman's shouting, "Hey, get off there!" and tries to pull the galoot off me. Another thug, a little guy with a pointy chin, enters the act, shoving the doorman. With a groan, the doorman's hustled off behind me, and after another groan I hear him thud to the ground. Pointy Chin joins Bulby Nose in wrestling the satchel from me. I can't take on both guys.

After a last smash of a fist to my gut, doubling me over, I finally lose my grip on the satchel. One of the thugs yanks it away, and both guys run into a waiting dark sedan and drive into the night. My Dancing Goddesses are gone.

My face stings. The pain in my gut churns all the way up through my chest. But I pull myself together, cursing the thugs, the pain, and the loss of my twenty-thousand-dollar treasure as I stumble over to the doorman, who's still on the ground. I say, "You okay, fella?" but the fella's not okay. He's been knifed. He's lying in a pool of blood, dead.

Poor schnook never figured he'd meet his end on his cushy job on fancy Fifth Avenue.

Hanging around over the guy's body, risking being seen by anyone coming in or out of the building, could jam me up when someone calls the cops—which someone certainly will—and the blue boys arrive like a swarm of stinging bugs. So I get off the street and into the lobby, a palatial affair with enough marble to build a library. I should probably take the service elevator at the back of the building to avoid being spotted, but the main elevator's already here, the door open. I don't waste time, just get in. The brass and mahogany elevator's as ornate as the lobby, but right now I'm less concerned with the elevator's hoity-toity decor than with the speed it travels to the penthouse. And I hope to hell it doesn't make any stops along the way. My battered face is in no condition to meet strangers. Not with a dead man at the front door.

I make it to the penthouse without interruption and ring the van Zell apartment. It's the only one on the floor.

A minute later, the door's opened by the butler, a dignified sort with neatly trimmed gray hair and large round eyes.

"Good evening, Charles," I say.

The normally unruffled Charles is ruffled plenty by the sight of the bruised and disheveled me. He tries with all his butler's dignity to control his eyebrows from rising nearly to his hairline, but fails, and his eyes open wider and rounder than usual. "You're hurt! Shall I—"

"I'm fine, Charles. Just take me to Miranda. She's expecting me."

"Yes, Mrs. van Zell informed me of your arrival. Follow me, please."

I follow Charles out of the vestibule and through the large, airy, walnut- and stained-glass-paneled gallery that leads past the dining room, living room, and solarium on one side, the tea room, music room, library, and study on the other. The bedrooms are upstairs, but I've never seen them.

Charles gives two discreet knocks on the study door and just as discreetly opens it. "Cantor Gold to see you, madam."

A low, throaty feminine voice, equally arrogant and playful in an I-dare-you sort of way, says, "Show her in, Charles."

He steps aside, I walk into the study. Charles closes the door behind me with a nearly silent click.

I'm in a small, cozy room filled with a couple of first-rate sofas and club chairs thickly upholstered in pale green velvet. The room's wrapped in silk-covered walls of deep blue, the color of a night sky in an exotic locale, the damask pattern catching flickers of light from the fire in a carved marble fireplace. The firelight shimmers on pricey paintings of country landscapes hung on the walls, none of the paintings newer than the late eighteenth century, and likely depicting the van Zell's ancestral holdings when New York was still green and hilly and Dutch. Muffling my footsteps is a dark blue Chinese silk rug whose colorful sprays of flowers are muted in the firelight. And in the middle of the grandeur, getting up from a delicate Louis XVI desk with gold trim at its dainty feet, is an elegant woman on one side or another of fifty. She's decked out in a light blue Persian caftan whose silver embroidery sends an aura around her. Light from the desk lamp brushes her strawberry blond hair falling in waves to her shoulders. The light also glints in her green eyes, which always seem to size you up. The light magnifies her know-the-score smile, which fades when she gets a full look at me.

"What on earth happened to your face?" She has one of those smoky aristocratic voices that treats trouble like an inconvenience that doesn't know its place. "You're hurt."

"Don't worry about me," I say. "I'm in better shape than your doorman."

"Frank? What's the matter with Frank?"

"He's dead. And your pyxis is gone."

She doesn't say anything, just stares at me, eyes narrowing. I fill the silence. "Miranda, I could really use a drink."

"What? Oh, yes. Yes, of course." Firelight slides along her caftan as she moves across the room to the bar cart, giving her the appearance of floating. I guess she does float above the rest of us up here in her penthouse in the sky. "Scotch, right?" she says.

"Yeah. Chivas. Neat."

She pours the scotch, hands it to me, and says, "You'd better sit down. You look like you're about to keel over."

One of the sofas accepts me in its tender embrace when I sit down and lean back. That's the difference between first-class furnishings and the cut-rate stuff currently filling up all those new suburban living rooms of the American Dream. The expensive stuff caters to the human body. The cheap stuff feels like it's doing your rump a favor, and not particularly happy about it.

The smooth scotch takes some of the sting out of my bruises. A cigarette helps settle me.

Miranda could use a bit of settling herself. She's pacing back and forth, her hands clenched, her mouth tight.

"Nervous?" I say.

Still wearing out the carpet, she says, "A man's dead on my doorstep. You've been beaten to a pulp. And a priceless object's been violently stolen from me. I'm not nervous. I'm scared, Cantor."

"And you should be."

"Well, thank you for making me feel oh-so-much better. Maybe you'd better tell me just who I should be afraid of. If I'm going to be looking over my shoulder for the bogeyman, I may as well know what he looks like."

"No time to go into that now," I say. "Listen, Miranda, someone's probably discovered the dead doorman by now and called the cops. They'll want to talk to everyone in the building. I can't be here when they knock on your door."

"Why not? I could tell them you were here with me when Frank was, well...you know. Unless...Cantor, you didn't—?" She abruptly stops pacing, stares at me, her body rigid, the idea she can't say stuck like a stone in her throat.

I say it for her. "No, Miranda, I didn't kill Frank. So, thanks for the offer of lying to the cops, but it wouldn't work anyway. I'm tops on their mug-they'd-most-like-to-frame list."

She gives me that size-me-up look again and chases it with her know-it-all smile. "Yes, I'm sure you are."

I finish off the scotch, crush my smoke in an ashtray on a side table, and get up from the sofa. "I can't linger, Miranda."

"Just a minute, Cantor. You haven't told me what's going on. Who killed Frank? And what happened to the pyxis?"

"I'll tell you, but not here, not now. The cops could be here any minute. I've got to get to the service elevator and out the back of the building before they're at your door."

"But when will I hear from you? I have a right to know what's going on."

On my way to the desk, I say, "I promise I'll tell you, but not now," and write an address on a notepad, tear off the sheet of paper and give it to Miranda. "After the cops leave, go to this address. I'll head over there now and wait for you. And don't have your chauffeur drive you. Take a cab. The less your staff knows, the better." On my way out the study door, I call over my shoulder, "And tell that butler of yours I was never here, understand?"

❖

The service door exits into a narrow alley that empties into Sixty-Fourth Street, a dozen yards from the Fifth Avenue corner. Out on the street, I hear a commotion of cops on the Fifth Avenue side, see their cars' twirling lights smear the street and the trees in the park red.

This is no place for me. I pull down the brim of my cap and walk into the shadow of East Sixty-Fourth Street.

CHAPTER TWO

It takes the cabbie quite a while to work through downtown traffic—Rosie would've had us out of the Times Square tangle in a few spins of the wheel—but since it'll be some time yet until Miranda meets me, I'm not too worried about it. The ride gives me time to think, even though I don't like what I'm thinking: somebody, some big shot with a long reach, a reach clear across an ocean, wants that little Dancing Goddesses pyxis, wants it bad enough to grab for it twice, and kill anyone who gets in the way. Bet they didn't figure their victim would be a Johnny Honest doorman. Bet they don't care, either.

I'm thinking over a list of possible big shots by the time the cabbie finally slithers through Times Square, past girls in ponytails and guys with slicked-back hair who dream of knocking 'em dead on Broadway or seeing their names on movie palace marquees, past tourists gawking at the lightbulb-animated billboards advertising everything from cars, to clothes, to Kleenex. By the time we cross Forty-Second Street, my list of big shots thins a bit as the cabbie cruises into the Garment District, its skyscrapers dark now for the night, the designers, fashion models, fabric cutters, seamstresses, and mobbed-up union bosses who squeeze every last dime from the rag trade all gone home.

Farther downtown, my list's gotten pretty skimpy as we slide past the Flatiron Building, its prow-shaped mass like a ship sailing up Fifth and Broadway. Soon we're through Union Square, where soapbox spielers still shout their grievances and shake their fists at capitalists and other annoying elements of the American hustle. We finally make it past Fourteenth Street and down into the Lower East Side. Down here, the streets still lilt to the singsong speech of the city's ethnic tribes, and the aroma of sour pickles and pastrami from the best delicatessens in the world spices the air.

But I'm no closer to figuring who'd kill for the pyxis, can't get a handle on who'd try to do me dirty. None of the names on my list would make a death play for the Greek stuff. I know a guy who'd gut you for a Michelangelo, and a dame who'd shoot you dead for the last Russian tsarina's jewels, but my clients for Greek antiquities tend to be patrician pussycats with lots of cash. Conniving, yeah. Killers, doubtful.

But you never know.

It's not quite nine o'clock when the cab pulls up in front of a brownstone on Second Avenue. Coming here always makes me queasy. I used to come here often, before it made me queasy. But ever since the old lady who lives here came clean a little over two years ago about how she really feels about me, which is none too sweet, I avoid the place. And it doesn't help that she's known as Mom—Esther "Mom" Sheinbaum—and that she really was like a second mother to me when I was a tomboy juvenile delinquent. It was Mom who served me honey cake and listened patiently to my teenage heartbreak over some girl I panted after. It was Mom who schooled me in my thieving ways and fenced my swag for our mutual profit. And all that time, as I wallowed in the warmth of her house and the wisdom of her tutelage, she considered me defective goods, even unnatural. My preference for custom-tailored gentlemen's suits, she told me later, only made it worse.

So I don't drop by much anymore, but there are times I can't avoid it. Tonight is one of those times, because if you want to know about the movement of stolen goods through New York—

who's buying, who's selling, who's moving it around—you talk to Mom Sheinbaum. There isn't a thief she doesn't know, a big shot she hasn't done business with, a politician she hasn't bribed, including the mayor. And it's been this way over fifty years, since New York did its shady deals by gaslight.

So if anyone can get a line on who's got the Dancing Goddesses, it's Mom; that is, *if* she's willing, and *if* there's something in it for her.

I run up the front stoop and press the doorbell, hear the old, familiar ring.

Here it comes: queasy.

Mom, white haired, button eyed, and built like a small boulder under a grandmotherly brown dress, greets me at the door with a look equal parts surprised, annoyed, and curious. "So," she says, one plump hand on her hip, the other on the door, no doubt ready to slam it in my face, "it's Cantor Gold." It comes out as *Kenta Gold*, the syllables rising and falling in her Lower East Side singsong. "To what do I owe this rare visit? And unannounced, yet. You don't call first? But you're here, so what do you want?"

"Information," I say, "and a safe spot for a meeting. Someone will be joining me here in a little while."

"You invite strangers to my house?"

"Something's been stolen from me, something I was supposed to deliver to a client tonight. She's meeting me here."

"This client, she knows it's gone?"

"Yeah, she knows."

Mom gives this information a slow nod, like a scholar working through an idea. "So you're going after it. And you want my help, yes?"

I give that a shrug. "Can you think of any other reason I'd drop by?"

She doesn't laugh at that exactly, more like a dry, scoffing *tsk*. But she opens the door.

Inside, the house is plush with the Gilded Age decor of Mom's youth, the heavy woodwork shined to a high polish, the furniture thickly tufted in dark wine-colored silk. The sweet aroma of honey cake wafts through the house, as always. And as always, it brings back memories I'd rather be rid of.

Tonight, the aroma comes from a loaf of cake on a silver tray on the lace-covered dining room table, the loaf a slice or two shy of complete. Mom seats herself at her usual place at the head of the table while I drape my coat and cap over the back of one of the mahogany chairs, polished to a luster, like everything else in the shadowy dining room.

Mom says, "That hair of yours, like an old broom in a stiff wind. And still with the men's suits, I see."

"What's the matter, Mom? Don't you think navy blue is my color?"

Her lips twisted in disgust, Mom waves off my little joke. You'd think I'd know by now not to make a play for even a shred of shared amusement with her.

Mom might be past any sweet times with me, but she's still an old-fashioned hostess, a trait bred in the bone. "Sit down, have a piece of honey cake, Cantor. It's good. From Weinstein's over on Rivington Street. I just heated it up."

"No, thanks," I say, and head for the liquor cabinet in the sideboard, where I pour myself a stiff Chivas. "You don't mind, do you, Mom?"

"A lotta good it would do me."

"No good at all." I swallow the scotch, pour myself another.

"Sure, go ahead, drink up my liquor," she says with a sarcasm so syrupy it could coat the walls. "You always were a little savage, Cantor. I tried to polish you up, but..." Another derisive *tsk* finishes her sentence.

"Sorry to be such a disappointment, Mom."

"So who says you're a disappointment?"

The doorbell saves me from a moment I can't figure out. "That must be Miranda," I say, and leave the dining room.

At the front door, there's almost more silver fox fur than Miranda, the coat wrapping her from head to ankle, the hood pulled forward, obscuring her face. She slides past me and into the house. "You certainly bring me to the best addresses," she says.

"Welcome to the place of my misspent youth."

She takes the hood down, looks at me with mild surprise. "I thought you were a boardwalk tough from Coney Island."

"I got around."

"Clearly, you still do."

"How'd it go with the cops?"

With a shrug, she says, "They came, they asked their questions, they went away."

"Yeah? And what were your answers?"

She gives me a shrewd smile, takes her time with it, lets its mischief play around with me. "Don't you trust me, Cantor?"

With a sly smile of my own, I say, "Any reason why I shouldn't?"

She meets my smile with an even slyer one. "No reason at all." The arrogance in that smoky voice of hers is as playful as the glint in her eyes. "I told them I had no idea the doorman was dead until they told me so, and oh, how terrible," she says with mock horror. "The poor man. And no, Officer, I didn't see anyone sneaking around."

"Good girl." I help her off with her coat. In her powder blue cashmere pullover tucked into a pencil-thin skirt—a deep maroon number that flows just below her knees on a pair of legs that no doubt still earn their share of wolf whistles—her hands graceful in maroon gloves, her hair pulled back into a smart little light blue hat, and a rose-petal perfume that drifts with the delicacy of a garden at a country house, Miranda fills the role of high society diva very nicely.

"Come with me," I say. "I'll introduce you to the lady of the house."

Mom's chewing a piece of honey cake when we walk into the dining room. She continues chewing as she looks Miranda up and down, Mom's small eyes like scalpels cutting down to Miranda's marrow, searching out her substance. Miranda doesn't flinch, even when Mom finishes her examination with a quick "Hm," then swallows the piece of cake and says, "Have a seat, Miss—?"

I make the introductions. "Mom, meet Mrs. Miranda van Zell. Miranda, meet Mrs. Esther Sheinbaum, also known in certain circles as Mom."

I pull out a chair for Miranda. Mom offers her a piece of cake, which Miranda declines. I offer her a drink, which she accepts.

"Bourbon, no ice. Why am I here, Cantor?"

I pour her a bourbon from the liquor cabinet, hand it to her, pick up my scotch, and after we each take a pull of our booze, I say, "Because you have a right to know what happened to your treasure, and Mom has the connections to help us get it back." I tell them about the thug who tried to snatch the pyxis in Piraeus. I tell them about Pointy Chin and Bulby Nose and how they grabbed it tonight, and how the doorman wound up dead. And I say to Mom, "That's why I asked Miranda to meet me here. When the cops got around to questioning her, I couldn't be in her apartment when they knocked at her door."

Mom gives that a nod and another short "Hm." I can't tell if she's backing my moves or annoyed that my moves intruded on her night.

"Look," I say, "someone with connections on both sides of the Atlantic knew about that pyxis, knew my plans for getting it to New York and where I'd be delivering it. So it might be just as well you don't have it, Miranda. They'd come after you if you did."

Even the whiskey can't keep the color in Miranda's cheeks. It drains from her face as the fear of being hunted rises in her bones.

I'll deal with Miranda's fear another time. Right now, it's Mom I need to win over, so I give her my best pitch. "Listen, nothing in this town moves without you knowing about it, right? You know every pinch-man and carrier in this city, and plenty of them owe you favors. Get me a line on who grabbed the pyxis, and I'll—I'll owe you a favor, too." Here comes queasy again. Who the hell wants to owe a favor to someone who thinks you're tainted goods?

"You'll owe me more than a favor, mommaleh. You'll owe me money, good money." Turning to Miranda, Mom says, "What's this…whaddya call it? A pixie?"

"Pyxis," Miranda and I say together.

"Okay, pyxis. What's it worth to you, Mrs. van Zell? What's Cantor charging you for this tchotchke?"

"Twenty grand," I say.

Before my very eyes, and for the first time in over two years, Mom smiles at me. It's not a big smile, and it's not warm, but it's got something familiar behind it, something I haven't seen in her since I was a kid: acknowledgment that I did good. Cupping her chin in one meaty hand, the rings on her fingers catching lamplight, she says, "Twenty grand? Not bad. I'll take ten of your twenty, Cantor."

"You'll take five," I say.

"For five, I only ask half the city. You want the other half, I take ten."

"Five or noth—"

Miranda jumps in, "*I'll* pay it," ending the negotiation. "*I'll* pay you ten thousand dollars, Mrs. Sheinbaum, if you help us recover the pyxis."

There are two kinds of rich people: the kind whose fists are so tight they get hand cramp if they have to part with a penny, particularly if that penny goes to the hoi polloi; and the kind I like better, the more confident kind who throw money around in any direction for anyone to catch, especially if it will help buy what—or who—they want. Miranda, bless her well-dressed heart, is the second kind.

But something's picking at me. "Thirty grand, Miranda? Twenty for me and ten for Mom? That's a lot of cash for that little jar."

With cool ease, Miranda polishes off her bourbon, takes a gold cigarette case from her purse, and puts a cigarette to her lips in the expectation I'll light it for her.

Never one to pass up a chivalrous moment, I take out my lighter, light her smoke, then light one of my own.

She says, "Cantor, how much do you know about fifth century BC Athenian pottery?"

"Enough. Why?"

"Then you know how rare it is to find an unbroken pot, completely intact, including its lid. And you also know how desirable Classical period red-figure Attic pottery is, especially by the Dancing Goddess Painter. The van Zell name is attached to the very best pieces in the museum's Greek collections, and I want to keep it that way. And you, Mrs. Sheinbaum, you can start earning your ten thousand dollars by contacting your connections tonight, start getting leads for Cantor." She stubs out her smoke, gets up from the chair, picks up her fox fur, and hands it to me, silently demanding another chivalrous moment.

I'm happy to oblige and help her on with her coat. "I'll call someone to drive you home," I say. "You'll never get a cab in this neighborhood at this hour."

"No need. I told my cabbie to keep his meter running and wait. Good night, Cantor, Mrs. Sheinbaum. You will keep me informed."

The scent of rose petals lingers after Miranda leaves the dining room.

Mom says, "Bossy, that one."

Chapter Three

Everything about this night is lousy: no Rosie, the loss of a twenty-thousand-dollar treasure, an innocent doorman dead in the street, and now even the weather's gone to crap. It's raining cats and dogs when I leave Mom's, with the cats clawing right through my cap, and splashing dogs nipping my ankles. I need a drink. I need the pleasure of women.

I know where to find both.

The evening paper I bought from a newsie outside the subway station at the corner of Fourteenth and Eighth isn't doing a helluva lot to keep the rain off me as I sprint the two blocks to an alley off Tenth Avenue. By the time I make it through the alley and down the stairs into the Green Door Club, a well hidden spot for women who like to sashay with other women, my cap and coat are soaked and I'm chilled to the bone.

But it's warm inside the club. Couples in red leather booths and at white-cloth'd tables give the place a cozy feel, even on this rainy Tuesday night, while the singles at the bar, ever hopeful, size each other up. Amber-shaded sconces on the walls and lamps on the tables throw a soft glow on everybody, highlighting lipstick on pretty faces, the bodices of colorful dresses, and the lapels of sharp suits on female bodies. On the dance floor, couples sway to the band's dreamy rendition of Hoagy Carmichael's classic, "The Nearness of You," some stealing dangerous kisses, ignoring the always hovering threat of a raid by the cops and a brutal night in the city lockup. The band's sax player, a blonde in a fetching red organza number, even gives her solo a little extra sass.

Bartender Peg Monroe, a big girl with caramel skin in a pink-and-green plaid shirt and navy bow tie, and whose dark eyes don't miss a trick, is busy mixing cocktails and setting up beers. She gives me a nod when I come in and has a Chivas poured for me by the time I slide onto a barstool. I signal to make it a double.

"Evenin', Slick," she says, using her longtime nickname for me. Soft remnants of her rural Georgia childhood drift through her speech, giving my nickname a courtliness I don't mind. "You're gonna get my bar all wet. Hand over your hat and coat, I'll put 'em back here to dry." I give her my soaked duds. She hangs them on an empty towel rack. "What're you doing here all alone on a rainy night? Where's Rosie?"

I answer with a shrug, say, "Not sure. Hauling some private fare tonight."

"Uh-huh. That why you're here kickin' back doubles alone?"

"It's not the first time I'm here drinking alone. What's with the third degree?"

"Because the last time you looked this miserable, everything about you droopin' like an old tree, you'd just lost—"

"Don't. Don't say her name, Peg." I don't want to hear Sophie's name. I don't need to pick at that wound after everything else that's gone wrong tonight. "Just keep the whiskey coming."

"Sure, whatever you say. But I'll cut you off, Slick, when I think you've had enough. Just like I always do."

"Uh-huh. I'm counting on it."

I down the whiskey in two pulls, feel it warm my bones, soothe my frayed nerves, relax me enough to look around, see who's here, examine the possibilities.

Peg says, "Anyone catch your eye?"

I answer through a snappy laugh, "Give me time," though the confidence behind it tonight is tepid as dishwater. Over the years, I've had my share of *No thank you*s, *Some other time*s, even a few *Drop dead*s, and if the pattern of my so-far crummy night is anything to go by, I won't be surprised if I'm in for more of those refrains.

Peg pours me another scotch. I take my time with this one, sip it slowly, let it ooze down my gut, enjoy its heat as it seeps into my sinew. I have a look at the ladies along the bar, especially a cute redhead at the far end, and try not to think about the night's losses or who stole the pyxis or how they knew my plans. That last bit really sticks in my craw.

"Martini, extra dry," comes from a lilting voice next to me, pulling me out of my thoughts. The voice belongs to a face that could cause heartbreak or cure it. The face has chiseled cheekbones, full lips glistening with you-can't-ignore-me red lipstick, a teasing curl at the corners of her mouth, and green eyes of the most dangerous kind. This knockout ensemble is capped off by short, wavy blond hair that would look terrific blowing in a breeze. As she slides onto the barstool next to mine and slips out of her evening coat—a white cashmere number that must've set her back a hefty handful of dollars—I see that the lower part of her ain't too bad either: creamy skin in a slinky purple satin dress that's cut low enough to be entertaining but still lets the imagination be creative about what lies beneath. When she crosses her legs, the dress ripples like a slow-moving river. I'd love to jump in and take a swim.

Peg pours the martini. The woman raises her glass in toast. "Cheers."

Maybe heaven is finally throwing a little something my way tonight. I could sure use it. I lift my glass. "Cheers to you, too." The woman sips her martini, I sip my scotch, then say, "There's a half dozen empty seats along this bar. You could have sat at any one of them. So to what do I owe my good fortune, Miss—?"

"Day. Lilah Day. And I sat here because I think you'll be interesting."

"Is that so? Why?"

"Because it will be interesting to figure out if you're sad or angry. By the look of you, you're one or the other."

"What if I'm a bit of both?"

"Then you'll be twice as interesting." She punctuates the idea by reaching a fingertip into her martini to scoop out the olive. Whole books could be written about the way she slides the olive into her mouth, the kind of books that come through the mail in plain brown wrappers.

She certainly has my attention. "Well, Miss Day, if I'm sad, then I could use a little tender loving care. And if I'm angry, then I could use a gentle touch to calm me. And if you still find all that interesting, then let's dance."

With a short, smart laugh, she takes my offered hand. I lead her to the dance floor, find our place among the couples, now swaying to a mellow version of "Bewitched, Bothered and Bewildered," an old Broadway tune with a pretty melody and chic lyrics that remind me why I don't dare fall in love again.

But dancing with Miss Lilah Day poses no risk to my heart, so I let myself enjoy the feel of her against me. She seems to know I'm enjoying it and moves her body in a way that allows me to enjoy her even more, fitting herself into me, swaying gently but seductively along the length of me, her back warm against my hand as I pull her even tighter to me.

"I knew you'd be interesting," she says.

She has charmingly curved ears, the type that beg to be whispered into. With my lips brushing her right ear, I say, "Anything else you want to know about me?" letting it ride on a breath.

"I'm getting there," she says, equally breathy. "Anything you want to tell me?"

"Maybe you're interested in my name?"

She gives my hand a quick, light, nearly imperceptible squeeze. A moment later, she says, "Yes, tell me your name."

"Cantor Gold."

"Interesting name. Anything else you want to share with me?"

"Sure. But not here."

She pulls away from me a little, tilts her head, and looks up at me in a way that could bring the Arctic waters to a boil. "Are you trying to pick me up?"

"I am. I think you're just what I need tonight."

"And what about what I need?"

"I'll do my best to figure it out."

She gives me a bedroom smile. "My car's outside."

By the time we run from a parking spot to my apartment building at the edge of the Theater District, we're both soaking wet from the unrelenting rain. Upstairs, walking into my living room, Lilah says, "Nice place. Love the red upholstery."

"Let's get out of these wet clothes."

"Aren't you going to offer me a robe, or even just a towel?"

"No." I say it as I slip her coat off, then slip off my own coat and cap, my suit jacket and my tie, tossing them all on the floor as I lead her to the bedroom.

Her eyes narrow when she sees my .38 revolver in its rig under my left shoulder.

"Don't let it frighten you," I say.

"It doesn't frighten me," she says, reaching for the gun.

I stop her before she gets there, grab her wrist. "What do you think you're doing?"

"I don't think we'll need this tonight. Do you? It might, um, get in the way."

She's right. I don't need my violent life intruding on us right now. I need *her*, Lilah Day, her body, her lust, to blot out the crimes that stalk me. I take the rig off, toss it on the floor with the rest of my duds.

As if reading my troubled thoughts, she turns and kisses me as soon as we cross the bedroom threshold, a long, warm kiss that savors me like a succulent hors d'oeuvre. When she's done, she turns around and gives me the gift of her back. There's a long zipper down her dress, starting about six inches below her shoulder blades and ending below the pretty curve at the base of her spine. I take my time with it, let my fingers glide along her skin as I slowly slide the zipper down, stretching out time and titillation. The dress falls to the floor. The graceful, seductive way she steps out of it would make a stripper faint with envy.

She doesn't speak, doesn't turn around to face me, just waits for me to unhook her brassiere, a lacy black strapless bit of fluff that slides off her body and joins the dress on the floor.

I whisper, "Turn around."

Now wearing only a black silk half-slip, she turns to face me. I'm not sure who's experiencing the greater pleasure: me, getting lost in the sight of her magnificent breasts, or her, watching me enjoy the sight.

She slides the slip down, kicks it away. Then does the same with her black lace panties, revealing a delectable blond patch that tempts me to part it. "So, Cantor Gold," she says. "What are you going to give me? Sad or angry?"

"Both."

She makes love to me like she knows everything about me: where to put her lips on me, where to stroke me with the tip of her tongue, when to let me fuck her, how slow or fast to move on her.

I make love to her like I don't know her at all, finding every inch of her like an explorer in exotic territory, my hands gliding along every curve and crevice, my mouth tasting her body's every offering.

And now, after our groans and the screams have quieted, I roll off of her, resist an urge to doze, but sit up and light a cigarette for each of us instead. Moonlight through the window catches the smoke, gives it a silvery tinge as it floats along Lilah's body, curls along her face, and trails upward, blurring the Cubist angles in the painting by Picasso that hides the safe in my bedroom wall.

I say, "So who sent you?"

Lilah raises herself up on an elbow, takes a long drag of her smoke, then sits up the rest of the way and looks at me as though nothing in life surprises her anymore. Moonlight shines like silver points in her eyes. "How did you know?"

"Come on. You're not stupid," I say, "and neither am I. In a bar full of empty seats, you sidled up to me like you had a longstanding reservation on that particular barstool. Then you flattered me with that line about me being interesting." I smile when I say it, because, yeah, the line she gave me was a good one, and I appreciate a good line. "I would've just enjoyed the flattery—I'd had a lousy night, and a little flattery from a beautiful woman did wonders for my spirits—but you slipped up when you didn't ask my name until I prompted you. And then you stiffened, like you knew you'd blundered. I'm guessing you already knew my name because someone told you. So who sent you? It had to be someone who knows my habits, knows where to find me, what I look like. So I ask you again: Why did they send you and what do they want?"

She stubs her smoke out in the ashtray on the night table, then pulls the blanket around her and gathers up her knees. With her arms around her legs, her chin on her knees, the blanket cocooning her, she looks more like a lost little girl than the sex-smart femme fatale who just took me to all the neighborhoods of Paradise. "My brother. Mickey," she says. If she sounded any more pitiful, I'd break down and cry.

"Nice brother you've got. Pimps you out for—well, for what?"

"I don't know. He wanted me to get close to you, get you to like me. The rest of it…how I did it…was my idea."

I don't know if I feel flattered or used, though I didn't mind the way she used me. "Okay, it was a swell idea, but it doesn't get me any closer to knowing what you and your brother want with me."

"I'm supposed to get you to come home with me, bring you to Mickey. He wants to talk to you."

"Wait a minute. If he knew to send you to the Green Door Club to find me, then he knows a few things about me, like who I am and maybe even how I earn my dough. Why couldn't he find me himself? Why send you?"

"You'll have to ask him."

"You bet I'll ask him. Get dressed and I'll take you home. Where's home?"

"Brooklyn. Coney Island."

If she'd said Timbuktu, I couldn't be any more thunderstruck.

Coney Island. The tawdry, colorful, raucous, seaside amusement carny of my youth, where the sideshow barkers and midway hucksters know all the angles and can figure more ways to finagle money from your pockets than a shyster lawyer. When I finally left, when I was an ambitious youth moving up in the world from my racket of stashing stolen trinkets under the boardwalk since I was a kid, to the high-priced treasures I deal in now, I rarely went back to the old neighborhood, just now and then to visit my mom and pop. With my mom and later my pop dead and buried, I haven't been back in years. But here it is, the past come to call, brought to my door by a cutie peddling a cute angle. Pure Coney Island.

"We'll take your car," I say. "I'll drive."

CHAPTER FOUR

During the summer nights of my childhood, the streets of Coney Island were crammed with people laughing it up and taking their chances at the shooting galleries, skee ball palaces, penny arcades, and other come-ons designed to pick your pocket while you're trying to impress your girlfriend. Children, staying up late, giggled through smiles sticky with sugary ecstasy sold by cotton-candy spinners. Couples made their way to and from the thrill rides and the great amusement parks—wild Steeplechase, magical Luna Park—where thrills and chills could be had for nickels and dimes. Squeals of delight and fright collided with the barkers' spiels and carny music echoing from every fun house, game stall, and girlie show, the noise floating in the air all the way to the beach. Zesty aromas of hot dogs, mustard, cotton candy, and saltwater taffy kept you hungry, hungry for food, hungry for all the pleasures on offer: pleasures for the family, pleasures for the flesh.

On winter nights like tonight, though, Coney is a shadowy town, its rides and amusements empty and still, most of its penny arcades, game stalls, and bathhouses boarded up for the season. But not all. A handful of die-hard Coney operators stay open all year, and well into the night, catching nearby Brooklynites who need a bit of honky-tonk after a tough day on a crummy job. So even on a damp night in the dead of winter, a few of Coney's neon lights throw their colors into the darkness. The thump of skee ball games, the rat-a-tat of pistol shoots, and the bells of pokerino machines jangle the air.

I'd always wanted to take Sophie here in Coney's off-season, show her where I grew up, the streets of neon and shadows that formed me. We never got around to it.

Lilah's leading me along Schweickerts Walk, an alley street that ends at the boardwalk. Except for Nathan's hot dog joint at the corner of Surf Avenue, there's nothing much along this stretch of Schweickerts, just some mom-and-pop game stall concessions and a bathhouse near the boardwalk, all closed for the season. A gaudy yellow glow from an all-night tattoo parlor in the middle of the block shimmers in puddles left by the earlier rain.

Lilah stops in front of the tattoo joint. "We're here."

Inside, the yellow walls are covered in colorful drawings of pinup girls, gypsy girls, movie stars—Rita Hayworth and Lana Turner are runaway favorites—sailing ships, anchors, broken or arrow-pierced hearts, and hearts with *MOM* written across the front in fancy letters. Otherwise, the place is empty except for a beefy ink artist dozing in a chair, his bare arms a gallery of pictures, most of them lightning bolts, skulls, devils, and a few flowers that seem like they've been sent to the wrong address. The guy wakes when he hears us walk in, but closes his eyes again when he sees it's Lilah and a friend, not customers interested in getting inked. The clock on the table next to him reads a few minutes before one a.m.

Lilah leads me to a dingy area in the back that's tricked out like a cheap living room. The floral wallpaper is colorful but shabby, the sofa and chairs lumpy, the worn-out upholstery a neither here-nor-there green.

The crummy decor doesn't jibe with Lilah's expensive evening coat and slinky dress. "You live here?" I say.

"Sometimes."

Before I get a chance to ask what sometimes means, a guy a few years Lilah's senior walks in from another room. He's a pudgy guy in dark chinos and a sweaty white shirt, the sleeves rolled up. His hard, gray, slit-like eyes keep his round face and thinning brown hair on his balding head from being laughable.

"You Mickey?" I say.

He looks me over with a spreading grin, toothy, like a monkey's. It gives me the creeps.

"Whaddya know," he says. "Cantor Gold, home again. The tomboy all grown up."

"You know me?" I take a hard look at the guy, at his monkey's grin and steely eyes, and they suddenly look familiar. I remember eyes and a grin like that from a wild time way back in my childhood, when a turf war for the Coney rackets left lots of tough guys bleeding to death all over the neighborhood, especially under the boardwalk. The owner of those remembered eyes and grin was the loser in the war. "Solly Schwartz," I say. "You're Solly Schwartz's kid." Fat Solly. The old-time rackets boss of Coney Island, until Sig Loreale muscled in with a modern and ruthless operation Fat Solly's old-fashioned gang couldn't defeat. "I remember now," I say. "I used to see you and your folks on the boardwalk before the turf war. You were—what?—four, maybe five years old? And, yeah, sure, your mother was holding a baby."

"Right. My sister. Only we don't go by Schwartz no more. It's Day. I'm Mickey Day. Aw, and don't gimme that look that says you think I'm ashamed of my name."

"Well, aren't you?"

"It ain't what you think. I ain't trying to fit in with the Smiths and Joneses like a lotta people do nowadays. It's just that after Pop lost Coney to Sig Loreale, the name Schwartz became a laughingstock around here." He reflexively balls his fists, like he's ready to throw a punch in the face of anyone who laughs at him or his family. Must be a habit, I suppose, after all these years.

"But people around here must know who you are," I say.

He shrugs. "Some do, some don't. Lots of new people coming in. The old crowd ain't what it used to be. But that's enough with the auld lang syne, Gold. I had Lilah bring you out here for a reason, and it's not to celebrate Old Home Week. And oh, by the way, little sister turned out to be quite a looker, yeah? From what I hear, I knew you'd like her." He says it with a smile that's more of a sneer, mean and grotesque through his monkey's grin.

"Is that why you didn't come find me yourself? How generous of you." I give him a sneer to match his own. Maybe not as grotesque, but just as snide.

"Why should I traipse all the way to Manhattan? Wasn't hard to figure you'd follow Lilah's skirt wherever it led you."

He gestures with a snap of his head that I should sit down in one of the ratty club chairs while he seats himself on the equally ratty sofa and puts his feet up on the coffee table. Then he barks, "Lilah, bring us a coupla drinks," before he makes slightly more polite noises at me. "What'll you have, Gold?"

I'm not crazy about the way this lout treats his sister, reducing her to a looker and bossing her around. I wouldn't mind swatting him across that monkey's mouth and washing that mouth out with soap, or maybe lye, burning out his nasty tongue. But then he couldn't tell me what I've come here to find out. So though it turns my stomach, I squelch my temper and let his savagery go for now, just take my cap and coat off, sit down, and light a smoke, letting a deep drag calm me. "I'll take Chivas, if you've got it."

"Woo-hoo! Aren't we fancy! You really left Brooklyn and old Coney behind, Gold. Bet you don't even go to Ebbets Field no more to see the Dodgers play." He eyeballs me while he says it, runs his eyes up and down my duds. He looks like he's not crazy about my color scheme of pale yellow shirt and pocket handkerchief with my navy suit. I guess he's just a sweaty white shirt kinda guy. When he's done looking me over, he says, "Well,

I got scotch. Doubt it's Chivas. Lilah, bring us a bottle of scotch." Pointing at my cigarette, he says, "Got another one of those? I'm fresh out. The candy store over on Mermaid Avenue won't open until seven in the morning."

I hand him one of my Chesterfields. He lights it with a match from a book on the coffee table, then sits back and blows out a stream of smoke, lord of his castle. Lowlife lord. Crummy castle.

But I didn't come here to be dazzled by his low-rent glory. Time to get down to business. "Well then, Schwartz—"

"Day."

"Sure, yeah, Day. You lured me out here, so suppose you tell me what this is all about."

After another lordly exhale, he says, "I want to take Coney Island back."

I nearly choke on my own smoke. But before I have a chance to clear my throat and tell Day he's nuts, Lilah's back with a bottle and two glasses, two fingers of whiskey in each glass. I all but gulp the scotch—a cheap but not overly rotgut brand—and let it open my throat again and help my brain sort out the crazy words Mickey's just said. I finally say, "You want to take Coney Island away from Sig Loreale? Do you have a death wish? Your father tried to tangle with him and the only thing he got for his trouble was a knife in the belly."

Watching the guy's round face harden is like watching milk congeal, his expression so sour I swear it smells. "That bastard Loreale left Pop to bleed to death right there on the beach for everyone to see. And did the cops do anything about it? 'Course not, 'cause Loreale owned the cops."

"He still does."

"Not all of 'em."

"As many as he needs."

"Yeah, well, leaving Pop to rot wasn't enough for Loreale. My mother and sister and me were left penniless. Yeah, that's right. Loreale didn't just steal Pop's rackets, he had his thugs brass knuckle the president of the bank where Pop kept his money until he transferred Pop's dough into Loreale's account."

That sounds like Sig. Bet he didn't even jostle in his underwear when he gave the order.

Day takes another slug of whiskey. It only fuels his bitterness, tightens the slits of his gray eyes. "My family lost everything," he says, "even our house over in Sea Gate. We wound up living in a shack in the Gut. Lilah and I are still there. Only thing he let Pop keep was his bathhouse locker." He's practically spitting it, and by the time he says, "How generous of Loreale to split Pop's dough with his thugs," the spit's so acid it could cut through the walls.

"All right, so Loreale did your family dirty," I say. "Loreale does everyone dirty. What's all that got to do with me?"

"Way I hear it, Loreale does you a little less dirty."

"Where'd you get that idea?"

"That same grapevine. Hey, you're famous around here, Gold. Local kid makes good, and all that. So I know you do business with Loreale, get fancy stuff for him."

"So he's a client from time to time. It's just business," I say. "But I know not to cross him, and I know not to trust him." The first would get me killed. The second would rip my heart out with broken promises, like the promise Sig made to use his web of connections to find out what happened to Sophie—who took her, and where the flesh boat went that sailed away with her—in exchange for handing him a priceless Renaissance watercolor I risked my life to bring into port. It's been over two years since the first time Sig made that promise. He made the promise again about a year and a half ago, and so far, he's given me nothing, not even a whisper. "You still haven't said what you want, Day."

"I want you to introduce me to Sig Loreale. You could do it. You could get me to him."

I polish off my drink, put the empty glass down on the coffee table with a hard thud, and get up from the chair. "Why?

So you can get your revenge and plug him? And you think either of us would live to tell about it? Neither of us would live long enough to get out his front door. His outfit would shoot us full of so many holes we'd shred where we stood. You're making the same mistake your father did, thinking he could deal with Sig Loreale."

"Sure, I'm my father's son. It's my job to restore his honor. I got roots here in Coney, Gold. A past. And by the way, so do you."

A past? Yeah. A life? No. "You want to stay trapped in your family's past? Be my guest. Sorry, Day. Count me out." I start for the door.

Day's up and at me quick, blocking my path. "Look, who said anything about plugging the guy? I just want to do business with him. I don't want any rough stuff, though I could if I had to. I've put my own outfit together, and if Loreale wants trouble, I'll give it to him."

I feel my eyebrows rise even before my mouth opens and the biggest laugh I've had in a long time comes barreling out.

"What's so funny, Gold? You think I can't stand up to Sig Loreale? Let me tell you, he's gone soft, from what I hear. More businessman than muscle. You know what he's planning on doing to Coney? He's thrown in with a bunch of real estate developers. Yeah. They're talkin' about tearing down the Gut, throw everybody outta the bungalows and shacks and put up a bunch of big apartment buildings. For the workingman, they say. Baloney, I say. They're out to make a killin' collecting rents from a coupla three thousand, four thousand people. Some say they even have their eyes on leveling Steeplechase Park!"

"Listen to me, Day," I say. "Loreale may dress like a banker but he's still hard as stone. There's nothing soft about him. He'll eat you alive."

"We'll see about that. But first I have to meet with him. Get him to deal."

"Deal? What kind of deal could a two-bit tattoo operator like you offer Sig Loreale?"

"Plenty." He says it with the grin of a schoolyard tough. "I've got inside dope on what goes on here. I know who owns what."

"And you think he doesn't?" I say. "Sig's got eyes and ears in every neighborhood in New York, including this one. *Especially* this one, since Coney Island was the first brick in his empire. He probably owns every nail and screw in this building, too."

Day sits back down on the couch, the lord of his castle again, his arms spread wide across the back, a know-it-all grin spreading across his monkey-like mouth. "Loreale ain't so smart. He don't own everything. And he's been selling off stuff, too, and now he thinks he knows the so-called Owners of Record. But he don't know beans. For that, he needs me. And lemme tell you, Gold, when he hears what I have to say, he'll fork over."

I give that the only response I can: a contemptuous chuckle. "Don't bet on it. Sig holds his dough very tight."

"I'm not talking about dough. I'm talking about the rackets and all the skim. My information will make him a fortune in real estate development, more than he could ever make on the skim. But handing those rackets over to me is my price." The guy's so bloated with himself I'm afraid he'll float up from the couch like a gassy balloon. "So c'mon, Gold," he says, "get me to Loreale, and I'll even cut you in for a piece. Whaddya want? A piece of the flesh action? Bet you'd like that." He says it on a smarmy laugh and a nod toward his sister.

Lilah's been the fly on the wall all this time, but no more. "Mickey, please! You can't just give me—" She almost chokes on whatever it is she can't say.

And then I get it: the sexy dress, the classy coat, her expertise between the sheets, her answer that she lives here sometimes. Lilah's a working skirt, selling her goods, not for Sig but for Mickey, and this hovel fronted by a tattoo parlor is what's known in the trade as a notch joint, a flesh parlor where her own brother set her up to do business. Mickey Day is slimier than a snake in a sewer.

My gut churns with an anger so cold that if I spit at Day he'd freeze solid. "I'm through with you, Day," I say, and move to leave. But not before I extend a hand to Lilah. "You don't have to do this. I can get you to—"

Day interrupts my bit of chivalry. "You want that old Greek jar back, Gold?"

I stop dead in my tracks.

"Yeah, that's right," he says. "Bet you didn't see that one coming, didya." He knows he's got me, his slitty eyes crinkling, his monkey's mouth grinning, enjoying his cheap victory. "Why don't you sit back down, have another drink while we talk business," he says. "Lilah, pour us both another scotch."

After Lilah, obedient again, pours the drinks, Day tells her, "And now scram."

I say, "She stays. She's got a right to hear what you've got her caught up in."

The grin folds up on Day's face. "She ain't none of your concern, Gold. Stay outta my family's business if you want to get your old clay jar back."

He's way ahead of me, at least for the moment. I nod at Lilah, letting my face pass the idea that sooner or later I'll get her out of here. I guess she got the message because she gives me a quick, careful smile before she walks out.

Another slug of scotch settles me enough to sit down again and talk business with the sleazy character whose whiskey I'm drinking. His round, ridiculous face only makes his self-satisfied grin look meaner. I resist the temptation to pull my gun and put holes in his teeth. "Okay, Day, that old clay jar is called a pyxis, and how do you know about it?"

"Yeah, right, a pyxis, I know," he says with a *tsk*. "Silly name. Anyway, you can thank Uncle Sam. Did you know your taxes paid for my, um, education?"

"Wouldn't be the first time the government had a thief on the payroll. Congress is full of 'em."

Day likes my little joke, raises his glass in toast. After downing the whiskey, he says, "It was the US Army that set me up. I was in the Quartermaster Corps during the war, made connections all over Europe, legit as well as black market. I got to know who has what and how to get it for the generals and all the other brass. And when the war was over, I stayed on a little while, kept those connections going. Could be that you and I know some of the same people, Gold." Day seems to like the idea.

I don't.

"Anyways," he says, "the boys over there keep me in the know about what's movin' around, know what I mean?" He says it with a conspirator's smile, like he shares a world with me. I don't smile back. "Of course, my racket's not as fancy as yours," he says, all smooth contrition. "Just a little side business of mine. There's still shortages of certain stuff in broken old Europe, stuff I can lay my hands on, or find people who can: a case of nylon stockings here, butter and sugar there, maybe some costume jewelry. Y'know, small stuff. But it keeps my ear to the ground, and when one of my guys heard about you moving this pyxis outta Greece, well, I knew I could get your attention, so I grabbed my moment, you might say."

"Yeah, you might say." It comes out dull and flat as stale crackers. I promise myself to make it my business to find out who did the talking in Greece, who ratted me out, but that comes later. Right now, I've got the annoying Mickey Schwartz Day to deal with. "So it was your guy who jumped me in Piraeus?"

"Sorta. One of my Europe guys owed me a favor, so I borrowed some of his muscle. But it was my local boys who jumped you on Fifth Avenue." There's that monkey's grin again.

"Uh-huh. And how'd you know where I was delivering?"

He gives me that in-the-know sneer again, says, "Loreale's not the only guy with sources, y'know."

I don't like the answer, but I have to live with it for now. But once I get the pyxis back, Mickey Day is going to spill his guts. I'll see to it. Meantime, all I say is, "Well, your thugs did a sloppy job, leaving a body behind. Did you know your boys killed the doorman?"

"Who cares?" He says it so offhand, and with such a casual shrug, it makes my bones freeze. "Look, Gold, I've got your pyxis. Got it where you'll never find it. So don't knock yourself out lookin' for it. But you can get it back real easy if you just set up a meeting with Sig Loreale. That's all there is to it."

I finish off my scotch in one gulp, hoping it'll loosen the knots Day's got me tangled up in, but all it seems to do is make those knots burn. "You're wrong, Day. That's never all there is to it with Loreale."

Without looking at me, like he's avoiding me, and looking at his hands instead as if admiring his manicure, he says, "Y'know, I think you're afraid of the guy, afraid of Sig Loreale."

"And if you were smart, you would be, too."

Now he gives me a tough guy shrug, or what he thinks a tough guy shrug should be. On him, it's just a shift of squishy flesh and bone. "Stop jerkin' me around," he says. "What'll it take to get you to set up a meeting?"

"Give me the pyxis back—now—and we'll talk about it."

"Talk now. Pyxis later. *After* I meet with Loreale."

"Not good enough, Day."

"Dammit, Gold! What'll it take? What'll it take for you to play ball? I didn't pay off a bunch of guys in Europe just for you to stonewall me."

An idea is creeping into my head, an idea I don't like and don't trust because I don't like and don't trust Mickey Day. But I learned a long time ago not to toss an opportunity out of my lap just because the opportunity has a coating of scum. And this opportunity may be too good to pass up. "There *is* something you can do for me, Day. You can use those European connections of yours to get me some information. I want to know about a boat. A flesh boat that sailed from Pier 8 on the East River docks in March of '48. I want to know who owned it, who skippered it, and where it went."

"March of '48? That's—what? Over three and a half years ago! It's history."

"That's the deal, Mickey. You get me information on that boat, I set up a meeting with Sig Loreale. Take it or leave it."

His pursed lips, tight with his annoyance at being outplayed, look even creepier than his monkey's grin. "Lemme see what I can do."

Chapter Five

It's nearly two a.m. when I'm finally free of Mickey's sleazy company and back out on the Coney Island streets. I'm tired, it's been a helluva night, and without my car I've got a subway ride of over an hour until I get home.

And then it sneaks up on me: I am home. Back home on the honky-tonk streets that formed me. These streets are different now, and not just because much of Coney is boarded up for the winter. The place is still sassy but a little sad, the way an aging Grande Dame is sad when her fancy clothes are not quite in style, clothes she cherishes that spark memories of youth and high times, a life now kicked aside by the more up-to-date new girl in her swirling skirts and tight sweaters who's moved in down the block. As I make my way along Schweickerts Walk, a distant bit of carny music and the buzz and jangle of game machines from an arcade on the boardwalk sound tinny and out of rhythm, a little desperate, like that Grande Dame in her determination to still dress up and have fun.

It annoys me to think that the stupid, gutter-crawling Mickey Day could be right about anything, but maybe he's right about what's going on in Coney Island. The idea of Sig Loreale trading muscle for real estate has a freakish feel to it, like putting a heavyweight boxer in a tutu and casting him in *Swan Lake*. But it wouldn't be the first time big money changes sides as it changes hands, and not the old kind of big money that had the greasy fingerprints of human greed and desire and corruption all over it, but a new corporate kind that has no fingerprints at all, and no human soul.

Well, Coney's troubles aren't my troubles anymore—I've got enough problems of my own to worry about—so at Surf Avenue, the dividing line between the amusement area and Coney's residential quarters, I cross the street on my way to the Stillwell Avenue train station.

But I don't head for the station. Some long buried instinct suddenly resurrects an equally long forgotten habit and turns me left instead, to West Sixteenth Street. I turn right on Sixteenth, keep walking past shuttered storefronts and car repair places, their owners and families asleep in cramped upstairs apartments smelling of crankcase oil. I cross Mermaid Avenue, keep walking along Sixteenth, past a remembered three-story walk-up apartment house at the corner, past boxy one- and two-story houses and bungalows that are as humble as when I left them, but now with television antennas sprouting like weeds on rooftops, and a few different sort of names on the mailboxes: what once was a neighborhood solid with Goldbergs, Scalisis, Kowalczyks, O'Reillys, even a handful of Smiths and Joneses, is now sprinkled here and there with Garcias and Hernandezes. But it's only the names that have changed, not the aspirations, the pride to keep the paint from peeling, keep the front stairs swept.

I stop at a small gray flat-fronted house with a well swept stoop of three concrete front stairs painted red. My mother would approve of the cleanliness, but not the red paint. She always insisted on white, making it easy to see if the steps needed scrubbing so my dungarees wouldn't get dirty when I sat on the stoop.

I'm not wearing dungarees now, and my coat will keep my trousers from getting dirty, so maybe my mother's spirit won't mind if I sit on the top step. I stay quiet, don't even light a cigarette, so the snap of my lighter won't wake the house's current inhabitants. I'd rather not go through the hassle of explaining my sentimental journey into trespassing.

It all comes rushing back: the noise of all us neighborhood kids on bicycles, playing stickball, running around, throwing pebbles at the few cars that came by—cheap boxy black Fords, mostly—interrupting our ownership of the street, our mothers and fathers hollering at us in immigrant English to come inside for dinner. The memories are sweet, and I can't help smiling, but these memories are incomplete. The rest of them are back among Coney's thrill rides and amusements, where the razzmatazz and the action seduced my young outlaw spirit. Back there is where the shadier amusement hucksters taught me how to be light fingered and shadowy, which helped me in my little racket of lifting trinkets and coins from people's unattended bags on the beach. I stowed the loot in a strongbox I kept buried under the boardwalk until I took it to the Lower East Side to fence, which was where Mom Sheinbaum grabbed hold of me.

I liked the trinkets. Some were pretty. It took me a while to learn—under Mom's tutelage—which trinkets could be turned into cash and which weren't worth my time. But it was their prettiness I liked, especially the ones with pictures enameled or painted on bracelets and necklaces, scenes of old stories or far away landscapes.

I remember one summer afternoon in Mom's dining room when I was about twelve or thirteen years old. My Coney Island loot was spread out on a velvet cloth on the table while she picked through the stuff and chose the pieces she wanted. I told her I liked the trinkets with pictures; they were prettier and she should pay me more for them. The way she looked at me, you'd think I'd told her I'd found a million dollars. Within seconds we were out the door to Second Avenue and into a cab, a square yellow-and-black box with a long front, whitewall tires, and driven by a guy in a yellow uniform and cap. It was my first time in a cab. My world suddenly got much bigger, got cleaner and classier, neighborhood by passing neighborhood, as we rode uptown. Except for Times Square, none of Manhattan's midtown streets were as wild as Coney Island, but every crisply colorful awning along Fifth Avenue hinted at the fancy life lived on the other side of those apartment and mansion windows, a high-class life I strained to see. I don't think I blinked the entire ride to our destination, to the biggest place I ever saw: the Metropolitan Museum of Art. It was even bigger than the Thunderbolt roller coaster. Bigger than the grand entrance to Luna Park. It looked like a royal palace to me.

It still does.

Inside, Mom traipsed me all around the place, which I was now absolutely sure was a palace, where lords and ladies in colorful silks and satins and jewels stared out from carved golden frames on the walls. On that day and in that place, I began my love affair with art, and with the money it commands. I made up my mind to learn all I could about both.

My own mom and pop—toiling away in their tiny second-hand bookstall on Mermaid Avenue, and then home, exhausted, in this little claptrap house behind me—never knew any of it, not even on the days they each died, which was just as well. They had a tough enough time tolerating my tomboy activities, at least the ones I let them see, like my insistence on wearing dungarees instead of dresses, or playing stickball with the boys. But the ones I didn't let them see would sure as hell have made my mother cry, and it would rip me up to hear her cry, the way it's starting to rip me up now, in my imaginings…

Except it's not in my imaginings. The sound of a woman crying is in the air. It comes at me from my right, about halfway down the block. I can just barely see her, a dark, bulky shape in the night, leaning against a car at the curb.

The woman's misery gets me up from my old stoop. Little by little, as I walk along the street, I see more of her, see her bundled up in a heavy coat, her hands to her face and leaning against a battered green '49 Chevy coupe. By the time I reach her, her crying has choked back to a whimper, the painful kind that claws the throat.

With her hands to her face, she hasn't seen me, and when I say, "You need any help?" her hands drop and she jolts out of her sobs, terrified. And then the terror dissipates. Her thick face, wet with tears, relaxes. Her eyes crinkle to get a better look at me in the meager light. "Cantor?" she says, her voice raspy with tears, cigarettes, and age. "Cantor Gold?"

I know that voice, and that face, older now, heavier than when I last saw her, when I'd said good-bye to her before I left Coney Island for good. She'd grabbed my arm that day and wouldn't let me go until she'd given me a tarot reading, a real one—she was a true believer from a family of practitioners stretching back centuries, or so she said—and at no charge, unlike the fortune-telling racket she ran for the marks in her stall near the giant Wonder Wheel ride on Jones Walk.

But what was she doing here on Sixteenth Street instead of in the rooms she shared with her husband above the fortune-telling stall? "Madame Mona?" I say. "Mona Carlotti?" I give her my pocket handkerchief to wipe her tears.

Wiping her eyes and cheeks, she strains to clear her throat of her sobs, then says, "What the hell you doin' here, Cantor, after all these years? And at this hour? Why you in the neighborhood in the middle of the night?"

"There's someone I had to speak to. But never mind that. What's wrong? Why are you out here crying?"

The question brings her sobs back, brings the handkerchief back to her eyes. "It's Miss Theresa. She's dying. She's in pain. I couldn't take watchin' her suffer no more, so I came outside for some air."

"I don't remember Miss Theresa. Is she a relative?"

"Miss Theresa's my dog. She's old. She don't hear good no more. She was outside tonight, she loves being outside, but she didn't hear…she didn't hear the car coming and didn't get outta the way." A miserable moan strangles in Mona's throat. "Oh, why did I come to live on this hard-hearted street? Didn't nobody see? Nobody help? Why did I leave Jones Walk? There's no cars on Jones Walk!" There's more than sadness in her plea; there's also bitterness at the loss of times past.

"So why did you leave, Mona?"

Her sigh is so heavy and so long I'm afraid she'll completely empty herself of breath. "It was time to pack up, Cantor. My husband Vito was gone. Heart attack got him. And new thugs with their hands out tryin' to get their share of the stalls and games. And then there's them real estate people snoopin' around, eyein' everything like it's just in their way. Ain't no fun in it no more. So I got out, I bought this place when old Mrs. Mangione died. You remember Rose Mangione? Her son sold it to me cheap."

I'm not interested in any more trips down memory lane tonight, so I just say, "New thugs?" though I can't imagine any new thugs moving in on Loreale, especially if Mickey's right and Loreale's cleaning up his rackets with real estate.

Drying more tears, her voice steadier now, Mona says, "You remember Solly Schwartz? Yeah, well, that scum son of his, calls himself Mickey Day, as if that's some kind of name. He's been trying to muscle in."

"I doubt Sig Loreale will let him get away with it."

"Loreale? The invisible man. Things used to run good when Loreale lived around here. Sure, we paid him plenty. You hadda give him a heavy skim or you suffered for it. But Sig kept things runnin' good, no trouble from outsiders or cops."

"Isn't that still the case? I mean, his outfit still runs things."

"Sure, but the games are a side issue for him now. He's even closed up some of the notch joints, if they're sittin' on valuable real estate. But now…" This last rides on the kind of shrug people give when life moves on without them, and they don't give a damn anymore about old friends or remembered places.

No wonder Mickey Day set up a joint of his own, and why Sig lets him operate—for now—or at least until Sig has other plans for Schweickerts Walk. "Mona, what can you tell me about Mickey?"

"Why you want to know about that crumb for? It'll only bring you trouble. Like father, like son, I say. Only he's even lousier than his father, and that's sayin' something."

"Listen, Mickey stole something of mine," I say. "Something I want back. The more information I have on the guy, the better. Maybe I can get some leverage."

Shifting her bulk away from the Chevy she'd been leaning against, Mona says, "Okay, Cantor, but let's go inside. I want to sit with Miss Theresa the rest of the night before I take her to the veterinary doctor in the morning. I guess he'll…" She's sobbing again, the words stuck in her throat. "I guess he'll put Miss Theresa to sleep. Well, okay, she'll be at peace. And anyways, I'll be able to contact her on the other side." I guess Madame Mona is still a true believer.

The hinges on the screen door to her bungalow could use an oiling, the squeak sending an eerie sound along the block. But inside, Mona's parlor is tidy and comfortable, with floral upholstery on a sofa and two big chairs. There's a television set in the corner, one of those consoles in a mahogany cabinet. I guess the fortune-telling racket was good to Mona, and I notice she keeps a remnant of that racket, a boxed deck of tarot cards next to a vase of flowers on the coffee table. But the little room, lit only by the soft amber light of a lamp next to the couch, is also the site of a death watch: on a bloodstained pink blanket on a pillow on the couch is little Miss Theresa, her body nearly crushed, her eyes closed, barely breathing, softly whimpering.

Mona takes off her coat and sits down next to the dog, pets her, but even that loving touch is too painful, and the pup's soft whimper cracks into a weak, strangled yelp, the more wretched for being barely audible. Mona takes her hand away, brings it to her eyes. She's crying again. When she lowers her head, her stringy black hair slides along her hands like spiders' threads. "I wish God would take her and end her suffering."

As tenderly as I can, I say, "Have you considered maybe helping her along?"

"I can't, I just can't bring myself to—to do it. And besides, what would I do? Strangle her? I don't think my hands even have the strength."

I need a drink if I'm going to get through this miserable scenario and coax Mona's attention from her suffering pup to talk to me about Mickey Day. "Mona, do you have any whiskey in the house?"

"There's wine in the kitchen. Help yourself."

After Mickey's mediocre scotch, I doubt the grape would mix well in my belly. "Thanks, but I'll pass." Instead, I light a smoke and sit down in one of the chairs opposite the couch. I start to say, "Okay, tell me what you know about—"

But Mona cuts me off. "Cantor, maybe you can do it? Maybe you can…maybe you can help Miss Theresa?"

"*Me?* Mona, I—look, I don't like killing. Even in my line of work, I try to avoid it."

"But it would not be a real killing! It would be *una benedizione*, a blessing. Please, Cantor. I remember that you always had a soul." She looks from me to Miss Theresa, desperate to pet her, but can't subject the miserable pup to even a light touch of pain.

Somewhere between numbness and pity, I more or less mumble, "Do you have a pillow you're willing to get rid of?"

"What? You're going to smother her? But that would take too long! It's cruel."

"I'm not going to smother her."

"You promise?"

"I promise."

"Okay." She gets up from the couch and leaves the parlor. My hand shakes when I take a deep drag on my smoke.

Mona's back soon, holding a limp bed pillow with no pillowcase, its striped ticking threadbare and stained. "Here, my Vito don't need this no more."

My hand's still shaking when I stick my cigarette between my teeth, take the pillow, and fold the old thing over on itself to give it more bulk. "Say your good-byes, Mona."

She stands over Miss Theresa, murmurs in Italian, "*Dormire ora, Signorina Theresa*," then crosses herself, eyes closed, and whispers, "*Nel nome del padre, e del figlio, e dello spirito santo.*" I place the folded pillow over Miss Theresa's head, take out my gun, put the barrel against the pillow to muffle the noise—the last thing I need is some nosy neighbor calling the cops at the sound of a gunshot—and pull the trigger.

Mona opens her eyes. "Bless you, Cantor. I'll get a shovel."

Digging the small grave in the bungalow's tiny backyard helps settle my shakes. Mona places Miss Theresa in the grave, settling her on the pillow and blanket. "They were her last comforts," she says. She crosses herself again, then nods at me, a signal to toss the dirt back into the grave.

That's two deaths in my lap tonight: the doorman at Miranda van Zell's place, and Miss Theresa. Except for my tryst between the sheets with Lilah, the night is not going well.

Back inside the bungalow, I nearly throw myself down in the chair, wishing I had a scotch, seriously contemplating Mona's wine, but my tightening stomach talks me out of it.

Mona sits on the couch, drying a few tears with my now balled-up handkerchief, but at peace for the first time since I found her crying in the street. "Thank you, Cantor. The Lord just made a spot for you in heaven."

"Tell him to keep it on ice. I'm in no hurry."

She actually laughs a little at that. It's good to see her laugh. "Ooo, be careful talking about God like that, you *il briccone*,

ANN APTAKER

you—what is it?—ah, rascal! So okay, what do you want to know about Mickey Day?"

"Well, how deep is he connected to whatever's happening in Coney? To hear him tell it, he knows who's who and what's what."

"He's a braggart with a big mouth," she says with a grunt that's part laugh and part Bronx cheer. "Someday that big mouth is gonna get him into real trouble."

"How you figure it?"

"He may be a chiseler, but he's still Solly Schwartz's son, which means he still has loyal people. All them sons and daughters of Solly's old gang, people worked over by Loreale when he muscled in, well, some of 'em might jump at the chance to help Mickey do *vendetta*. And that's where Mickey's big mouth is gonna get him into trouble. He's been tellin' everyone how he wants to take Coney back from Loreale and the real estate people. Sooner or later—"

"Loreale will shut him up." If Loreale wants to knock off Mickey, I hope it's later rather than sooner, not until Mickey gives me back my Dancing Goddesses pot, *and* does his bit to get me information about the flesh slavers who stole Sophie. After that, it's between him and Loreale. They can knock each other off, for all I care. "What about Mickey's sister, Lilah? She seems like she's an okay bill of goods."

Mona looks me up and down, at my suit under my open coat. A sly little smile curls at the corners of her mouth. "Oh, so you've met the pretty one," she says. "You like her?"

"Like I said, she seems okay." I'm not about to tell tales of the sexual fantasia Lilah and I performed in my bed.

But by the cagey glint in Mona's eyes, it's obvious she's wise to me and Lilah, if not in fact, at least in assumption. Yeah, Mona Carlotti is vintage Coney, all right: adventurers of all kinds welcome, no questions asked. The glint in her eyes fades, though, and the sly smile disappears. "If you like her, Cantor, you'll get her away from her brother. He's no good, treats her lousy."

I give Mona a nod, but that's all. My plans for Lilah, if I even have any plans, are better kept to myself for now. I just get up, say, "Okay, Mona, I've got a long ride back to the city. I'd better get going."

"Wait. Not yet. If you're dealing with Mickey Day, then you're lookin' at somethin' rough and dangerous. You maybe oughta know what's coming." She takes the deck of tarot cards from their box. "Sit down, Cantor. I'll give you a reading."

I'm not a believer, but after Mona's gratitude for ending Miss Theresa's suffering, and her obvious concern for my well-being, I'm not about to insult her by turning down the only kind of help she knows how to give. I sit down.

She moves the vase of flowers and the ashtray to the end of the coffee table, making space for the tarot spread.

Mona's hands, thick and blunt, move with practiced grace as she expertly shuffles the cards. She turns one over, says with slow, quiet authority, "Ah, yes, the Queen of Wands. This is for you, Cantor. The card speaks truth: you are seeking answers, and the Queen is a seeker. See? She holds a sunflower, which always turns its face to the sun. It tries to find the light. You are trying to find the light, Cantor."

I have to admit, there's definitely something uncanny about asking a guy named Day to find out information about the light of my life, my Sophie, Sophie de la Luna y Sol, Sophie of the Moon and the Sun.

I'm not about to go down that road, though. Life and I have an understanding: no fairy tales, no guy with a beard on a throne in the clouds, no guardian angels. They probably wouldn't give me a break, anyway.

But I'm not about to stop Mona's routine with the cards. She needs to do this. She needs to make sense of life and death the only way she knows how.

She lays down another card, places it at a right angle on top of the Queen, making a cross. "The Tower," she says. "A card of danger."

Considering everything that's happened tonight, no surprise there, with or without any woo-woo power.

Mona says, "But see the lightning bolt in the sky? Lightning is always sudden. We never know where it will flash in the sky, or when it will strike, or where it will hit the ground. The lightning is like the danger you will face, Cantor. Sudden, and unexpected."

I guess you could say I never expected to be robbed outside Miranda van Zell's apartment building, or get a doorman murdered.

Mona's still fingering the Tower card. "And look. Look at the people falling from the burning Tower. They were arrogant, building their Tower into the sky, and now they are doomed. You cannot escape fate, Cantor. You cannot outthink it." She looks straight at me, making sure I get her meaning, then looks down at the cards again. "These two cards, the Queen and the Tower, are your present, and they speak of danger. But a Queen is powerful and always decisive, as you must be, Cantor. So now let's see what awaits you."

She deals out four more cards, placing one above the crossed center, one below, and one each to the right and left.

Mona places a finger on the left-hand card, a scene of some blindfolded dame bound in ropes and standing in front of what looks like a fence made of swords. "Here is your past, Cantor, the Eight of Swords. This past may be long ago, or maybe more recent, but it says you are caught in falsehoods. You must cut those ropes of falseness that bind you, Cantor, if you want to find the truth you're looking for."

Mona moves her finger to the card below, a picture of a moon in a night sky, with a dog and a wolf howling on the ground. "Darkness and deceit are the root of the danger you face, Cantor. It is here, in the Moon's card. Sure, okay, there is a path ahead between these two towers here, but that path is not clear in the moonlight. The howling dog, usually so faithful—" She chokes up a little, talking about the dog so soon after the loss of her own faithful companion. But she gathers herself, wipes her eyes, and struggles to keep going. "The dog can't find the way, but lucky for you, neither can the howling wolf, the trickster who wants to lead you astray. So it is up to you to find your own way in the darkness."

I'm tempted to tell Mona to hurry it up. I'm tired, I haven't had any rest since I got back from Athens, and the cards aren't telling me anything I don't already know; it's always been up to me to find my way through my dark life. But Mona's concern for me is too real and too tender to brush aside. So I just take a deep breath to catch a second wind and listen as she reads the cards. I wish I had that scotch, though.

She puts a finger to the card above, a scene of someone sitting up in bed, hands on their face and swords across the wall behind. "The Nine of Swords shows a goal for you. The number nine means the end of a cycle. Something is changing. You will awake from a nightmare, but you will still be haunted by that nightmare, haunted by questions from your past, your present, and about what waits for you in your future."

With a deep and solemn breath, Mona puts her finger on the final card, on the right, a picture of someone in a red cape walking along a rocky road, with a bunch of wine goblets stacked behind. "Your future," she says. "The Eight of Cups. Another card of the moon and the night. You have many cards of night, Cantor. Your path will take you through much darkness. There will be challenges from inside yourself that you will need to conquer. And see? Those eight cups are your emotions. They are neatly arranged, but look, you are walking away. You must walk away to find your direction along this dangerous road if you want to find the answers you seek. And you *will* find them Cantor, but they will come with a cost. A terrible cost."

❖

It feels good to be back at Surf Avenue and finally heading for the Stillwell Avenue station. I've had all the fortune-telling and Coney Island nostalgia I can take for one night. All I want now is to get to the station, board the train, and grab a little shut-eye during the long ride home.

But a scream, shrill and raw, cuts through the night. The screamer screams again, and again, her terror barreling out from Schweickerts Walk.

I can't ignore it. I can't ignore the possibility that it's Lilah.

If Mickey's hurting her, if he's pushing her around…

I run back along Schweickerts, the screams getting louder the nearer I get to the tattoo parlor. I push my way through the small crowd that's gathered outside, shout "Lilah!" when I burst in.

The ink artist who'd been dozing in his chair is now dead in the chair, his throat cut, his blood splattered on the drawings on the walls. The guy must've been sleeping when it happened. Never saw it coming.

I run into the back room where I'd talked with Mickey Day. Lilah's standing in the room, tears and mascara running down her face. Mickey is draped facedown over the coffee table, blood soaking his white shirt, a knife in his back.

Chapter Six

L ilah stands stone still over her dead brother. Even her face muscles barely move with her sobs. Her mascara-smeared tears drip onto her white coat, seeping into the cashmere.

"Lilah?" The sound of my voice shocks her into the here and now. Her sobs catch in her throat, her eyes widen as she turns to me. "Lilah, what happened?"

But she's not looking at me, she's looking over my shoulder. I turn around and see a few of the bystanders from outside now inside the room.

One guy, a skinny, grizzled old coot in a green lumber jacket and brown chinos, and who looks like a weak breeze could blow him over, says, "Ain't you—yeah, ain't you Cantor Gold?"

"Who's asking?"

"Eddie Janko. Don't you remember me? I run th—"

"Sure, I remember you. You ran a spook-house ride down the block."

"Still do, in summertime," which in Eddie's thick Brooklyn-ese comes out *suhmmuh-dime*. "Off-season, I run the Good Time Arcade up there on the boardwalk while the owner's in Florida. I was makin' change for a mark losing his shirt to a pokerino machine when I heard the screams, so I came runnin'."

I remember Eddie as a right guy, so I say, "Do me a favor, get everybody outta here, then come back in. I could use your help."

"Sure. You'd better get Lilah outta here, too, if you catch my drift."

I catch it all right, give Eddie a nod to let him know. As he hustles the rubberneckers out the tattoo parlor, I say, "Make sure they understand they were never here. They never heard any screaming." Eddie and I both know the Coney old-timers won't talk when the cops come around, and any new people wouldn't know what to talk about, anyway.

I'm alone with Lilah. Softly, carefully, I say, "What happened?"

She practically collapses against me, buries her head in my neck. "I—I found them, Mickey and Gus…"

"Gus is the ink man?"

She nods her head. "I went out after you left," she says, choking on it. "I took a walk on the beach. I had to get away from Mickey for a while, away from all his—" But she can't finish. She can barely stand up. I take hold of her, let her support herself against me.

Eddie walks back in on us, gives us a glaring eye but says nothing about Lilah draped all over me. He says only, "You really gotta get her away from here, Cantor."

"Yeah. We're going," I say. "Look, I heard Lilah's screams all the way to Surf Avenue, so it's a good bet someone's called the cops by now. When the Law comes around, tell the cops—"

"I know what to tell 'em. That I heard screams, came down from the boardwalk, and found Gus and Mickey dead."

"Good. And if they ask about Lilah—"

"Never saw her. Nobody here but them stiffs."

I give Eddie twenty bucks and hustle Lilah out of the tattoo joint.

❖

By the time we're back at Mona's door, Lilah's not crying anymore. Her face is blank, numb.

Can't blame her. Mickey Schwartz—oh, yeah, Mickey Day—might've been a heel, treated his sister like chattel, but he was family, her last link to her once powerful Coney Island family, and now he's dead. Lilah's life has been bookended by murder—first her father, now her brother, with her mother passed on somewhere in between. Poor kid's alone.

Mona's house is dark, she must be asleep. Even the creaking hinges on the screen door don't wake her. It takes several rings of the doorbell for a light to come on and for Mona to finally call through the door, "Who's there?"

"It's me, Mona. It's Cantor."

She opens the door. She's wrapped in a robe, but silhouetted in the lamplight from the parlor, I can't really see her shadowed face. She says, "What's goin' on, Cantor, that you show up after three o'clock in the morn—?" Then, "Lilah? Lilah Day?"

Lilah says, "Hello, Mona," a little less numb now.

"Let us in," I say. "I need to get Lilah off the street."

With a tilt of her head, her stringy hair flopping, Mona signals us to follow her inside.

When we're in the parlor, I try to help Lilah off with her coat but she resists, wraps it tighter around her, says, "No, please, I'm cold." It's warm in Mona's living room, I take my own coat and cap off, but I guess Lilah's got the chill of shock. Her face is pale as milk, whiter than her cashmere coat, now smudged with mascara even at the sleeves, which she must've used to wipe her tears. The fancy coat's ruined.

I settle Lilah on the couch and ask Mona, "Still have that wine? Lilah could use some."

"Sure. One for you, too, Cantor?" I shake my head. Mona heads for the kitchen.

I take out my pack of smokes, offer a cigarette to Lilah. She takes it, her hand shaking as she brings it to her lips. I take one for myself, light hers then mine. Lilah's deep pull on the smoke settles her a little. She leans back on the couch.

I sit down next to her, realize I'm sitting in the spot where Miss Theresa lay crushed and dying a little more than an hour ago. It occurs to me that the same time I was digging the pup's grave might've been when someone slashed Gus-the-ink-artist's throat and stuck a knife in Mickey's back. How much death is going to cling to me tonight?

I squelch that morbid thought, and try to ignore the tarot cards on the coffee table, the deck back in their box, Mona's dark fairy tale about my future shuffled away.

Better to keep focused on the hard reality of the night's business. "Lilah, Mickey stole something from me, a small clay jar. It's called a pyxis, and I have to get it back. I risked my neck bringing it to New York for someone who's paying a lot of money, so I'm not about to just let it disappear. You have any idea where Mickey might've stashed it?"

She shakes her head, slowly, her awareness still dull.

"Think," I say. "He said it was in a place I'd never find it, but you knew Mickey better than anyone, knew his habits—"

There's a sudden snap in her, the dullness nearly gone, pushed to her edges, letting a bright, hard hurt shine through. "I knew his habits, all right," she says, her voice cold, sharp. "I was on the business end of those habits." The next drag of her smoke is long and deep, as if she's trying to obliterate memories of Mickey's pawing *habits*, but she can't. Her body, cringing, remembers.

Pimping his sister is suddenly only one of my reasons for hating Mickey. Too bad his death is an inconvenience to my business, otherwise I'd spit on his grave, or maybe dance on it.

Mona walks back into the living room with a bottle of red wine and two glasses. She pours a glass for herself and one for Lilah, who ignores it, lost in that protective numbness again.

I take the glass, say, "Here, drink this. It'll help," and hold the glass to Lilah's lips.

That supple mouth, which only hours ago roamed my body with confidence, now just reluctantly obeys and takes a sip of the wine.

Mona says, "What's going on, Cantor? I don't see you for twenty years and suddenly you're on my doorstep two times in one night. And why is Lilah here? Poor thing looks like she's about to fall over."

"There's trouble at the tattoo parlor," I say. "She can't be there."

"What kinda trouble?"

But it's Lilah who answers. "Murder," she says, her voice a monotone, dark and wispy as a shadow. "Bloody murder."

Mona looks as if every ghost she's ever conjured has just shown up, uninvited, crowding her parlor. "Mother of God... Mickey, he's dead?"

I nod.

"And that other guy, the tattoo guy? What's his name?"

Lilah mutters, "Gus."

I say, "Yeah, him, too."

Mona, serious as rosary beads, sits herself on the couch, puts an arm around Lilah. "You poor child," she says. Lilah doesn't resist, doesn't even react when Mona runs a hand through Lilah's hair, combing the short blond strands as if preparing her for a viewing.

I say, "Keep her here tonight, Mona, okay? She's in no shape to face the cops. Listen, you know Eddie Janko?"

"Yeah, sure."

"Good. I'll have him come around in the morning and take Lilah back to the tattoo shop before the cops get there."

"No, it's okay," Mona says. "I will take her."

"Uh-uh, I'd rather Eddie handled it."

I guess I insulted Mona's Coney Island pride, because she stiffens, gets a little huffy that I brushed her aside in favor of Eddie. "And what about you, Cantor?" she says. "Remember what the cards told you?"

"Yeah, yeah," I say, more dismissive than polite, while I put my coat and cap on.

Mona's voice follows me to the door. "There's danger in your path, Cantor, and darkness, and a terrible cost. Remember."

❖

In a phone booth on Stillwell Avenue, I find the number, drop my dime in the slot, dial, and get Eddie on the line. He's annoyed that I got him out of the bed he'd just gotten into. "It's Cantor, Eddie. Listen, I've got Lilah stashed at Mona Carlotti's. Know her place?"

"Yeah. Over on Sixteenth."

"Go over there in the morning and walk Lilah back to the tattoo shop before the cops get there. Okay?"

"Sure," he says, sounding like he's just been chosen to escort the prettiest bathing beauty on the boardwalk. "Glad to."

"G'night, Eddie," I say, and hang up.

My legs feel like rubber, my knees cranky, and all of me is exhausted as I climb the stairs to the Brighton Line platform at the Stillwell Avenue station. Lucky me, there's a train waiting to pull out, and I make it into the last car just as the doors close. I have no trouble finding a seat: at nearly four a.m., I'm all alone in the car.

I don't take the subway very often anymore, not since I started earning the kind of dough that allows me to buy a new car whenever I want—like the '52 Buick I picked up before I left for Athens—but the schoolroom-green walls of the train and the white enameled standees' straps and poles greet me like old friends wondering where the hell I've been. I park myself in a corner seat whose woven cane isn't too badly shredded. I've heard otherwise prim sweeties curse like a sailor when they sit down in the subway after a tough day at the office only to have a broken strand of cane tear their nylon stockings.

When I was a kid, I used to enjoy the ride on these elevated tracks, keeping my face pressed to the window, watching low-slung Brooklyn roll by, with high-rise Manhattan looming in the distance. But tonight—actually, this dead dark predawn morning—I'm too bushed to care about the scenic tour. It's not long before my head lolls…and I'm asleep.

CHAPTER SEVEN

A shower at my apartment and a change of clothes into a fresh shirt and a favorite deep green silk suit nearly bring me back to life. The strong black coffee poured by Doris at Pete's luncheonette finishes the job. Pete's is my favorite cheap eats joint, a sliver of a spot with a green-and-black checkerboard linoleum floor scuffed by the shuffle of actors, musicians, songwriters, whores, hustlers, gamblers, and gangsters who live in my neighborhood. We come for the good food, strong coffee, and the easygoing attitude among ourselves that stops short of asking the wrong sort of questions. Out front, the busted neon sign reading PE E'S instead of PETE'S keeps the tourists away, which is fine by everyone—Pete, his help, and the regulars— because Mom and Pop Cornstalk order cheap, tip cheap, and linger too long.

After a mug of hot black brew and a warm bagel with cream cheese and lox, my brain's restored and I can finally think, though it ain't easy. It's just a little after seven and the only sleep I've had was my lurching shut-eye on the subway, and before that on a damp, lumpy mattress on a tramp freighter from Athens. Things have only gone downhill since: my goods stolen, three murders, and oh, yeah, a dead dog.

And then there's Rosie, tossing me over for her regular fare, though that loss was nicely soothed by Lilah's sexual ministrations.

Thinking about Lilah leads me to think about the hell she must be going through. Mickey might've treated her like dirt, but he was family. Seeing her brother in a pool of blood with a knife in his back is a horror that will linger in her soul for a long time, maybe forever.

Thinking about Mickey with a knife in his back leads me to think again about what a louse he was, pimping his sister, pawing her for his own pleasure, stealing from me, which leads me to think about the places he might've stashed the pyxis—a safe deposit box? in a sandpit under the boardwalk? under a mattress in his tattoo parlor/brothel?—but I come up empty. He said it's in a place I'd never find, and I believe him. I'll need help puzzling it out.

But all those thoughts can't silence the other persistent whispers and visions inside my head: memories. Memories of the Coney Island life that made me, those snappy times of my naughty childhood and hooligan teens; scary times when I thought the Law or a gangster's gun would get me; heartbreaking times when some girl would slap my face under the boardwalk because I wasn't allowed the same koochie-koo privileges the boys had. Sure, I've come out on top since those days, I live and love the way I want, run a classier racket than cheap trinkets snatched on the beach, but being back to Coney hit me with a truth I'd been running from for years: the honky-tonk is still with me, inside me, *is* me, the shady operator in colorful clothes.

I'm brought back to the here and now by the rattle of nearby dishes being cleared by Doris. Always attentive to the needs of her customers, Doris strolls in my direction while she wipes the marble counter with a rag in one hand and holds a pot of coffee in the other. Her pink uniform is still clean and crisp. By afternoon it'll be wilted with sweat and spotted with mustard. But her permed salt-and-pepper hair will stay coiled around her thin face all day, and her friendly brown eyes and toothy smile will retain their wisdom and warmth, though her red lipstick is already seeping into the age lines around her mouth. "Can I hotten your cup, Cantor?" Even her cigarette-croak voice is warm and wise, like the voice of your favorite aunt who thinks you're swell but your parents are boring. "You look like you could use another jolt," she says. "Tell you the truth, you look like you could use a lotta jolts, maybe even spiked with a hooch pick-me-up."

I nod that she should pour the coffee, and as the black gold swirls in my mug, I say, "You remember that book several years ago, *You Can't Go Home Again*?"

"Can't say I heard of it, but I heard a lotta people say that line: you can't go home again. Always wondered why they think that. Of course you can go home again. Hell, I go home every night to the same old walls and same old husband!" Doris's merry chuckle could pep up the sorriest soul, but as the chuckle fades, her brown eyes narrow, probing me gently. "You been tryin' to go home, Cantor?"

"Wasn't planning on it. Anyway, it turns out actually *going* home's got nothing to do with it. Home caught up with me."

"Too many ghosts, I guess."

That gives me the first laugh I've had since I got back from Greece. It's not a big laugh, just a sharp blurt that finally shreds my unwanted nostalgia. "Yeah, ghosts! And new ones all the time, even canine ones, and they seem to follow me around. So keep your husband and your household pets locked away, Doris, if the Grim Reaper of Coney Island ever shows up at your door."

She puts the coffeepot down, leans on the counter, and looks at me like she can't make up her mind if she wants to slap sense into me or pat my head and say *there, there*. Finally, with a shrug, she says, "Listen, you ain't no Grim Reaper. I ain't scared of you, Cantor Gold, despite your peculiar—um—y'know, romantic…tastes."

"And I thought you put up with me just because I'm a big tipper."

"Okay, yeah, there's that. But also because you talk to this old hash slinger like I'm a person. Figure I owe you the same. So what's troublin' you?"

I wouldn't mind that hooch pick-me-up Doris mentioned, even at this early hour, but a draw on the strong coffee is all I've got. I let it warm my insides, further loosen my tongue, and as I put the mug back down on the counter, I say, "Since last night, even after all my careful plans, everything that *can* go wrong went wrong."

Doris treats that with a canny smile. "That's just God havin' a laugh."

"Didn't know you believe in God, Doris."

She pours herself a mug of coffee while she considers the idea. After a sip of the brew, she says, "Don't know that I do, don't know that I don't. You?"

"Count me out."

"I guess you need some sorta proof, huh? Maybe a sign from above?"

"Just a fair shake down here would be helpful."

Mom Sheinbaum's not crazy about seeing me at her door, but she lets me in anyway and leads me into her dining room, where she finishes a cup of tea and a bowl of fruit. The clashing floral patterns of the fruit bowl, teacup, and her housedress could give a person a headache. After a last swallow of tea, she says, "If you got useful information, have a seat, Cantor. If not, you're just spoiling my breakfast, and I got enough stomach trouble already." She punctuates this with a belch, as if to prove her point, and follows the belch with a woeful, "Oy."

I take off my coat and cap, say, "I should be the one asking for useful information," and sit down at the dining table, light a smoke. "After all, my client's paying for it."

"True," Mom says. "But I got nothin' new yet. I asked around, but I'll get you something. I got people all over the place, they'll dig good."

"Don't worry about it. There's been a change. Ever hear of Mickey Day?"

She takes a minute to think about it, then she flicks her hand as if shooing a fly. "A *kleyn shpiler*, y'know, a small player. Operates out in your old neck of the woods. Used to be Mickey Sch—"

"Schwartz. Yeah, I know. Solly Schwartz's kid."

"Yeh, that's him," Mom says, wrinkling her nose as if a bad smell seeped into the room. "Sig tossed Solly and his gang outta Coney Island like old rags. But you were just a little kid back then. What's Solly Schwartz's boy got to do with you?"

"Mickey's dead. Took a knife in the back."

All that gets is a light shrug, her bulky body as unyielding as a steel safe, allowing no pity for the murdered dead, not even the customary underworld distaste for the sneaky method of murder. "Not surprised," she says. "A schlepper like him invites trouble. So what's your interest?"

"Seems Mickey wasn't such a small player after all. He's the guy who arranged the attempt on the pyxis at the Piraeus docks and the successful grab for it last night. It was Mickey's thugs who stole the goods and killed the doorman." I slide Mom's empty fruit bowl over to me, use it as an ashtray.

Her button eyes narrow into dark points of disgust. "Don't be a savage," she says, sneering.

Scolded into obedience, I get up from the table, get an ashtray from the sideboard, but while I'm there I open the liquor cabinet and pour myself a Chivas, that hooch pick-me-up I've needed since Doris poured me coffee. After a night of no sleep, and murder coming at me from all sides, whiskey is one of the fortifiers I'll need to get me through the day. Another is the .38 under my arm.

Mom says, "It's not even eight in the morning and you're drinking, Cantor? Go ahead, kill yourself."

"Since when do you care?"

That doesn't get an answer, not even a look in my direction, just a deep breath over her pursed lips.

I take my drink, my smoke, and the ashtray back to the table but I don't sit down. A pull on the scotch keeps my blood pumping while I wait for Mom to decide to talk to me again.

It doesn't take long, though she still isn't looking at me. "So this Schwartz kid stole your pixie—"

"Pyxis."

"Yeh, pyxis, and now he's dead, and you can't find your goods. Is that it?"

"That's it. I came here figuring maybe you've heard things about his operation, maybe get a line on where he's stashed it. Don't forget, Miranda van Zell's ten grand is still on your table."

The mention of money warms up Mom's attitude. "I'll see what I can find out."

"And there's one other thing. I think it might've been Sig who ordered the hit on Mickey."

Mom's warming cooperation cools again, but there's no real ice behind it, just a chill in her eyes, a stiffening of her posture, which surprises me. Mom Sheinbaum is the only person I know who isn't afraid of Sig Loreale, because Mom is the only person Sig indulges, even defers to. For all his hard ways, Sig is an old-fashioned guy who built his empire in an old-fashioned world, where even gangsters deferred to their mothers. Mom's not Sig's mother, but she's underworld royalty, part of the old-time criminal legacy he's part of, and she's the mother of his beloved dead fiancée, Opal.

So why the sudden chill in Mom at the idea that Sig might have ordered a murder, one of dozens he's ordered—or committed—over the years?

"If that's true," Mom says, "if Sig is in back of it, he'll—" She waves her hand as if dismissing an irritating thought that's spoiling her morning. "He'll get rid of any buttinsky who pokes around in his business. Even you, mommaleh. It won't matter how far back you two go. It won't matter that you and your trinket racket amused him when you were a little pisher under the boardwalk. It won't matter how many paintings and fancy tchotchkes you've gotten for him since those days. Sig will kill you."

If Sig's going to kill me, if he orders one of his assassins to blow my head off, I hope it's not in my new car. She's a beauty, the latest Buick Roadmaster model, her maroon curves shapely as a lover's thighs, her cream convertible top sexy as a blonde in the sun, her cream leather interior soft as a woman's lap, and her customized maroon, cream, and chrome dash classy as a yacht's pilothouse. I haven't had much chance to drive her since I picked her up before I left for Greece, so getting blood and brains all over the pretty interior before she's even had her first oil change would be a cryin' shame.

But it's a chance I have to take if I want to figure Sig's angle in Mickey's killing; that is, if Sig has any angle at all. He certainly had motive. Mickey's shenanigans in Coney Island might've been getting in the way of Sig's real estate plans, and if Sig Loreale has plans, he sees them through, smoothly if he can, brutally if he has to. Interlopers and pests like Mickey Schwartz Day are efficiently removed.

I find a parking spot in front of Sig's building on Fortieth Street, a classy black brick Art Deco office tower crowned with Gothic-style gilt work, and where Sig maintains a penthouse residence. The building is across the street from Bryant Park and the main branch of the New York Public Library, the famous one with the two lions out front facing Fifth Avenue. I'm sure Sig's enjoyed a stroll through the park. Not sure he's ever been in the library.

Inside his building, the black marble lobby is filling up with nine-to-fivers shivering after their walk from the subway at the Sixth Avenue corner down the block. Businessmen in wool overcoats and gray fedoras, women in colorful coats, some in the new princess style pinched at the waist, walk briskly to the elevators. I like the princess style. I like any style that accentuates a woman's body.

I don't join the crowd at the bank of public elevators. I keep walking to the end of the row, to the private elevator to Sig's penthouse, guarded by a thug the nine-to-fivers pointedly ignore. They know who lives in the penthouse. Their fear of the crime boss upstairs is greater than their thrill at occasionally being in the presence of the most powerful man in New York when they see him walking through the lobby. Maybe the businessmen tip their hats when they pass him, maybe the women give him a polite smile. None of them know he doesn't give a damn.

I don't know the thug guarding the private elevator, but then again, I haven't been to see Sig in quite a while. So the galoot doesn't know me, either. He eyes me up and down. It takes him a minute to figure me, then looks at me like he's examining me for germs. "What's your business here?"

"Tell Sig that Cantor Gold wants to see him."

I have to wait while the lobby galoot calls on the intercom beside the elevator and gives the upstairs galoot my message, and that galoot in turn gives the message to Sig's personal galoot. I use the time to enjoy the lovely sight of an especially pretty office girl reading the front page of her newspaper while she waits for an elevator. But as much as I'd like to linger along her angelic face, have a little fun imagining what's under her coat, my attention's diverted when she opens the paper and I can see the whole front page. I'm grabbed by a particular story—down below all the headlines about President Truman and the Red Scare, the shoot-'em-up in Korea, and the never ending bedlam of city politics—printed way down at the bottom of the page, like a cockroach that slipped under the door: JUDGE ACQUITS GUZIK.

So Jake "Greasy Thumb" Guzik, the Chicago Mob's payoff man, a confidante of Capone during Al's heyday, beat another rap. It was Guzik who peeled off the bills that went into the palms of Chicago's cops and politicians, a job which earned him the Greasy Thumb moniker. I met the guy a coupla times on his trips here after Capone bit the dust back in '47, and gangster power coalesced in New York.

The pretty office girl catches me smiling, which makes her cringe, and she turns away. That might hurt my feelings except I'm not smiling at her. Nope, I'm smiling because my chances of not being killed today by Sig Loreale just went up. He'll be in a good mood.

Or in as good a mood as a killer can be. By the time the elevator reaches the penthouse floor, I'm asking myself whether coming here was such a hot idea after all. Probing Sig for his secrets is a dangerous play, whether he's in a good mood or not.

But there's no turning back. Sig wouldn't let me, anyway. He knows I'm here and he'll want to know why. I'd never make it out of the building.

One of his galoots greets me at the apartment door, tells me Sig is waiting for me in his den. "Through the livin' room and to the left. And I gotta hold your piece." The guy has all the charm of a shark chewing a leg.

I'm not crazy about handing over my gun, but Sig demands all visitors check any hardware at the door. He likes his guests defenseless. Resistance would only get me a fist in the gut, and frankly I'm just not in the mood. I give the galoot my gun and walk in.

The last time I was in this living room was a night in March of '49. Crammed among the fine furnishings, English landscape paintings on the walls, and various antiquities here and there—a number of them supplied by me for hefty sums of Sig's cash—were bushels of flowers for a wedding that was abruptly cancelled:

Opal died that night, her wedding night. Sig took his revenge the next morning, soothed his broken heart with murder. I was there. I saw the woman Sig blamed for Opal's death fall at my feet, a bullet in her skull. I saw Sig and his gunman drive away.

But before he drove away, Sig made a promise, the same promise he made again a year and a half ago when I handed over a Dürer watercolor that should've gone to a dead client's heirs, or at least a museum. It was his promise to look into what happened to Sophie, a promise he hasn't kept. Sig prides himself on his word, so either he really has no information, or his fabled square dealing is just that: a fable, a story line to calm unsuspecting marks before he cleans them out, runs them outta town, or kills them.

If it turns out Sig sees me as one of the marks, or even just a pest, then Mom's right; he'll kill me. Maybe not today, but when a moment comes up that suits him.

Bringing these thoughts into a meeting with Sig is a bad idea. Worrying over my own demise will blunt my energy, and any encounter with Sig Loreale requires operating at full spark. A deep breath and a swallow are the only weapons I have to squelch my dangerous thoughts. They do the trick, because they have to.

I knock on the door of the den.

"Come in, Cantor," comes through the door in Sig's terrifyingly quiet, scratchy voice, like claws scraping the wood, each word slow and precise, nothing sloppy, the same scalpel-sharp way Sig does business. He's cultivated his manner of speech and his method of business to obliterate the messy, immigrant Coney Island background we both came from. I wonder, if I look hard enough, if I'll see any of the same honky-tonk remnants in Sig that still lurk inside me. I doubt it. Sig's too disciplined, his soul too cold to cozy up to any nostalgia, a soul grown only colder since Opal's death.

He's at his desk, a large burled maple affair in a burled maple paneled room that's as much about power as taste, though the taste, I think, isn't entirely Sig's. Like the elegantly furnished living room, the den appears to be the work of the dearly departed Opal, whose mother, Mom Sheinbaum, bred Opal to marry into the American Dream. Mom sent her to all the right schools to acquire the culture and taste that come with them, rid Opal of the salami taint of the Lower East Side. To Mom's disappointment, Sig Loreale, the up-from-the-gutter crime lord and killer, was the beneficiary of all that culture, instead of the square-jawed, blue-eyed American dreamboat Mom wanted for her precious Opal.

Sig, in shirtsleeves, a half-finished cup of coffee on the desk, is reading a newspaper when I come in. What for other people would be an otherwise benign activity is, in Sig's hands, a tableau of his ruthlessly efficient control of life: his, and while I'm here, mine. His white shirt, crisp in the light from the windows and the glass-paned door to the terrace, doesn't have a single wrinkle, and wouldn't dare. The gray-and-white houndstooth pattern of his tie is precisely aligned with the knot. The pinstripes on his charcoal suit-vest, fully buttoned, are in military straight lines. And though the cigar smoke curling around his face softens his jowly cheeks and the baggy pouches under his eyes, the smoke can't hide the predatory menace in those eyes, despite his smile. It's not a big smile, just a small sneer of satisfaction as he reads the same article about Greasy Thumb Guzik beating the rap that the pretty office girl read downstairs; only the office girl has no connection to Guzik or the judge who dismissed the charges against him. Sig, no doubt, does. Sig, no doubt, owns both Guzik and the judge. The judge, having done what he was told to do, will continue to live his plush, well-paid-for life for the foreseeable future. Jake Guzik will owe Sig his freedom. Both men will keep their mouths shut about anything they know regarding what goes on in the underworld. And Sig, to my relief, is in his ice-cold version of a good mood.

Without looking at me, he rests his cigar in a crystal ashtray on his desk, closes the newspaper, folds it neatly, and lays it beside his coffee cup. "Have a seat, Cantor," he says. "If you want a cup of coffee, I can have it brought in for you." It's not a courteous offer. Just an agenda item he'd like to settle one way or the other.

"No thanks," I say, and take off my coat and cap and lay them over one of the club chairs opposite Sig's desk before I sit down in the other. The chairs, big, square, upholstered in steely gray leather, are more intimidating than welcoming, just like Sig.

He takes a sip of coffee, puts the cup down as meticulously as a surgeon positioning a scalpel on flesh, then finally looks at me, his ruthlessness all too visible in his narrowing eyes and the remnant of his sneer. "So, Cantor, why are you here?" Typical Sig. Right to business. No *Good morning*. No *It's been a long time*. No *How've you been*. None of the pleasantries between people who've known each other nearly thirty years, since I was a little kid and he was a young tough muscling into the Coney rackets.

Lighting a smoke gives me time to gather my wits before I start the conversation that could either lead to my enlightenment or my demise. Sig's watching my every move: my inhale, my exhale, the snap shut of my lighter. I don't dare try his patience any longer. "Solly Schwartz's kid, Mickey—Mickey Day, he called himself—"

"Is dead. Yes, Cantor, I know." Two things make what he'd just said scary as hell: the fact that he already knows about Mickey's death, and the slowness with which he said it. About the first: maybe Sig's behind the killing, and poking my nose into it might be my death sentence, or maybe Sig's web of connections just keep him informed, but poking my nose into anything in Coney Island could be my death sentence anyway. About the second: If he'd said it any slower, he wouldn't have to kill me. I'd be dead of old age, my face frozen in a grimace of fear.

He picks up his cigar again, puffs it slowly while he keeps looking at me, the glowing tip of the cigar throwing a red flicker around his eyes, deepening the shadows under their pouches, making him look like a monster in a horror picture. I can't tell if he's waiting for me to speak or waiting to give me permission to speak. I go for the former, because I've never known Sig to waste time. "Mickey stole something from me," I say, "and I need it back. It's worth a lot of money to me from an important client. And it's bad for business if word gets around that goods have been lifted right under my nose. But I don't know where he's hidden it. And I don't know if he was killed for it or"—I've got to clear my guts out of my throat before I can finish the sentence—"or for some other reason."

Sig's cigar goes back into the ashtray again, mercifully taking the red glow from his eyes. But the cold smile is back, and it's shaping itself into another of Sig's terrifying habits. His head tilts back, his eyes crinkle, his mouth opens. He's laughing but no sound comes out, a silent laugh that's been making my skin crawl since I was a kid. As the laugh shrinks again into his chilly smile, he says, "And you want to know if I am responsible for the hit."

I give him a nod. "If you are, it's for your own reasons and I can assume it's got nothing to do with my missing treasure, so I'll need to look elsewhere for information. But if you're not, then we both have a problem."

He doesn't look like a movie monster now, more like a professor who has a reputation for sadistic punishment if a student comes up with the wrong answer, and I'm the student.

But I can't shrivel from the guy, can't back down if I want Sig's cooperation, or even just useful tidbits of information. So I stub out my smoke in the ashtray on the little glass table next to my chair, give Sig a show of confidence I barely feel, and keep talking. "Mickey told me he knew all about your real estate plans in Coney Island, and he didn't like what you and your business partners have in mind, especially in the Gut. He figured you're going to level every shack and bungalow in the neighborhood to make room for your apartment houses, throw everyone in the Gut out in the street." Nothing's moved on Sig's face, no telltale tightening at the corner of his mouth, no inadvertent crinkle of his eyes, nothing to concede even the slightest guilt at throwing a couple thousand people out of their homes. He doesn't care.

I keep going, even though I feel like I've been forced to swallow sharp shards of ice. "But just because Mickey didn't like your plans didn't mean he couldn't see a way to profit by them."

"And just how did Mr. Day expect to profit?" His acid tone could shred whole trees.

"He was hoping to be your man on the ground," I say, "the inside guy in Coney who could feed you the real who's who and what's what among Coney's real estate people, in exchange for taking his father's rackets back. He…uh…lured me out there to ask me to set up a meeting with you, lay out his offer."

Sig brings the cigar back to his mouth, but after a single puff he stubs it out, as if disgusted not just with the cigar but with me. "May I ask how he lured you? Was it money?"

"No, not money." A dangerous little smile curls at the corner of my mouth. I try to snuff it, because the last thing I need is for Sig to think I find anything he says amusing. But the memory of Lilah's body against mine ambushes me, and I can't muzzle the smile the memory provokes.

All Sig says is, "Oh. Of course. His sister. I am told she is good-looking."

My only response is an awkward nod and finally losing the silly smile.

"Cantor, I do not care who you—" he stops as if he's tripped over something he doesn't recognize and can't figure out, then dismisses it and moves on—"well, whatever it is you do. But when your rutting collides with my business interests, then you are correct, we both have a problem. So to answer your question: No, I did not order Mr. Day's death. He and his…his shabby operation were too small even to be annoyances. But his death, Cantor, that is another matter. His death will attract the notice of the police, which I will of course do my best to control, make sure their investigation is correctly focused. But there are new people on the force out there who are proving less cooperative than their predecessors." His jaw tight, his eyes narrowed, the businessman in Sig has just made a mental memo to deal with those new people. "In the meantime," he says, "I assume you will be going back to Coney Island to see if you can locate your lost article?"

"Yeah. Any idea where I might start?"

"I can't help you there. The last time I saw Solly Schwartz's boy was at his father's funeral."

I start to blurt, *You went to the funeral of the man you killed?* but immediately think better of it, just let Sig keep talking.

"I've been aware of Day's business," he says, "but not his personal habits, so I don't know, or care, where he hid things. But I advise you to keep your head down, Cantor. I have people in Coney Island protecting my interests. They will be making sure Day's killing doesn't affect my business. Do not get in their way."

"Wouldn't dream of it."

"Good. So if there's nothing else—"

"There is something else, Sig." This is it. This is the moment that's been gnawing at me for too long. If it goes sour, if I annoy Sig, I could wind up buried in some obscure landfill in an out of the way corner of Staten Island, maybe even Jersey. But I can't let the moment pass by. I may not get this chance again anytime soon, or ever. And besides, risking my life is a small price for any scrap of information about Sophie. The loss of her has been eating me alive for too long. "When are you going to make good on your promise, Sig, to find out what happened to Sophie? When are you going to come through?"

He leans forward, slow as a locomotive gearing up its massive power, and I feel myself leaning back to escape his relentless force. I brace myself for whatever threat he's getting ready to push at me.

I do everything I can to hide my tension. I cross my legs, flick a nonexistent speck of dust from my knee, take a deep, long breath.

But no threat comes. Instead, to my surprise, he leans back in his chair again, his body relaxing, his expression softening, which for Sig means he looks only slightly less deadly than a rabid dog. "You are still very much in love with this woman, yes, Cantor?"

"Do you really need to ask, Sig?"

"You know I always keep my promises, Cantor, always pay my debts. But you must understand that finding one boat in a very big ocean is not an easy business."

"You want me to believe you've gotten no hints in all this time? There isn't a dockworker who doesn't owe his livelihood to you, Sig. There isn't a dockside Mob boss who isn't in your pocket. Someone must've seen *something* that night."

He doesn't argue, just stays frighteningly relaxed. "Whatever outfit runs the flesh operation that took your girl is very slick, Cantor. They've hidden themselves well. But I promise you I will track them down. Sooner or later, I will track them down. You must be patient."

"As patient as you were in avenging Opal's death?"

I've crossed a line. I know it even as the words fall out of my mouth.

Sig's face goes back to stone. His eyes darken. He's so still I'm not sure he's even breathing. When he finally moves, the only sound I hear is the crackle of the pages as he picks up the newspaper and opens it.

I've been dismissed.

I gather my coat and cap, and head for the door.

In back of me, I hear Sig's rasp. "In thirty years, I have never been angry with you, Cantor. Do not make me start now."

Chapter Eight

My office is more than just my base of operations. It's also my retreat, the quiet place I go to when I need to get away from the noise of the world, think things through, figure my next moves. My office is also my hideaway when I need to lay low, stay out of sight of the Law, or babysit a treasure that's too hot to move. Only four people in the world know about this place: Rosie, who ferries me in her cab on the sly when I'm carrying goods so the cops or other nosy types who know my car never know I'm on the move; Judson Zane, my young office guy, whose commitment to secrecy is as great as his talent for crime's details, and who does me the great honor of checking for leads on Sophie first thing in the morning and last thing at night, but until he hears something, we just don't talk about it; Red Drogan, the tugboater who's my eyes, ears, and legs along the harbor; and my lawyer, a smart and polished operator with more connections into New York politics than the electric company, and who buried my name so deep in the ownership paperwork even a dredging machine wouldn't find it. Only those four people know that the small, nondescript corner building in the shadows below the elevated West Side Highway and across the street from the midtown Hudson River docks hosts a big money smuggling racket and a room-size basement vault containing treasures people have killed for and died for, and still do.

The only way to enter my little building is through a back door in the maze of alleyways behind the warehouses and piece-goods factories along Twelfth Avenue. After I park my Buick up the block in Louie's garage, I make my way through the alleys, pull my cap low and the collar of my overcoat tight against the winter wind coming off the river. The icy chill seeping through me is almost as cold as Sig's warning.

The noise of city traffic on Twelfth Avenue echoes through the alleys; all those delivery trucks, taxicabs, and pushcarts fighting for dockside space under the highway, their horns honking, tires screeching, men yelling. Sounds of river traffic make their way back here, too. The melancholy clang of buoy bells, nearly drowned out by the bleat of ships' horns, never fails to break my heart, their slow toll cruel reminders of Sophie kidnapped and carried out to sea.

Rosie's cab is parked in the alley outside my office door.

She's chatting with Judson when I come in, leaning against his desk. She looks tired, like she didn't get much sleep. Judson, his eyes alert in his boyishly chiseled face behind his wire-rim glasses, his hair trim, his white shirt and dungarees crisp, looks worried. Worry never looks good on a guy under thirty, especially on Judson, who prides himself on keeping his emotions in check.

I'm pretty sure I know why Rosie's tired, so I skip the question I really don't want to ask anyway. But I need to know why Judson's worried. "What's up? You look like you just lost your last dime."

"Red Drogan called," he says. "You didn't show up this morning with his cut of the van Zell payoff. You've never skipped out on Drogan, so we both figured something's not kosher."

"I don't have anyone's cut, not Red's, not yours, not Rosie's, not even mine, because Miranda van Zell didn't pay off."

"What? All that money in the bank," Judson says with as much of a sneer as his steady nature allow, which isn't much, "and she stiffed us? She's never stiffed us."

"She didn't stiff us, Judson. She never got her goods. All she got was a body winding up on her sidewalk."

Judson's eyebrows rise up above his wire rims.

"Yeah," I say, "I guess even fancy Fifth Avenue's going to seed." But my deadpan joke falls flat, earning only lowered eyebrows from Judson and a *tsk* from Rosie. So I just bring them up to date on all the goings-on—the theft, the deaths, my meetings with Mom and Sig and Mickey—but conveniently leave out my bedtime activity with Lilah.

As I spill my story, concern crowds the fatigue in Rosie's eyes. She puts her hand on my cheek, says, "New bruises, I see," and strokes the place where Bulby Nose slugged me. "No new scars this time, though."

Her touch is tender, caring. I don't deserve it.

And she doesn't deserve the guilt that's slowly poisoning her concern for me. I see it creep into her eyes. But it shouldn't be there at all, because even if Rosie hadn't driven away to meet that regular fare, she probably couldn't have done much to stop the attack that came out of the darkness. Rosie's not weak, and she's no coward. But the thugs came on fast. They were brutal and ready to kill.

And I'm a heel for enjoying Rosie's guilt.

Someday I'll grow up. Someday I'll grow up and understand just how savvy Rosie really is. She shows me some of that savvy now, as the guilt fades from her eyes, replaced by annoyance. She's caught me in my selfish pleasure.

Her hand drops from my cheek. She leans against Judson's desk again, her arms crossed, her face down, anger and sadness each vying for possession of her.

But Rosie's feelings—and mine—will have to wait. I've got business to take care of, a client to satisfy, money at stake.

I walk into my private office. In the corner of my eye, I see Rosie's eyes follow me. I feel the chill when she looks away.

My private office is the sanctum sanctorum of my operation. I've outfitted it with grade A furnishings, luxuries I've awarded myself for surviving my dangerous life. There's an antique walnut desk, a pale green leather club chair smooth as flesh, and an oxblood leather couch. I've stocked the place with a supply of scotch, a refrigerator with plenty of food, a hotplate, a shower stall, and a closet with changes of outfits for those days and nights I sometimes spend here.

But I'm not here to linger among my trophies. I'm here to make a quick but important phone call.

The number's answered at the other end. "Van Zell residence."

"Good morning, Charles. Please tell Mrs. van Zell, Cantor Gold needs to speak with her."

"Just a moment."

While I wait for Miranda to come on the line, I tuck the phone between my chin and my shoulder, and swing aside the painting that covers the wall safe behind my desk. The painting's a moody arrangement of brown, green, and black fuzzy-edged rectangles and squares by Mark Rothko, one of the modern rebels blowing up all definitions of art. I like the painting, and the attitude.

Miranda comes on the line as I open the safe. "Cantor, have you found the pyxis?"

"Not yet, but I found who took it."

"I see. Well, what will it take to get it back? How much money do they want?"

"The guy has no use for money, Miranda. He's dead. Murdered."

There's a silence while Miranda handles this twist of events. I use the time to take spare cash and extra rounds of ammunition from the safe, put the cash in my wallet and the rounds in my pants pocket. I also grab my case of lock picks, slip it into my inside jacket pocket, in case Mickey's stashed the pyxis in a strongbox or locked room I'm lucky enough to find.

Miranda comes back on the line. "Before he died, I guess he didn't tell you where he has the pyxis?"

"No, but I'm working on it."

"Yes, no doubt." There's a snide tone to that remark that I can do without. But considering everything that's happened, I guess Miranda's entitled to it. "I have news, too, Cantor," she says, her friendly attitude restored. "The police have come 'round again."

"Yeah? What do they want this time?"

"They say they have a witness who saw what happened last night. Someone was coming out of the building next door and saw the whole thing, even saw the doorman's death. But it seems you're in luck, Cantor."

"If I get any luckier, I'll need a cemetery plot."

"Please do not die on me until you've recovered the pyxis. In the meantime, according to the police, this witness said they saw a man in a gray coat and cap attacked by two other men." Miranda's throaty chuckle is met with my own dry laugh because, yeah, I get the joke. In fact, I'm still wearing the joke.

Miranda says, "The police asked everyone in the building if we were expecting a gentleman guest in a gray cap and coat."

"And what did you tell them?"

Through another throaty laugh, this one enjoying its walk on the wild side, she says, "I told them I wasn't expecting any gentleman. 'Bye, Cantor. Keep me informed."

My day just got a tiny bit better. Any day I'm not in the Law's notepad is a better day.

After Miranda hangs up, I turn back to the safe, ready to close it. But before I do, I take out a framed photograph, drawn to it like a magnet to metal. The photo used to sit on my desk until it became too painful to look at it every day. It's a picture of Sophie and me, taken the morning after our first night together. The picture, and the memory of that night—Sophie's long dark hair falling softly along her face, brushing mine, the heat of her damp skin, the feel of her on my mouth, her kiss, her love—nearly drop me.

I hear Rosie say, "Oh, for heaven's sake, put it back on your desk already." I look up to see her in the doorway, zipping her cabbie's jacket in one fast, sharp stroke. "You're still in love with her, Cantor. You'll never love anyone else until you find out what happened to her."

But I can't put the photo on my desk, not if I want to keep my sanity. I put it back in the safe, close the door, the click of the lock followed by a *tsk* from Rosie as she walks away.

I'd like nothing better than to fold up in a chair and cry my eyes out, but those days are gone. Rosie's right; I won't love anymore. I can't. The loss of Sophie nearly deep-sixed me, and until she's found, I can't let my heart rule me. My instinct for survival rules everything now, the same instinct that guides me through my outlaw world and criminal life.

It kicks in now. Before I leave my office, I go to my closet, take off my gray coat and cap, and put on a black coat and fedora.

Chapter Nine

If Coney Island lures in summer with cotton candy and sun-warmed flesh, in winter it bites with steel teeth. I'd forgotten how cold and sharp the salty wind off the ocean could be. Even now, at noon, with the sun glaring off the sea, the wind up here on the boardwalk is hungry for the uncovered flesh of my face.

It's warmer inside the Good Time Arcade, half empty with an off-season daytime crowd of nickel-and-dimers, but still noisy with skee ball thumps, carny music, muffled laughter of teenagers behind the curtains of twenty-five-cent photo booths, and occasional grunts from players who keep feeding coins into game machines, lured by flashing lights promising thrills.

Eddie Janko's in the middle of all this, still wearing last night's green lumber jacket and brown chinos, but the jacket's open for quick access to the coin changer hooked to his belt. He nods when he sees me walk in, and when I approach he says, "Everyone in Coney's talkin' about what happened to Mickey and that tattoo guy, Gus somethin'-or-other. We ain't seen blood like that since the old Schwartz-Loreale War back in the '20s. People wonderin' if the war's comin' back."

"Sig says he had nothing to do with the killings."

"He told you personal-like?" Eddie blurts it like he can't believe I was really in the king's presence.

"Yeah, personal-like, like he's not happy about the whole damn thing and how the consequences might interfere with his business. Look, how'd it go with Lilah this morning? You got her home before the cops showed up?"

"Yeah. I got Lilah back to the Gut maybe five minutes before the cops dropped in. Said they came lookin' for her last night, too."

"Figured they would, but she wasn't in any condition to talk. What story did you give them?"

"Me? I didn't tell 'em a thing. But Lilah told 'em plenty. Surprised the hell outta me, lemme tell you."

Eddie's just surprised the hell outta *me*. "What are you talking about? What did Lilah say?"

But there's a sallow-faced kid of maybe ten or twelve playing hooky from school at Eddie's elbow. The kid's waving a grimy dollar bill in his equally grimy hand. "Hey, mistuh, gimme five dimes and ten nickels, and make it snappy."

Typical Coney kid. Stuffed with attitude. Nothing's changed since my own wild childhood.

Eddie thumbs the levers on his coin changer, gives the kid his nickels and dimes. When the kid's gone, Eddie says, "So Lilah says she—whoa, tell ya later." He releases a few more coins from his changer, stuffs them into my hand. "Go play some pokerino. Way in the back."

By Eddie's tone, I figure cops came in, or maybe Sig's enforcers making rounds, collecting the midday cut. Either way, folding myself into the crowd is a good idea.

I park myself at the end of a row of pokerino machines, open my coat, get comfortable, and insert a nickel to release my five little rubber balls. When I roll the first ball along the alley, it scores a hole for a jack of diamonds. A second ball lands another jack, this one in spades. The poker pair makes a bell ring, and since the last thing I need is to ring any more of the machine's bells and attract attention, I push the remaining balls without much zest, let them roll around aimlessly.

So I'm not too concerned that after two more nickels and more minutes of play, I've only dealt myself losing hands. But I'm damned concerned about the sudden tap on my shoulder and a smooth male voice saying, "We've got a few questions for you."

Cops.

I turn around, see two guys, one clearly in charge, the other an underling. The in-charge guy is only a little taller than I am but built like a bulldog. Under his gray fedora, his chubby olive-skinned face has fleshy lips and soft dark brown eyes that might fool you into thinking the guy is a pussycat, but his steady gaze gives him away as a predator on the hunt. The other cop, his underling, is taller, but with his long face and dull eyes he's less imposing, except for his big ears, which seem to be holding up his hat, a stained brown fedora that's somewhere between beat-up and dead.

A quick glance past the cops shows me Eddie across the room, his palms up, his shoulders hunched in a couldn't-do-anything-about-it apology.

The bulldog says, "So you're Cantor Gold."

"According to my friends. Are you one of my friends?"

"I could be, if you play along." In a slick move, he slides a gold shield out of his inside pocket, holds it up to my face. "Lieutenant Esposito. And this here's Sergeant Pike." Pike gives me an expressionless nod. "Listen, Gold," Esposito says, sliding the shield back into his pocket, "we can all avoid a lot of aggravation if you just tell me everything you know about Mickey Day's murder."

If the lieutenant and I are going to do the who-knows-what dance, I figure maybe I oughta take the lead, see where he follows me. "I heard there were two killings. What about the other guy? The ink artist?"

The phony softness in Esposito's eyes becomes a genuine, icy suspicion. "How do you know about Gus?"

"Everyone knows, Lieutenant. The whole island's talking about the killings."

His, "Uh-huh," is sour as stomach acid. "Yeah, well," he says, "I doubt Gus was the target. Who'd have it in for a cheap tattoo guy? Poor lug must've just been in the way." He says it like he's talking about a piece of furniture someone's merely tripped on.

But he's likely right. There were probably lots of reasons to knife a creep like Mickey Day, lots of people who'd want to do it, and not leave any witnesses. Good-bye, Gus.

Sharing my thoughts with the Law, though, is not a practice I indulge in. That badge gives cops the power to decide life and death and freedom, mine and everybody else's. I don't count on them being merciful.

So all I say is, "I don't know anything about Day's killing."

"Then why are you in Coney Island? You left the neighborhood years ago, or so they tell me."

"Who's *they*?"

He pulls out some coins from his pants pocket, gives them to Pike. "Go get us some coffee, Sergeant. How do you take yours, Gold?"

"None for me, thanks." I don't accept free coffee or booze or anything else from cops. I don't want to have to say thank you.

When Pike's gone, Esposito gives me a smile that could charm the panties off a virgin. Except I'm not a virgin, and panties aren't my preferred underwear.

"Gold, Gold," he croons through his squishy lips, his bulldog posture still rigid but leaning in, a pretense of friendliness. "Believe me when I say I don't want to make trouble for you. I just want to clean this case up, get it off the books, and go take my two weeks' vacation in Florida. I mean, who needs all this cold weather, right? Look, I know you saw Mickey's sister last night, which means you know something about what's going on. So I ask you again: What are you doing in Coney Island?"

"Well, Lieutenant, if you really must know, I had to attend a burial." I throw that out as a step in the dance, a do-si-do to get information, like how he knew I saw Lilah last night, who told him.

He gives me a doubting eye. "Uh, aren't you a little early? Mickey's still on a slab in the morgue."

"It's not his burial I attended," I say.

"Attended? As in already been?"

"Uh-huh."

"So who else died, may I ask?"

"Miss Theresa."

"Who?" He looks at me like I've suddenly started speaking a foreign lingo he doesn't understand. "Who the hell is Miss Theresa?"

"It was a private affair. Mona Carlotti and I were the only attendees last night. Go talk to her. She can tell you all about it."

"Last night? But Miss Day says you were with her last night."

Bingo.

Now I know why Lilah surprised Eddie when she talked to the cops this morning.

While I try to work out why Lilah would spill that story to a cop, and just how much of it she spilled—what was her description of *with her*?—I realize Esposito is looking me over. Actually, he's just looking over part of me, my midsection, from the lapels of my suit, down my arms to my hands, and landing at my crotch. His sneer, oozing as much curiosity as disgust, might make my skin crawl if I hadn't seen that sneer a million times before on a million other sanctimonious faces, sometimes followed by a punch to the gut I long ago learned to either avoid or bear. But Esposito's sneer answers my question about what Lilah told him, or at least intimated. Which leaves me with two other questions: Why would she tell a tale that risks getting us arrested on a morals charge? Unless she said I forced her. And if that's the case, why isn't Esposito arresting me?

My dance with Esposito has gone suddenly out of step. It seems we've each been dancing to different music, and I've only heard mine. What's his tune? And who's playing it?

The arrival of Sergeant Pike with two mugs of coffee brings our do-si-do to a stop.

Pike gives a mug to Esposito, who makes a face after his first sip, his pudgy lips like two long balloons twisted into an unnatural shape. "When did Eddie brew this stuff? Last week?"

"Coney Island requires strong bones, Lieutenant," I say.

"Don't you worry about my bones, Gold. Worry about your own. We wouldn't want them to crack."

"You telling me you care for my safety?"

"Sure." His smile has all the sincerity of a devil promising salvation. "I'm a nice guy, haven't you heard? C'mon, Pike, let's go." As they leave, Pike actually touches the brim of his fedora in a gesture of toodle-oo. Esposito doesn't bother.

When they're gone, I wander back over to Eddie, ask him to tell me just what Lilah said to Esposito.

"She gave him an earful, that's what. Said she was with you last night, that you were, y'know, a client."

"Did Esposito buy it?"

"Don't ask me. When she told him that tale, I was too busy picking myself up off the floor. Listen, Cantor, sorry about sending Esposito over to you. Said he was looking for you, and I was afraid he was gonna take me in if I said I didn't know where you are. You know how it is, once you're in the hands of the Law, you ain't never gettin' out."

"Yeah, Eddie, I know."

"That Esposito, he thinks he's a big cheese since he got his lieutenant's stripes. Too bad he didn't earn 'em."

"Most of them never do, Eddie. They may pass an exam, but they flunk honor questions."

"No, I mean he *really* didn't earn his stripes. He never took no exam. Catch my drift?"

Eddie knows damn well I catch his drift. "So who's his sugar daddy? Who owns him?" My question doesn't surprise Eddie. It scares him.

When I was a kid, my mother wouldn't let me wander into the Gut, though obedience was never one of my habits. The place had its lures for a ruffian child like me. Back then, it was still a ramshackle neighborhood of rotgut speakeasies defying Prohibition with brass knuckles and tommy guns, rough-'em-up gambling joints where losers paid up or were cut up, and larcenous notch rooms where johns had their pockets emptied while they were emptying something else inside a hooker. Wild times had been the neighborhood's lineage since the 1880s, or so the old-timers said. During my kiddie days, the Gut's shady profits went into the pockets of Solly Schwartz and his cutthroats, until the even more cutthroat Sig Loreale grabbed those profits for himself.

The neighborhood's still ramshackle, though sturdier residences with solid families have since taken root. Small brick houses and more durable bungalows share this block of Second Street with the old shanties still standing. Looking around, seeing the television antennas now sprouted on rooftops, and the line of cars—mostly inexpensive Ford or Chevy coupes, some pretty beat-up—parked at the muddy curb, it's clear the Gut, like every place else since the end of the Second World War, is making its grab for the American Dream, but it's still home to a lot of Coney's hard knuckles and threadbare pockets.

The wooden porch stairs of the Schwartz-Day bungalow on Second Street could use repair, the red paint faded and chipped.

The house's white siding and red trim are in no better shape, the splintered wood poking through the paint like bristly warts. If Mickey Day was making money off Lilah's back, he certainly wasn't spending any of it on providing brother and sister with a decent place to live.

Second Street is two blocks inland from the boardwalk and beach, so the wind back here is less biting, but not by much. I pull down my fedora, but the wind pushes itself under the brim, does a good job of chewing my face while I wait for Lilah to answer my knock on the door. The wind feasts especially on my scars, as if the Coney wind is trying to taste all the life I've lived since I left.

Lilah finally opens the door. She's wearing a white terry robe, her head wrapped in a terry towel, which slips down to reveal freshly washed hair. Even limp and damp, her short blond waves give Lilah the windblown look of an adventuress, though one who's had a rough night. Her eyes are red rimmed, sleepless, but with a glint that hints she's happy to see me. I'm happy to see her, too, which takes me by surprise, and worries me. Desiring Lilah is one thing; feelings for her could get in my way.

"Come in out of the cold, Cantor," she says in that lilting voice that won me over last night at the Green Door Club. And she smells good, fresh with soap and radiant skin, as I walk inside.

The air in the living room is warm, stuffy warm in that overheated way a small room can be when the heat's cranked up to keep drafts from seeping through the cheap walls. And the fussy floral wallpaper, its fading pinks and blues and greens all tangled up in each other, makes the place feel even stuffier, the thick foliage seems to squeeze the air out of the room. I take off my hat and coat, lay them on the back of the worn-out couch, a dark purple velvet number that was fashionable when I was still a schoolyard tomboy. The mahogany coffee table in front of the couch is of equal vintage, its long, hard life etched in scratches and cigarette burns on the tabletop.

"My mother picked them out," Lilah says. I must have a puzzled look on my face. "The coffee table and couch. My mother picked them out. They came with us from the house in Sea Gate. We had lots of nice furniture in Sea Gate. At least, that's what Mickey said. I was too young to remember. I only remember growing up here."

"Yeah, you were still a baby when—"

"When Sig Loreale took everything from my family." There's enough edge to her voice to slice a throat.

"You sound like your brother," I say.

Her green eyes are suddenly too bright, her jaw tightens, straining the lovely curl at the corner of her mouth. "Listen, Mickey might've been a heel," she says, the edge in her voice replaced by a hiss worthy of a coiled snake. "Okay, sure, my brother *was* a heel, but he was right about what Loreale did to us. Loreale won the turf war. Wasn't that enough? Did he have to send my family into the poorhouse?"

"Ask yourself this," I say. "If your father had won the war, don't you think he would've done the same to Sig? Taken him for all he had?"

"No. No, my mother told me my father was tough, but he wasn't that kind of man."

She's right. Solly Schwartz wasn't the same kind of man as Sig. He wasn't as smart or cunning. He wasn't a man who wins.

But I drop the issue. I'm not here to drag up old Coney history, though enough of it has been clawing at me since I wandered around the old neighborhood last night. Instead, I take a seat on the couch, say, "Lilah, we need to talk."

She gives me a nod. "I know," she says, and sits down next to me. Her voice is sweet again, the hiss gone, her usual alluring lilt finding its natural place in her body. And that body, shaping her terry robe into a sculpture as sinuous as any classical Venus, is sweet, too, her freshly showered scent brushing my face like warm fingertips.

No sense kidding myself, I want more of Lilah in my future. Yeah, the body, sure, but there's an inconvenient sentiment picking at me, some sort of caring I hadn't counted on when we were tossing around in my bed. Maybe it's because she's just lost the last of her family. She's a woman alone in a dangerous game. And I'm a sucker for women in dangerous games.

But whatever future is in our cards will have to wait. There are crimes between us that need sorting out: I have a stolen treasure to find; Lilah has a murdered brother to bury.

With a smile as grateful as it is sexy, she says, "By the way, thanks for taking care of me last night. I don't know how I could have gotten through it without you."

"You can thank Eddie Janko, too."

"Okay," she says without any warmth behind it, "but it was you, Cantor, who set things up so I could avoid the police."

There it is, the thing that twists my sense of logic.

I take my pack of Chesterfields and lighter from my inside pocket, say, "Yeah, about the police." I offer a smoke to Lilah, shake another out for myself, light them both, then say, "I understand you told the cops we were together last night."

"Well, yes. I had to."

"Yeah? Why? Why'd you put us both at risk of being hauled into the city lockup on a morals rap?"

"Because I needed an alibi, that's why. I don't trust that Esposito. He—he actually insinuated that maybe *I* had something to do with Mickey's killing! As if I'd kill my own brother, and Gus, too. Gus, who'd never hurt a fly."

"Yeah, but Mickey hurt a lot of flies," I say. "He sure as hell hurt you. Pimping his sister isn't a particularly loving thing to do."

I've plucked a nerve, the one that loves and hates her brother at the same time. Her jaw tightens again, turns her supple mouth into a hard crease. But a deep drag of her cigarette gives her a moment to untangle, eases her, and she eventually slides me a glance that acknowledges we're in this mess together, whether we like it or not.

She says, "Look, this Esposito—he just seemed too anxious to pin it on me, just so he could close the book on it real fast, report it to his higher-ups."

"Sure. The cops always look to family first for suspects." And with good reason. Family members have been killing each other off since the invention of the throne. Seems everyone wants to sit in it. "Maybe Esposito figured you wanted to take over Mickey's operation."

"Which is why I needed an alibi! And since I really was with you last night, it was the first thing I thought of."

The memory of it rouses my lust, brings my hand to her face, my fingers brushing her cheek. She seems to like it. "But our little tryst was hours before Mickey's death," I say. "You must've really twisted up the time when you sold that bill of goods to Esposito."

"I twisted more than the time, Cantor. I never told Esposito about your earlier meeting with Mickey. See? I protected you, too." She takes my hand from her cheek, brings it to her lips, kisses my palm. I don't pull my hand away, let it linger and enjoy her smooth mouth, its warmth, its need. I want this woman now as much as I did last night, maybe more, despite the crime and murder between us, or maybe because of them. Crime heats the blood. Coney Island crime heats the senses.

With a sideways glance that promises a stimulating journey to wherever she's leading me, she says, "And we were never in any danger of jail, Cantor. Esposito wasn't going to arrest either of us on a morals charge. Not without permission."

I must look even more puzzled than I did when she blurted that business about her mother and the furniture.

"Don't you know?" she says. "Esposito is one of Sig Loreale's boys. He can't arrest a flea without Loreale's say-so."

A Sig-and-cops cocktail will kill a mood faster than a cold shower. I slide my hand from Lilah's cheek.

Everyone knows Sig stirs badges from every precinct in the city's five boroughs into his brew of rackets, and it usually works to the underworld's advantage, keeps things from being looked at too closely, or keeps our time in the slammer from going on too long. But sometimes the cocktail's deadly. This one feels deadly, with Esposito dropped in as a poison pill.

Lilah says, "What's going on, Cantor? You look frightened."

"Is night shift homicide Esposito's usual beat?"

"What's that got to do with anything? He came around this morning."

"Yeah, but he came around last night, too, when I had you stowed at Mona's."

Lilah's softly beautiful face slowly, slowly hardens as she figures out the danger behind what I just said. When her features finally settle, Lilah looks frightened now, too.

CHAPTER TEN

How do you know Esposito is on Sig's payroll?" I say. Lilah's dismissive *tsk* seeps through her fear and reminds me that I've been away from Coney Island for a long time, not up to date on who owns who around here. It also reminds me that when I spoke to Sig this morning, he conveniently left out the names of his Coney operatives. Any beat cop on any corner could be in his pocket. For that matter, *anyone*, any Joe or Jane playing skee ball or walking around on the boardwalk, could be taking orders from the crime lord in the golden penthouse.

Sometimes I think Sig puts me in the crosshairs just for sport.

Lilah says, "Ask Eddie Janko. He can tell you all about it."

"I will, but I have other business first." And if I solve that business, I can finally get the hell out of Coney Island for good, escape its grip on my memories, escape Loreale's schemes. Mickey's murder can go unsolved, for all I care, though his sister's a sweet number, a woman who's reached deeper into me than I'd bargained for. I guess she wants Mickey's killer found, but I'd rather someone else do the looking. I have my own business to see to, and a rich client ready to cross my palm with a wad of cash the sooner I see to it. "Listen, Lilah, can you think of anyplace in this house where Mickey would hide something? Some hole in the wall? A secret spot in the attic?"

"Uh-uh. I know every inch of this shack, and there's nothing like that."

"Mind if I have a look around?"

"Suit yourself."

An hour later, after I've gone through the bungalow from back to front, searched through closets, bedroom furniture, kitchen cabinets, under creaky floorboards, over, under, and behind every stick of furniture in the living room, and knocked on its walls until I'm dizzy from all that floral wallpaper, I've come up with zip—just loose change, hairpins, Mickey's lost socks, a pair of nylon hose I assume belong to Lilah and which set my fantasies going, and a lot of dust. But no ancient Greek Dancing Goddesses pottery.

I was so busy searching the place, I didn't notice that Lilah wasn't near me, wasn't even in any room with me, until now, when she walks back into the living room, her hair dry and styled, her face carefully made up with mascara and a bright red lipstick that goes nicely with her brown and red striped dress and a pair of red plastic flower-shaped earrings she holds up as she considers them. The dress, belted at the waist and cut low, could give a biology student a damn good education in the structure and motion of flesh. "I'm not complaining," I say, "but that dress ain't exactly mourning weeds."

She shrugs, says, "Mickey's body hasn't been released from the morgue, so I can't bury him yet. Meantime, I still have to make a living, and a client's meeting me in twenty minutes. One of my tattoo shop regulars."

Every inch of me, inside and out, feels a sudden chill, an icy draft blowing through my bones, nipping my heart along the way. "Lilah, you don't have to do that anymore. Mickey can't force you anymore."

"Who says I have to be forced?" she says, putting her earrings on. The two red flowers are like blood drops on either side of her face, contrasting her creamy skin, accenting the red lipstick across her mouth. "Besides, this john's not so bad, a real—What's wrong, Cantor? You look like you just heard that your mother died." Finished with her earrings, Lilah slowly lowers her arms to her sides as she looks at me, the expression on her face changing from chatty nonchalance to canny awareness and then to something that might be taken for tenderness if it wasn't so streetwise.

Walking toward me, she says, "Oh," her voice gentle and low. She puts her hand on my cheek. "So many scars," she says, tracing them with her fingertips. "Am I giving you more, inside you, where they can't be seen?"

The touch of her fingers is warm and soothing, but not soothing enough to blunt the truth of what she just said. The idea of Lilah's body—a body I explored and whose heat I shared— soon pawed over by some ravenous john, cuts right down to my guts.

And then I take control, pull her to me, kiss her, gently at first, then harder and deeper, and with an appreciation for Lilah's gifts no john could ever imagine.

She stays with me, presses against me, even as she releases from my kiss and whispers my name. The emotion she brings to it surprises me, digs into me.

"You don't have to earn your living on your back," I say. "I can get you away."

"What are you saying, Cantor? That you would take care of me? That you'd love me? I've needed someone to love me for so long." She rests her head against my shoulder as if it's a pillow on a bed of peace.

And then I guess she feels my body stiffen, because even though she's still in my arms, she's no longer pressed against me. The look on her face isn't tender anymore, it's pleading.

I know I can be a heel. Sometimes it bothers me, sometimes it doesn't. It bothers me now, but lying to Lilah would be worse. "I care about you, Lilah. I care what happens to you, want to help you. And you excite me, I want you right down to my marrow. I can make love to you day and night, as much as you want, whenever you want—"

"But you can't love me." She releases from me, steps back with a sigh so deep I'm afraid it will drag her heart out of her chest and drop it on the floor. "Yeah, I've heard that line before. They're happy to take my body but can't love a whore's heart."

"Stop it. That's not what I meant. It's just that love's not on my menu. Not just with you, not with anybody."

"Then I feel sorry for you, Cantor. You've got stone for a heart."

Maybe I should explain to her that my heart's not stone. It's just been pummeled to pulp when I lost Sophie, and the only way I can keep my heart alive, keep it beating, is by locking it away in a steel cage.

But I don't mention it.

All the way back to the boardwalk to see Eddie at the Good Time Arcade, I try not to think about Lilah down there at the tattoo parlor, where the walls and floor are still stained with blood, and Lilah's servicing a john. Brooding about Lilah wrapped in blood and sex would drive me crazy and distract me from my real purpose here: to find where the late not-so-lamented Mickey Schwartz Day hid Miranda van Zell's treasure. To do that, I have to avoid getting tangled up in Sig Loreale's shenanigans, and to avoid Sig's shenanigans, I have to know what they are and who's operating them. I can't get free of Coney Island until I do.

Eddie better have some answers.

What Eddie has, as I walk into the arcade, is a cop in his face. It's Lieutenant Esposito, and he's jabbering at Eddie, poking a finger in his shoulder while Eddie sags like an old mutt being punished for peeing on the floor.

I can't hear Esposito through the racket of bells, whistles, and carny music in the arcade. But it may be just as well, because if the lieutenant really is Sig's henchman, it's probably not healthy for me to butt in on his rant.

I have to risk it, though, if I want to find out what's going on, why he's pressing Eddie. So relying on the iffy idea that if Sig wanted me dead, I would be, I amble toward the conversation, until there's an arm across my chest, blocking me.

It's Esposito's lackey, Sergeant Pike of the long face, big ears, and misshapen fedora. "Don't go over there," he says, his voice low. This is the first time I've heard him speak. He's got a rough, nasal voice, like a bear trying to whisper through a nasty cold.

"Is that an official police order?" I say.

"Keep your voice down, dammit. Look, I just figured you were smart enough to know a friendly suggestion when you hear it."

I can't help smiling. It's not a warm smile, not chummy, but the kind of tight, silly smile that spreads across your mouth when you can't believe your ears. "Well now," I say, dropping my voice when Pike makes a shushing gesture, "that's a new one, a cop giving me a friendly suggestion. And just what did I do to earn your friendship, Sergeant Pike?"

"It's not what you did. It's what you're gonna do. You're gonna scram."

"I don't take orders from cops."

"Fine. So step on the lieutenant's toes. See if I care. He'll just toss you in the tank, maybe even gimme the go-ahead to rough you up." His smile through his nasal whisper makes the threat even more irritating.

"Maybe you'd better tell me what's going on, Sergeant."

"I don't have to tell you anything, Gold. But I'm gonna be a nice guy and give you a piece of advice. Leave the lieutenant alone."

"Fine by me. I came here to talk to Eddie."

"Yeah? What about?"

If Pike wants to hold tight to his information, I'll hold tight to mine. "Old friends. I want to ask him about old friends. I grew up here, y'know," is all I give him.

"So I've heard. Neighborhood's changed since your day."

"So have a lot of things, like who's taking whose money around here."

Through a grin that's more sneering than friendly, his long face puckered like a squeezed lemon, he says, "Yeah."

Whatever Pike's up to, whatever toying around with me he has in mind, it's cut short by the arrival of Esposito. "Well, look who's back, like that bad penny everyone talks about."

"It's a public place, Lieutenant," I say.

"Uh-huh. Y'know, I could haul you in right now."

"Yeah? What for? I didn't rob anybody, or kill anybody, either."

His thick-lipped sneer is almost as sour as Pike's, but not quite, more like chicken fat gone rancid. "I could lock you up for that hat," he says, "that fancy fedora. And for that suit you've got on under your coat. You're in violation of the Criminal Code—the one about hiding your genuine…um…identity."

"Yeah, I know that one by heart. You guys like to hit me with that one every chance you get."

"Don't give me lip, Gold. It's against the law to be all tricked up like the opposite sex."

"Opposite which one, Lieutenant?"

That actually gets a laugh from the guy. "You sure take chances, Gold! Besides, I'd love to see you in a skirt. I bet you'd look good in a skirt. I bet you have great knees."

"They do the job, Lieutenant. They bend when I walk up and down stairs."

Another laugh, even smarmier. Those fatty lips are sure getting a workout. "I bet that's not the only time they bend!

C'mon, Pike, let's get outta here." Esposito's laughter gets lost in the arcade's bells and carny music as he and Pike make their way to the door.

When the Law boys are finally gone, I approach Eddie, who looks exhausted.

"Hiya, Cantor," he says, as if the two little words are all his mouth and tongue have the strength for.

"What did Esposito want?"

"Why you askin' me that, Cantor? Why you want to make trouble?"

Eddie's singing a whole different tune than the one he sang last night and earlier today, when he was Johnny-on-the-spot to help me. But he wasn't scared then. He's scared now. "Look, Eddie, I'm not here to make trouble for you. If you're scared of Esposito because he's Loreale's man—"

"You got it all wrong. I ain't scared. Not yet, anyways. But I'm gonna be plenty scared if you keep pokin' around in things certain people don't want you pokin' around in. So I'm endin' this conversation right now. I gotta get back to work." He starts to walk away, nervously thumbing the coin changer on his belt.

I grab his arm, stop him. "Then let's talk about something else. If you can help me solve another problem, then I can stop poking around in all those things certain people don't want me poking around in. I can get the hell away from Coney Island, and you'll never see me or hear from me again. So tell me this, Eddie: You have any idea where Mickey would hide something?"

"Like money? Where he'd hide money? Offshore, maybe, or—"

"No, not money. An object. About this big." My hands indicate about six inches tall.

"Nah," Eddie says, waving the idea away. "I wouldn't know nothin' about that. You should look through his bungalow."

"Already did."

"What about the tattoo joint?"

"It's on the list."

"Then why you wastin' my time here?"

I let his arm slip from my grip. I don't explain why. I don't have to. I guess the look on my face says it all.

"Oh," he says through a slow grin, the kind that savors smut. "Yeah, sure. That seat is occupied." He slips some coins from his changer, tries to put them in my hand. "Need to kill some time? Here, play a little pokerino."

I don't want to play pokerino. I want to get far away from Eddie's ugly grin.

❖

Outside on the boardwalk, the sun is still glaring off the ocean, and the salty air is still cold. Steely weather for me to stand around and do what Eddie made sound so crummy: kill time. Kill about an hour, I guess, unless I want to walk in and interrupt Lilah's trade.

That idea goes nowhere.

So instead I'm stuck here on the boardwalk, pulling down the brim of my hat, shielding my face from the wind and my eyes from the glare off the ocean, looking along the beach, remembering the beach packed with summertime bodies in the old-fashioned bathing jerseys of my youth. The women looked like adorable kewpie dolls, the men looked like they wore their long underwear to the beach. Memories of luggers, sweating teenage guys hired to lug rented beach chairs and umbrellas to good spots. Memories of little tomboy me in my dungarees and ratty plaid short-sleeved shirt as I meandered through the crowds, pilfering watches and bracelets from the unwatched bags of smooching couples, or the satchels of old ladies cooling their thighs in the surf. Memories of stowing my loot in my strongbox buried in the sand under the boardwalk.

My eyes and thoughts are pulled down to the boards, see the sun filter between the seams, and wonder if maybe Mickey had the same idea and buried the pyxis in the sand.

And then I doubt it. He said it was in a place I'd never find it, and he knew, if he remembered my old ways, that if it was under the boardwalk, I'd find it.

My old ways. I see them in my mind's eye when I turn away from the ocean and look at the amusements, arcades, bath joints, and rides lined up along the boardwalk and beyond, a seaside extravaganza of wild colors and thrills. I learned a lot in those old days from Coney's carny men like Eddie, fortune-tellers like Mona, and all the other Coney characters who strutted and strolled in top hats and straw boaters, or the sideshow performers in feathers and finery that would make Barnum and Bailey jealous. They taught me courage, and to show it with style. And I learned the patter of the operators, all mostly legit, but some palming your change from a buck, shorting you two bits and giving a sly count to make it tally for the suckers who believed it, or were too timid to challenge the more than slightly shady Coney Island sharpies. I learned plenty from gangsters like Sig and, before him, Solly.

Solly Schwartz, Mickey's disgraced pop. Before his downfall, he ran the place like he owned it, and in a certain way, he did. He took his cut from every hot dog, every oyster and clam sold in the neighborhood, every palm reading, every amusement ride, every kid on a carousel horse, every teenage Don Juan terrorizing girls in a bumper car, every shpritz, towel, and massage in the bathhouses. Solly even owned a bathhouse farther down the boardwalk, Shore Baths, a large, stuccoed building with a glass skylight arching across the roof. The place is closed now for the winter, like the other bathhouses. Sig probably took it over with the rest of Solly's empire, leaving the poor guy with just a locker. I get a laugh trying to picture Sig using its steam room: a schvitz bath, the old timers used to call it. I stop laughing when the idea crosses my mind that maybe Sig used the steam room whenever Solly did, just to show off his triumph over the fat old gangster.

But maybe not. Sig's not the gloating type. He's too smart to make unnecessary waves.

None of these memories are getting me anywhere—

Until they do. Until I realize that even if Mickey had lived to have his meeting with Sig, he'd never win Coney Island back because Sig is smart and Mickey was stupid. Sig never lets any information of any kind slip uncontrolled from his lips. He's skimpy with his words, tells you only what he wants you to know. Mickey, though, babbled like a housewife over the backyard fence.

We didn't have a backyard fence last night, just a crummy coffee table between us, but if what I'm thinking is right, then the babblings of a jackass could lead to the jackpot.

Chapter Eleven

The door to the Shore Baths is locked, the big, arched windows with their pink and blue painted mermaid moldings boarded up for the winter. I've got my lock picks and could pick the lock, but there's just enough passersby on the boardwalk to make that risky.

Around back, facing an alley that serves as a cemetery for dead tires, broken thrill-ride hardware, and faded old signs with peeling paint, the back door's boarded up, too, the lock blocked, so I can't get at it. But the workers weren't so thorough in their hammering and nailing along back windows. A board across one window is just loose enough at a corner for me to pry off using a piece of the castoff hardware as a tool.

But the window's locked from inside.

The quiet of the alley is shattered when I break the glass, the shards crashing onto the bathhouse floor with a brittle clatter. But Coney's off-season is my salvation: there's no one else in the alley to hear the noise, or see me reach inside, unlock the window, open it, and climb through.

Inside, I land in a back hallway that gets just enough light from the edge of the skylight for me to see my way to a door.

The door leads into a blue tiled room, bigger than your average bus station washroom, smaller than a high school gym. With its drains on the floor, and spigots and rubber hoses protruding from the walls, you might confuse it with a torture chamber, but it's not. It's a hosing room, where attendants hose you down with needle-sharp sprays of warm water, a therapy believed to invigorate the circulation. My pop was an enthusiast of these hose downs. I always knew when he'd had a shpritz. He was extra frisky with my mother when he came home.

I don't bother looking into the drains; they're small, too small to hide the pyxis, so I move on into other rooms. The drains are just as small in the hot bath pool and cold bath pool—the former tiled in fleshy pink, the latter tiled in aquamarine—so I don't bother with them, either, though the swimming pool drains look promising. I hear my own breathing, deep and anxious, echoing around the cavernous blue and white tiled room and the empty pool as I unscrew the drain covers with my penknife, but the effort yields nothing.

A place I'd never find it, Mickey bragged. So far, he's right. But these were only just-in-case searches before heading for the place his loose lips let slip. So I forget about searching the men's and women's steam rooms and what the country club crowd would call a sauna, but the Coney denizens just call dry heat. And I breeze past the kitchen, where beer and sandwiches are served up in summer to a bathing-suited clientele on a boardwalk patio. I'm headed to the last private place Sig allowed the joint's previous owner: the men's locker room.

Rows and rows of lockers face me when I walk in, some tall, the kind where you can hang your clothes, some little more than cubbyholes with doors. If Mickey's using the locker he inherited from his father, and if Sig let Solly keep the locker he'd always had since he built the place, then I can forget about the little cubbies. Solly would've claimed a full-size locker for himself. And it would be in a prime spot, away from the drafts of the door and at an end, handy to the rear aisle.

The lockers at the far end fit the bill, but which one? Which locker at the end of which of the ten rows is now Mickey's?

I head for the last locker in the last row, pull out my case of lock picks, choose a small pick and tension wrench, and go to work. The locker door opens. Nothing in there but a moldy towel, and nothing to identify the locker as Mickey's. The next two are empty, the one after that has another towel and an abandoned pair of canvas beach shoes, which look too big for Mickey's feet. I move on to the locker at the end of another row: bingo. It's Mickey's. I know because there's a mustard-stained sandwich-and-beer order receipt on the floor with Mickey's name scrawled on it.

I found Mickey's locker, but all I have to show for it is a mustard-smudged receipt. No jackpot.

I take a last glance at the receipt, laugh—bitterly, I suppose—at this mustard-stained slip of paper that mocks me. *Shore Baths Café*, it says, *Where the elite meet.* Yeah, sure, some elite. Sweaty guys with pot bellies, workingmen with rough knuckles, tired wives, noisy kids.

I was one of those kids once, though my family preferred Stauch's Baths to Shore. But since Shore Baths was built and owned by Solly Schwartz, a gangster with strong lines to boot-leggers, when Prohibition hit, everyone in Coney knew you could still get a beer and whiskey at the café at Solly's bathhouse. The contraband came in on the ocean, picked up from freighters and trawlers by hard guys in small boats, and brought ashore in the middle of the night to out-of-the-way inlets along Coney Island Creek. Solly's trucks—and later Sig's trucks—bristling with gunmen met the boats and drove the booze to the bathhouse kitchen, where it was stored in tunnels.

Speakeasy tunnels.

I head to the kitchen.

Since the end of Prohibition, most of New York's speakeasy tunnels are used for extra storage, everything from supplies of napkins and tablecloths, to glasses, silverware, and boxes of matches. Some saloons still use the tunnels to store extra booze. To satisfy their original purpose, the entrances to the tunnels were carefully hidden, but once found they were easily entered and exited. The last thing the bootlegging bunch needed was a hard to climb through hole in the wall while lugging cases of whiskey.

I'm sure Solly hid the entrance to his speakeasy with that in mind: hard to find, easy to move through.

It takes me a little while, but I find it behind a rack of hanging tablecloths inside a steel cabinet built into a wall. Telltale screw holes give away that the cabinet used to have a false back hiding the door. Tilting back my fedora, keeping my head down, the door's big enough to walk through.

The cold and pitch-dark tunnel hits me with the limey smell of damp rock, the gritty scrape of sand, and the sting of salty air. I feel around near the door for a light switch, find one, flip it, but nothing happens. The electricity must be turned off for the winter.

I pull out my lighter, flick it into flame. All I see in the weak light is a narrow path between racks of shelves on either side of me, and the white edges of dishes and curved cup handles stacked on the shelves. I never knew dishware could give me the ghostly creeps.

The flame blurs as I walk between the shelves, turning the lighter left and right, looking for my jackpot bundle. The path's treacherous with loose pebbles, and I trip more than once, banging against the shelves, rattling the ghostly dishware.

My lighter's getting hot, the chrome-plated steel burning my fingers. I snap it shut, let it cool. I'm in the dark.

The mind does funny things in the dark. Since it can't look out, it looks in, rummages around in memories, finding ones that fit with whatever sensations seep in from the air. The gritty sand, the stinging smell of saltwater, coax from the darkness fragments of carny music and shuffled images in swirling colors. I'm inside those colors, feeling the windy thrill of wild rides, seeing the wide grins of wild people who taught me how to beat the world at its own game. I see myself move through the slatted shadows under the boardwalk, where I'd bury the loot I stole from the beach, and bury, too, my hurt feelings when a pretty girl would shrink from my longings. I'm on the Thunderbolt coaster, screaming with giddy fear. I see myself hanging around Mona's fortune-telling booth near the Wonder Wheel, watch Mona dig deep into the marks' minds and pockets with just a word, a hint that their future hangs in the balance. I'm at a shooting gallery where I was better than any ten-year-old should be in shooting a moving line of painted tin ducks. I'm in my gaudy once-upon-a-time days and neon nights tangy with salt air and my shoes full of sand.

My soul's never gotten rid of any of it.

I force myself out of the reverie. My lighter's cooled down enough for me to snap a new flame. The flickering light replaces the memories and visions. I'm back in my *now*, back in my need to find my stolen treasure and pick up my life in the bright lights and dark alleys of Manhattan, back to making peace with Rosie, and pressing Sig to make good on his promise to find Sophie. I need all that but can't get it back until I find what Mickey Schwartz Day stole from me, a treasure older than any of my memories.

So I start moving through the tunnel again, past the white glimmer of dishware.

My lighter picks out a dark, slouching shape next to a stack of dishes. Reaching for it, I feel a leather strap and a damp, bulging stretch of canvas. I bring the lighter close: it's my satchel.

If my heart beat any harder it would crack my bones. My palms are suddenly sweaty despite the tunnel's salty chill, because finding the satchel won't matter a whit if the pyxis isn't in it or if it's broken. I can't count on Mickey's thugs, or Mickey himself, for taking good care of my stolen loot.

Putting the lighter on the shelf, I take hold of the satchel, reach inside, feel the bulky padding I'd wrapped around the pyxis. The shape under it feels intact, as if Mickey never bothered to unwrap it for a look, but I won't know what's what until I examine it for damage. Miranda van Zell expects me to deliver a perfect specimen, and she'd probably keep her money in her handbag if there's so much as a scratch. Slowly, carefully, I unwrap the bundle, then bring the lighter close to examine the surface.

In the flickering light, I'm again thrown back in time, but now it's far, far back to the ancient moment when the dancing ladies on the surface of the pot were first seen by torchlight, their lifted legs and swirling chitons of red-ochre against a black background, their heads thrown back in pagan ecstasy. I'm pretty sure I would've enjoyed attending their feasts.

I don't see any cracks in the surface, at least not in the meager light of the flame. Even the lid, with its sunburst pattern bordered by the traditional meandering Greek key and surmounted by a small ringlike handle, seems to be intact. I can't be sure, though, until I get it out of Coney Island and under good light.

But I found my Dancing Goddesses. I can get out from under the secret, watchful eyes of Sig's local henchmen, out from the cops nosing around in my business, out from the mess of Mickey's murder, out from Coney Island's sweet grip.

Chapter Twelve

I didn't say good-bye to Lilah, didn't bother with any toodle-oo to Eddie, or check in with Esposito and Pike to let them know I'll be out of their hair, their precinct, and their gun sights. I drove right back to the city. As I walk through the back alleys from Louie's garage to my office, the noise of my dockside neighborhood gathers around me like a comforting shawl, helps shake off Coney Island's fevered dreams.

Judson's hanging up the phone when I walk in. "That was Mrs. van Zell. She wants to know—" He sees the satchel. "You found it?"

"Yeah. But I need to check its condition before I deliver it to Miranda. It's had a rough ride since I brought it ashore. C'mon, let's look this baby over."

Inside my private office, I take two magnifying glasses from my desk, give one magnifier and the lid of the pyxis to Judson, keep the body of the pot and the other magnifier for myself, and turn my desk lamp on. I've done this dance with Judson before, each of us checking the condition of an artwork or artifact, then confirming what the other found, or didn't.

"Wow," Judson says when we're done. "It's a beauty, and not a scratch on her."

"She's a beauty, all right. Twenty thousand dollars worth of beautiful." I wrap it back up, put it in the satchel.

Judson says, "So where'd the guy stash twenty grand of gorgeous?"

"In a booze tunnel in a bathhouse kitchen."

"Huh. Not bad. Pretty smart."

"The choice of spot was smart," I say. "The guy wasn't. Okay, let's get Miranda back on the phone."

Judson dials the phone on my desk, says to Miranda's butler Charles, "Cantor Gold for Mrs. van Zell," hands me the receiver, then goes back to the outer office.

I hear Miranda's throaty hello.

"It's Cantor," I say. "I have your little piece of ancient Greece."

I hear her quick, sharp intake of breath, then, "Intact?"

"Intact."

Her breath flows out again, slowly. "Well done, Cantor. Very well done, indeed. How soon can you be here?"

"How soon can you have twenty grand?"

"As soon as I open the safe."

"I'll be right over."

❖

It's nearly three in the afternoon when I arrive at the van Zell penthouse, and Charles escorts me to the same study where I delivered the bad news about the pyxis last night.

Miranda, dressed in a pencil-thin gray skirt and a severely cut, severely expensive belted black jacket, is enjoying a drink at her desk when I walk in. "Join me?" she says.

"Chivas, neat."

The way she gets up from the desk and walks to the bar cart, serene as a smooth lake, you'd never know she's about to receive a fabulous treasure. But that's one of the differences between people whose money is old as quill pens and people whose cash is newer than yesterday's gossip columns. The old-money crowd doesn't grab for things. They're accustomed to things coming to them.

Miranda hands me the scotch, and with a wave of her hand invites me to join her on the couch. After allowing me the courtesy of enjoying a deep swallow of my drink, she nods discreetly toward the satchel. "So, is it as beautiful as I imagined?"

"You tell me." I remove the bundle from the satchel, unwrap it, and give the pyxis to Miranda, whose green eyes suddenly shine. Not with grasping greed, but with a kind of scholarly lust. She has a collector's appreciation for beauty: finely sophisticated, and utterly primal.

"This is it," she says. "This is the treasure that will finally convince the museum to name their ancient art galleries the van Zell wing."

So much for the pure love of beauty.

"Thank you, Cantor," she says. "You've succeeded admirably."

"I've earned my money," I say. The hint's not especially subtle, and not meant to be.

"Ah yes, your twenty thousand. Just a moment." She says it with the easy confidence of someone for whom twenty grand is just pin money as she gets up from the couch. Putting the pyxis on the desk, she walks around to the landscape painting on the wall and pushes a button camouflaged by the blue silk wallpaper. The painting slides up, revealing a wall safe. With a glance back over her shoulder, no doubt making sure I'm too far away to see—and memorize—the combination to the safe, Miranda twirls the dial. I just smile back at her. My smile hides my annoyance at being distrusted.

My annoyance melts when Miranda hands me two tight stacks of cash.

Twenty thousand dollars in hundred dollar bills makes a bulge in my inside jacket pocket, but my black overcoat hides it. "Thanks," I say, taking my satchel and starting to leave, "until next time."

"Yes, until next time."

I'm just about at the study door when another bit of business turns me back. "By the way, have the police been around again about the dead doorman? What was his name? Frank?"

"Oh, that," she says, as if I've brought up a minor irritation and not a man's murder, a murder I was privy to. "The police won't be around anymore, Cantor. That matter's been taken care of."

"They've arrested someone?" That could jam me up, since the thug who killed the doorman was one of the thugs who grabbed the pyxis from me. The guy was one of Mickey's boys, and if the two murders, Frank's and Mickey's, get roped together, I could find myself tangled in so many police knots I'll be picking threads of rope outta my skin for years. "What do you mean, taken care of?"

"Just that," she says as she sits down at her desk with the nonchalance of someone who has nothing much of importance to do, except maybe write a cocktail party guest list. "There won't be any further inquiries in the matter. When I spoke to the police commissioner this morning, we agreed the guilty party must be a common thief who tried to rob poor Frank and wound up killing him when Frank resisted. And you know, anonymous muggers are rarely, if ever, caught. Don't you agree, Cantor?"

I don't know if I've ever been reminded so diplomatically that I owe someone—in this case, the well-connected Miranda van Zell—a favor. "Yeah, that sounds about right," I say.

"Good-bye, Cantor. Until next time."

"Until next time, Miranda."

❖

Back out on the street on this beautiful day, I take my time walking along Fifth Avenue to my car. The sun is shining, the air is winter crisp, and my recent troubles are done with. I'm even tempted to cross the street and stroll in Central Park. But walking around New York with twenty grand in my suit pocket is not the best idea, so I figure I ought to get back to my office and my own wall safe behind my own desk.

In my good mood, I'm not particularly uneasy about Miranda's cozy relationship with the police commissioner, or her power to cover up a crime, but I feel a little guilty about Frank being cast aside as just another poor shlub too unimportant to get justice. Still, that's the way of the world. If it wasn't for the money I make so I can afford one of the best lawyers in town, and having fixers like Miranda van Zell and Sig Loreale on my dance card, the Law would treat me as less than human, too. It already tries. And not because I steal things.

Meantime, though, I'm free as a bird. I've got money in my pocket, and time on my hands to spend it. I wouldn't mind spending the time, and a chunk of the cash, with a beautiful woman on my arm. I wouldn't mind spending it with Rosie.

I'm not in my office five minutes, giving Judson his three grand cut of the twenty Gs and then putting the rest in the safe—where I glance, as always, at the photo of Sophie and me—before Judson comes into my private office, his face pale and pasty as wet bread.

"Loreale's on the phone for you. How come he's calling here? He never calls here."

Sig's a man of habits, and when he breaks a habit, the world gets nervous. I get nervous. But I also get curious. "Close the door on your way out, Judson."

When Judson's gone, and I'm alone, I pour myself a scotch, sit down at my desk, take a long pull of the whiskey, and wonder if this could be it, if this could be the phone call when Sig tells me he's found Sophie.

I've got a belly full of butterflies when I pick up the phone, say, "Hello, Sig," and hear the click of Judson ringing off.

"Good afternoon, Cantor. I assume that click is your boy hanging up?" His slow way of speaking makes everything he says, even a casual question, sound like a death knell.

"You assume right. What's on your mind?"

"I heard you left Coney Island without even saying good-bye."

I don't waste my breath asking who told him.

"That was wise, Cantor," he says. "Leaving was wise, and the way you left was wise, too. No fuss, no messy ends regarding the death of Mr. Day."

"I found what I was looking for, so his death no longer concerns me."

"Yes, that is wise, too. That matter will all be taken care of." There it is again, the second time today I've heard the language of the privileged or the powerful, the language of matters taken care of. If the average Joe and Jane ever found out just how many people were pulling life's strings, they'd break down and cry over the lie that's the American Dream. Or maybe they'd just keep barbecuing in their new backyards, numbed by a juicy steak.

"So why are you calling, Sig?" The heart-pounding hope I started this conversation with is fading, but not gone. No, not entirely gone. "Do you have something to tell me?"

"No, I have something to ask you."

My last bit of hope just crumbled. "Sure. Go ahead."

"In the aftermath of Mr. Day's death, I assume you had dealings with his sister."

"I wouldn't say dealings. Just a chat. What you might call a condolence chat."

"I see. All right, during your condolence chat, did she say what her plans were for Mr. Day's property and any of his businesses? Not that he had much."

"No." I almost gag on the word, remembering that the only thing Lilah was concerned about was servicing her next john.

"Of course, you will keep me informed should you hear of her—"

"Look, Sig, I don't expect to hear from Miss Day, and I have no plans to be in touch with her. My business in Coney Island is finished. But my business with you isn't."

"I wasn't aware we had any current business, Cantor." He couldn't sound any colder if he spoke through a mouthful of ice.

"Sophie." I say. "The business about Sophie. About who took her and where. Look, I've paid for big ears all over the place, listening for any whisper of information. But my contacts, extensive as they are, are nothing compared to yours, and we made a deal to use your contacts to help find her. For a man who thumps his chest about keeping his promises, you sure aren't living up to your billing."

The silence on the other end of the phone is as thick and heavy as the air before a dangerous storm. "When I have something to tell you," he says, every slow word like the deep rumble of thunder, "I will tell you. Good-bye, Cantor."

Doris is pouring a mug of coffee for a guy down the line when I take a seat at the counter of Pete's luncheonette. Finishing up with the guy, Doris brings me a mug and the coffeepot, and pours me coffee. "Late lunch?" she says. "Or early dinner? Or maybe just a piece of pie?" The friendly warmth of her cigarette voice is a welcome change after Loreale's cold rumbling. "We got a nice apple today. I could heat it up for you."

"Chicken on rye," I say. "I haven't eaten a thing since I was here this morning, and I'm hungry, so make it a double-decker."

"Double-decker chicken on rye. Mustard, right? Slice of tomato?"

"You know me too well, Doris. Marry me."

"Not in this lifetime." Then she adds, "But maybe the next."

"I'll look for you."

I take off my coat and hat, hang them on the rack, then sip the good black coffee while Doris orders up my sandwich.

The day was okay until Sig put his chill in it. I'll need a lot more than just hot coffee to warm it back up. My spoiled mood must be all over my face, because when Doris comes back with my chicken sandwich, she says, "So who the hell hurt you in the five minutes I was gone?"

The only things Doris knows about Sig Loreale are the same things everybody else reads in the paper, hears on the radio, or sees on the television news: crime stories or gossip squeezed between the latest battlefield news from Korea and items about some Hollywood pinup girl's latest playboy romance. None of them gets Loreale's story right, anyway. But the less Doris knows about the real Sig, the better. And it's better if she has no idea that I know Sig at all.

So with as much cheery nonchalance as I can muster, all I say is, "Hey, life hurts sometimes, Doris."

"Eat your chicken sandwich. You'll feel better. And when you feel better, you'll be able to lie to me better."

"I'd never lie to the woman who brews the best damned coffee in America."

"Listen, smart aleck, lyin' to me ain't no skin off my back. I'll pour your coffee anyway. But lyin' to yourself, well, that'll catch up with you and kill you. Eat you alive from the inside. So whatever's botherin' you, you don't want to tell me? Fine. Maybe it's none of my business. But do yourself a favor and own up to what hurts you. You'll live longer."

❖

Home now, standing at my apartment window in my shirtsleeves, a smooth Ellington tune on the radio on low, I sip a drink in one hand, follow it with a pull on a cigarette in the other, smoke curling along the window as evening descends on the towers of the city. The lights of my Theater District neighborhood glow into life. The drink, the smoke, the music, the sweet view vanquish Doris's finger wagging about owning up to what hurts me. Sure, the loss of Sophie hurts. But that always hurts. I'd have to be numb, or dead, to deny it.

Rosie sure pegged me this morning: I'm still in love with Sophie. I'll always be in love with her. She was my joy, the passion in my loins and the sweetness in my soul, my smile in the morning, my peaceful sleep at night. With or without Sig, I've got to find her.

As much as I love Sophie, I also love life. My life. My crazy, brazen, thumb in the Law's eye life. That life was good to me today. So why do I feel so crummy tonight?

CHAPTER THIRTEEN

Rosie's phone rings half a dozen times before I accept there's no answer, accept she's not home. I wonder if she's with that regular fare again tonight. Serves me right if she is. Rosie's too smart to keep waiting around for what I can't give her.

I grab a quick shower, spiff up in a fresh suit—a navy double-breasted with pinstripes over a pale green shirt, navy tie with pale yellow chevrons, finish it off with a pale green silk pocket square—and figure I'll take in a slow fox-trot with a sweet stranger at the Green Door Club. That oughta pep up my mood.

I'm just about to grab my overcoat and fedora from the closet when there's a buzz at my apartment door.

My heart beats fast again, just like it always does when there's a buzz at my door, ever since the night Sophie disappeared. Scenes of reunion play in my head, scenes of embraces and kisses and tears, my face buried in Sophie's dark hair, my arms around her, while she whispers my name. Those scenes play in my head now, I hear her…*Cantor*…when I open the door.

It's Rosie.

My heart slows down, resumes its mundane function of keeping me alive.

Still, it's good to see Rosie. It's always good to see Rosie, and the way she looks right now, all dolled up in a black velvet cocktail dress, a strapless number, heart-shaped at the top and curvy the rest of the way down to just below the knee, her coat thrown over one shoulder, makes seeing her even better.

"Oh," we both say at the same time.

"Oh," she says again, "you're dressed like you're going out."

"So are you."

She gives me a shrug and a smile. "Can I spoil your plans?"

"You can improve my plans."

I have to admit, I love Rosie's smile. It's sweet and tart at the same time. It hints at ecstasy, promises an adventure in finding it.

Her smile shrinks a little, a touch of regret settling in the corners. "I'm sorry, Cantor. I was...a little rough on you this morning. Forgive me?"

"Always."

❖

The feel of Rosie against me as we sway on the dance floor of the Green Door Club is the best medicine I could have tonight. Warmer than swaying with a stranger, more stimulating than any amount of booze I could swallow. I could be content in Rosie's arms forever, if only...

"Mmmm," she purrs, "if I didn't know you as well as I do, I'd say you're actually enjoying yourself."

"Of course, I'm enjoying myself. Dancing with you is always a pleasure, Rosie."

We dance a little more, sway around the dance floor to the swoony music. Indulging myself in Rosie's warmth, her body in rhythm with mine, I'm barely aware of the crowd in the room, barely notice the drinkers at the bar.

She says, speaking slow and low, "I almost didn't come over tonight. I almost took a fare."

"Same one as last night?"

"Oh...well, yeah. She's a regular, and—"

"You don't owe me any explanation, Rosie. I shouldn't have asked."

"Maybe I'm glad you did."

I have no response to that, at least, not one that would make her happy. I could tell her I was jealous last night, and it would be the truth, but not the happily-ever-after kind of truth.

But the way she moves with me, the way her body curves into mine, is a truth, too. So I hold her a little closer, move a little more smoothly to the music, just let myself enjoy Rosie, trust our friendship on whatever terms we live it. Tonight, at least, here on the dance floor, I'll let myself be happy.

Except it's a rotten happiness. It's rotten because as Rosie and I circle around on the dance floor, I catch sight of Peg Monroe serving drinks to a couple at the bar. The couple's on the same bar stools where Lilah and I sat last night.

I don't want to think about Lilah, have no reason to think about her now that I've recovered the Dancing Goddesses. My work in Coney Island is done.

But it isn't done, because Mickey's killer is still out there, and the killer may have designs on Lilah. And now I know that Sig Loreale has his own interest in Lilah.

She might be in the crosshairs of killers.

I stop dancing. "I'm sorry, Rosie. I have to go."

The way she pulls away from me, quick and stiff, you'd think I'd slapped her. And in a way, I did.

"Good-bye, Cantor." It's as if she's slapped me back.

I stop by my place, strap into my shoulder holster, slide my .38 into the rig, put extra rounds into my trousers pocket, and grab my lock picks. Breaking and entering is often on my menu.

It's almost ten o'clock by the time I arrive back in Coney and park outside Lilah's bungalow in the Gut. The place is dark, probably no one home, but I knock on the door anyway.

No answer.

I walk around the bungalow, check for light or sounds of life in a back room.

Nothing, which worries me. The possibility of Lilah dead on the floor worries me.

Back on the porch, I pick the front door lock and walk inside, switch on a living room lamp. All that floral wallpaper almost dizzies me.

The kitchen and two bedrooms are tiny, tidy, and with walls of a cheerless, dull beige.

No one's home.

I drive over to Surf Avenue, park the Buick, then walk along Schweickerts to the tattoo parlor. It's dark, too. Against my better judgment, I knock on the door, pound on it, not giving a damn if I'm disturbing Lilah and some john in the back room.

No answer.

I pick the lock and walk inside.

Finding a light switch, I flip it on, call out, "Lilah!" and move through the still blood-spattered tattoo joint and into the back room where I met with Mickey. It's empty, so I walk into a side room, flip on a light there, too. It's a cramped, dreary bedroom with an empty, unmade bed, the sheets tangled, the air tinged with the smell of flesh. I don't want to be in here.

I'm grateful for the salty ocean air when I get back outside and walk up to the boardwalk. The nippy night clears my head of the fleshy misery of that bedroom.

But the familiar Coney breezes do nothing to calm my worry for Lilah's safety. Where the hell is she?

Eddie's emptying coins from a shoot-'em-up machine when I walk into the arcade. The nighttime crowd's thick with locals, plenty of people feeding the games, making them clang and whistle and shriek.

Eddie's not happy to see me. "I can't be talkin' to you."

"Who're you afraid of, Eddie?"

"That's not a smart question."

"Maybe you'll like this one better. Where's Lilah Day?"

"How should I know? What am I, her babysitter?"

"You were happy to babysit her last night, make sure she was safe."

"Yeah, well, that was last night. I'm busy tonight. Take a look around, lots of people for me to handle. I can't be bothered about one dangerous little girl." His grizzled face is suddenly all pasty, like he's been caught in a spotlight with nowhere to hide.

"That's a strange thing to say, Eddie. I figure Lilah's more in danger than she is dangerous."

"Sure, that's what I mean. If she's in danger, I don't want her bringin' that danger in here. I don't need the aggravation."

"And I thought you're a nice guy, Eddie. I guess I was misinformed."

"Go away, Cantor. I got work to do."

"Sure, I'll go away," I say. "Next time I see Sig Loreale—remember? I know him *personal-like*, just like you said this morning—I'll be sure to mention your name, tell him you're a good soldier after all." The old geezer's gone from pasty to green. "Uh-huh, I get the picture now. You're one of Sig's Coney locals. But you're way down on the ladder, Eddie. He doesn't chat personal-like with you. So you must be getting your orders from…um, let's see, how about Esposito? Is that why he was all over you today?"

Eddie suddenly looks a little less trapped, even gives a small laugh, sort of a nervous spit. "Sure, Cantor, I'm way down on the ladder. And if you want to tell Mr. Loreale I'm a good soldier, that's fine by me. But I don't know where Lilah Day is."

"Then you're not such a good soldier after all, Eddie. But maybe you can make it good. What do you know about Mickey Day's operations?" He starts to walk away, I grab his arm. "He told me he'd been putting an outfit together, young toughs who are probably the angry sons of Solly Schwartz's old gang. I, uh, had a little run-in with two of them last night."

"I don't know anything about that," he says, yanking his arm, but I don't let go.

"No, I wouldn't guess you do. But are there any little tidbits about Mickey's operations you *do* know, Eddie? I figure you're supposed to snoop and give the information to Esposito, who gives it to one of Sig's henchmen, who gives it to Sig. You're not gonna get rid of me, Eddie, until you spill."

There's that nervous spit of a laugh again. He wipes his mouth with the back of his free hand, a way of buying a few extra seconds of not talking to me, maybe put a wall between him and me. But none of it works, the wall crumbles, and he finally says, "Yeah, Mickey was puttin' an outfit together. He really thought he could go to war with Loreale if Loreale didn't accept his business offer to get Coney's rackets back. Jerk. Loreale had damn good reason to kill him—"

"But he didn't."

"Right, he didn't. So who the hell did?"

"I was hoping you could tell me, because whoever killed Mickey may want to kill Lilah. The killer might figure Mickey's sister would inherit his operations. Somebody might want the last of Solly Schwartz's kids out of the way."

Eddie's stiff attitude loosens a little, and I let go of his arm. Maybe I hit some out-of-the-way sentimental spot in the old Coney coot, maybe the mention of Solly's family stirred a nostalgia for the old days. "I hope you find her, Cantor."

Chapter Fourteen

I drive over to Sixteenth Street, and I'm not crazy about it that the only parking spot on the block is in front of my old house. Last night's trip down memory lane while lounging on the stoop—just like I did as a kid—was enough. Being back in Coney's sugar-sticky grip, wallowing in all the memories, could get in my way. I have even more dangerous things to do.

So I make it snappy down the block to Mona's bungalow, walk past a patched-up Chevy truck, a pre-war but newly shined Ford, and a fairly recent model dark Dodge. I never liked a Dodge. Its chrome grille, stretched across the front, makes the car look like it's in a bad mood.

Mona's front parlor light's on.

The squeaky screen door announces my arrival even before I ring the doorbell. Mona's "Who's there?" comes through the door.

"It's Cantor."

It takes a little longer than I'd like before she opens the door, her aqua terry robe catching streetlight, throwing a watery pallor onto her puffy face and stringy black hair. "Come in, Cantor. Quickly." When I step inside, Mona shuts the door fast.

"Why the fast slam? What's going on, Mona?" But the answer is right in front of me: Lilah.

She's seated on the couch, dressed more like a jazz denizen of Greenwich Village than a Coney Island cutie in black high-heeled shoes, a black high-necked sweater, and a green-and-black plaid pleated skirt that's at war with the couch's floral upholstery. The skirt is winning.

Lilah's nervous when she sees me, runs her hand through her hair, making it even more adorably tousled, as she gets up from the couch. "Cantor, what are you doing here?" The usual lilt in her voice is gone. Instead it's tight and scratchy.

"Making sure you're all right," I say. "I've been looking all over for you. Tried you at home and the tattoo parlor. Only other place I could think of was here."

"That's—that's very kind. But I'm fine."

"Yeah. So I see. You're as nervous as a rat in a streetlight, Lilah. What's going on? What are you doing here at this hour?"

But it's Mona who answers. "She's helping me, Cantor. She knows how upset I am about the loss of my precious Miss Theresa. Lilah's keeping me company."

"Mona," I say, "you were a better liar when you were in the fortune-telling racket. You weren't sad when you came to the door, you were jittery. So drop the death-in-the-family act and tell me what the hell is going on."

Lilah sits back down on the couch, Mona sits next to her. Neither of them looks comfortable.

I let their discomfort fester, waiting to see which one will finally break and tell me what's what.

After a few awkward moments, Mona sits up, and when I think she's about to talk, she just dully primps the same vase of flowers next to the same deck of tarot cards that were on the coffee table last night. She doesn't say a word.

The stillness in the parlor is heavy enough to flatten every wave in the ocean.

It's Lilah who finally breaks it. "It's because of me, Cantor. Mona's scared because of me. I came here because I'm terrified, and I hoped Mona would…well, take me in for a while. My house and the tattoo parlor aren't safe anymore. I couldn't think of anywhere else to go, who else to call."

A twinge of—hurt feelings? jealousy?—sneaks up on me. We'd shared a bed. We'd shared a murder. And now I'm not even in Lilah's phone book. Maybe I should just walk out of here, go back to the city, back to Rosie, try to patch things up with the woman who could teach Miss Lilah Schwartz Day a thing or two about being on the level.

But if I turn my back and go home to Manhattan, and something happens to Lilah, if a killer finds her, could I live with that? I don't want to find out. "Who's scaring you, Lilah?"

"That's just it," she says, sitting up, eyes wide with fear. "I don't know. But someone's after me, Cantor. Someone's been to my house and the tattoo parlor. When I went home this afternoon, things were out of place, like someone looked through my stuff, through Mickey's stuff, too. I think they tried to put everything back the same way, but I could tell. Same thing at the tattoo parlor when I went there tonight. Things were moved around like they'd been handled. I was so scared, I had to…I had to send a client away."

Lilah's not the first hooker I've bedded or befriended. The ladies and I share some of the same turf. Their lives, like mine, are acts of giving the middle finger to the Law that kicks us around. Their clients, like mine, provide the cash to keep a roof over our heads, food in our mouths, and if we make a few extra bucks, well-tailored clothes, like mine, like Lilah's. It's just business. So why is it that whenever Lilah talks about her clients, my stomach tightens and my throat threatens to close up?

After a "Hmm," meant to sound like I'm thinking but really to get my insides to settle down, I say, "Anything missing?"

"Not that I could see," she says.

"What about Mickey's business records? Are they in the house or at the tattoo parlor?"

"I don't know."

"What do you mean, you don't know? Didn't you ever see him write a check, or cook the books?"

"Look, Mickey wasn't big on sharing anything with me about his business, except when he collected money from a client and gave me my cut." She takes a deep breath, the kind that tries to flush out a memory, then says, "A lousy, chintzy cut. Mickey could sure be cheap, even though he was my brother. The only time he forked over more cash was for my clothes. He wanted me to look nice. He said it was good for business." She says it like the words are spiked with bitter juice. But then something in her softens, something inside works its way outside, and she winds up looking like a little kid wondering whether she's allowed to go into the candy store. "Cantor, I don't remember my father. I was just a baby when Loreale murdered him. My mother always said my father was a hard man but a generous one, that's why his friends—well, okay, his *gang*—were so loyal to him. Do you remember him that way?"

"I didn't really know him all that well," I say. "I remember him as the boss of Coney. I remember seeing him around. Don't forget, Lilah, I was a kid myself when Sig and your dad battled it out. And like everybody else in Coney Island, I just tried to stay out of their way. Maybe you should ask Mona. She was around then."

Mona waves away the question like she's shooing a fly. "Yeah, sure, I was around, but what good is talking about it? Solly is dead and gone, and now Mickey is dead and gone, and if we don't want Lilah dead and gone, we need to forget about all that old stuff and think about what's going on now."

"All right," I say, "let's talk about what's going on now. Like what was Mickey involved in, besides putting a new gang together? What was Mickey's racket?"

The way Lilah looks at me, and laughs at me, you'd think my pants suddenly fell down. "You're really asking *me* how he made money, Cantor?"

It's another gut-tightening moment. "Besides that," I say.

"Gee," she says, playing at a smart-aleck attitude, "I'm sorry if you don't approve. But don't worry. I've been sneered at before. I'm just surprised to be sneered at by you." Those gorgeous green eyes which last night looked at me with so much lust, and later with a plea for protection, look at me now with a disappointment that makes me ache.

I push aside the vase of flowers and deck of tarot cards on the coffee table, then sit down on the table, knees to knees with Lilah, and take her hands. "You've got me all wrong, Miss Day," I say. "I'm not sneering at you, or how you earn your daily bread. Hell, last night I was the grateful beneficiary of your talents."

Mona's gaudy laugh breaks my tender moment. "You always did like the professionals, Cantor. You remember? When you were a rowdy young dandy, just before you left Coney Island for good, you used to drop by the notch joints. Loreale owned them by then."

It's not a tidbit I particularly want brought up, but I'm not especially embarrassed by it either. It actually seems to make Lilah friendly toward me again, if the smile she gives me is any indication. There's surprise in her eyes, but enjoyment in her smile. The two sentiments merge into a gentle laugh rich with wisdom.

"Mona," I say, "you sure can pick 'em."

She shrugs that off, says, "I just don't want you to forget where you come from. You left in such a hurry today—yeah, word got around that you just up and left—it was like you washed your hands of us. Scrubbed us outta your fancy new life, dumped the sand outta your shoes. Not even an *arrivederci*. Maybe you shoulda stayed away, Cantor. You bring trouble."

"I'm here now."

"So you're here now, so what? So why? Suddenly you're back? Who sent you? Maybe it was that *bandito* Loreale. I hear you're close with him."

"You heard wrong, Mona."

"Maybe. But you two got history. You think I don't know you worked for him before? Hey, I was around then, like you said. Remember?" She says it through a sneer that hints she has beans to spill and she's going to spill them. "Those visits to his flesh joints weren't just because you had hot pants, Cantor. You weren't only a customer. Word has it you picked up cash for Loreale."

Lilah's smile disappears. She slides her hands away.

"Like I said, Mona, you sure can pick 'em. But you don't always know what you're picking." Lighting a smoke gives me a minute to soothe the hurt under the scab Mona's just ripped off.

Lilah whispers, "Got another smoke?"

I shake out a cigarette. She puts it between her lips, I light it for her.

Through a slow exhale that sends smoke around her face like one of Salome's veils, she says, "I think it's time for you to come clean about your connection to Loreale, Cantor."

"I'm not on his payroll, if that's what you mean."

Mona says, "But you were."

"I was young and trying to stay alive, Mona, that's all. And like you said, it's no good talking about the past. We have enough to worry about in the here and now." I close down Mona's inquisition by taking Lilah's hand again and moving the conversation back where I want it. "Look, Lilah, getting tangled up in Sig's business is the last thing I want to do. That's why I left this afternoon. After I got what I came for, all I wanted was to get Sig's hired Coney Island eyes off me, get back to my own racket. But life isn't that simple. Stuff pulls at you. Stuff was pulling at me."

Some women stroke your cheek when they think you're talking sweet about them. Some give you a charmingly innocent smile or the come-hither variety. But Lilah Schwartz Day doesn't stroke my cheek or give me a smile. She starts to cry, a silent sob carried on a long, slow tear that rolls down her cheek and settles in a corner of her mouth.

She looks almost as defenseless as she did when she saw the knife in her brother's back, only now there's no fear mixed up in it, no horror, just a weary hope that someone actually gives a damn about her.

I say, "I came back because I figured you might be in danger, and I couldn't put it out of mind. With the cops snooping around, and Loreale's people looking into Mickey's business—yeah, it might've been one of his people poking around in your things, looking for Mickey's books—you may have a target on your back. Whoever killed Mickey may figure you'll take over his operation, and they'd want you out of the way, too."

Mona jumps on that. "So maybe it was Loreale who had Mickey killed?"

"Sig had no reason to kill him. Mickey was a fly Sig could swat out of the way when the time came. Mickey's murder makes things messy for Sig's business plans now, and Sig doesn't like things messy."

Mona says, "So you're not close to Mr. Loreale, huh? How come you know so much about what he thinks? You a mind reader?"

With a laugh more annoyed than jolly, I say, "I leave the mind reading to you, Mona. I spoke with Sig this morning, that's all."

"You spoke to Loreale? I thought you don't work for him."

"Just because I don't work for him doesn't mean I don't talk to him, even when I don't want to. And believe me, I usually don't want to. Listen, both of you, you're just going to have to trust me. Mona, I have to assume that you have Lilah's best interest at heart. You have to trust that I do, too."

She reaches for the deck of tarot cards. "We'll see."

I take the deck from her hands. "Forget about the cards. I don't need them to tell me what to do. And what I have to do now is get Lilah to safety until I figure out Mickey's murder. C'mon, Lilah, get your coat. I don't know how much longer you'll be safe here. Esposito knows I was here last night, so sooner or later he'll be around again, and then whammo, your cover's blown."

"I don't know, Cantor. I'm not sure I should leave."

Standing up from the coffee table, I tower over Lilah, still seated on the couch. Reaching for her hand, I say, "I'm not giving you a choice."

She stands up without resistance, her black high-necked sweater catching light, her plaid pleated skirt swaying, her green eyes narrowing. "Where are you taking me?"

"Out of Coney Island."

Lilah pulls her coat more tightly around her as we walk out Mona's door and down the front stoop. She looks along the street, turning her head left and then right, watchful.

"Don't be scared," I say. "We'll be gone in a minute. My car's just down the block. We'll be back at my place in an hour." I take her arm, lead her toward my car.

But someone takes *my* arm from behind, grips it hard. A thick voice says, "We'll take things from here."

The voice comes from a jowly face with hooded eyes and a red nose under a dark fedora. Bulby Nose. The thug who grabbed the satchel with the pyxis last night outside Miranda van Zell's place.

The *we* he referred to is his murderous pal, Pointy Chin, who's got Lilah's arm in his grip.

"Well, well," I say, "if it isn't my new friends from last night. What gives, boys? Your boss is dead, so you operating on your own? Nah, you don't have the brains. So who you taking orders from now?"

Lilah says, quietly, like she's trying not to wake the neighbors, "Maybe you shouldn't push them, Cantor."

"I'm not letting them take you."

Pointy Chin says, "Get in the car, Miss Day," and tugs her to the dark, bad-mood Dodge sedan parked at the curb.

I pull Lilah back with my free arm. "Don't get in that car."

Bulby Nose yanks my arm loose from her. "You're not givin' the orders here."

"Yeah? Well, who is? Loreale? Is it Loreale? Did he get to you? Make a deal with you? Are you his boys now?"

Bulby Nose snorts. "Shut up, Gold. Miss Day, get in the car."

"She's not going anywhere," I say, surprising everyone by pulling my gun. "Let her go," I tell Pointy Chin. "And you, Bulby Nose, let go of *me*."

"What did you call me?"

"You heard me. And if you don't want to hear the muzzle of this gun blasting in your ear, you'll let Miss Day and me go." I don't see Lilah, and I don't see Pointy Chin, but I feel a gun muzzle suddenly rammed against my back.

Pointy must've moved around back of me while I got gun cute with Bulby. "Drop it, Gold," he says. "Drop the gun."

"And if I don't?"

His laugh is as sharp as his chin, a brittle cackle like cracking plaster. "Well, then someone's gonna die."

He probably means me. But he might mean Lilah. I won't be happy with either result.

But I know he's a killer. He's the thug who knifed Frank the Doorman at Miranda van Zell's.

Pointy Chin's in back of me. Bulby Nose is in front of me. Which is why the elbow of my free arm lunges backward, smashing Pointy's gun out of my back, while my gun hand slams forward, right across Bulby's face.

I make a grab for Lilah, try to make a run for it to my car, but Bulby Nose recovers fast and yanks me away from her. I can't see Lilah now, don't know if Pointy's got her. I'm too busy trying to get Bulby Nose off me, to keep him from wrenching my gun out of my hand. He's a big guy, strong as an ox, and I swear he's trying to pull off my whole hand from my wrist, just to get my gun.

We tug back and forth, pain shooting deep into my hand, my wrist, and up my arm. Bulby's eyes glare under his fedora, his teeth bared in a rage that he can't wrest my gun from me. But I don't dare let go, even after the gun goes off, scaring the crap out of everybody. The bullet hits the sidewalk. Lilah screams.

Pointy Chin yells, "Let's go!"

I spin around in time to see him get behind the wheel of the Dodge, Lilah beside him. Bulby gets into the backseat, slams the door shut as Pointy Chin drives the car away.

CHAPTER FIFTEEN

House lights that flicked on briefly during the tumult go off now. None of the neighbors ever came outside, nobody lent a hand, didn't even look through their windows. Same old story: there's nothing like a little fear to kill off neighborliness.

I go back to Mona's, knock on her door. But even she doesn't answer. I guess fear can kill even the most tender friendships. It certainly seems to have killed Mona's friendship for Lilah, and whatever nostalgic friendship she may have had for me.

I'm scared now, too, scared for Lilah. I have to find where they've taken her. I have to get her out alive.

I walk over to a hard-drinking saloon I used to frequent on Mermaid Avenue, hoping the place is still there. I need the walk to calm me, shake off my fear, try to figure my way through the spook-house ride I've been on since I came back to Coney Island. It's been tough enough to avoid the ghosts in the darkness, and now the crazy car I'm riding risks smashups with murder and kidnapping and sex, the sex I had with Lilah for pleasure, and the sex she has for sale. I wonder if sex is Lilah's way of navigating through her own spook-house life, the way crime is mine. I suppose we all choose our survival gear, our weapons to fight our way into the American Dream: sex, guns, money, a wife and two kids, a husband and a two-car garage.

By the time I reach the saloon—still open, to my relief—I need a drink and a phone more than I needed the walk.

Inside, the saloon hasn't changed much since the last time I was in here over fifteen years ago, except the bar stools—once green—have been re-covered in red vinyl, and the song playing on the jukebox is a Johnnie Ray tearjerker instead of a Benny Goodman swing. Otherwise, the air still smells of beer and cheap whiskey, the dark walnut bar's still scratched, and the sawdust on the floor still reeks of salt air, vomit, and beer. The four guys at the bar, two of them drinking alone, pay no attention to any of it.

The song finishes up on the jukebox, but nobody gets up to put in a dime and play another tune. The fellas are too busy watching me. The saloon's quiet as a tomb as stares follow me to the bar.

I've seen these kinds of stares plenty. They could mean trouble, or just the cold shoulder. Since no one's moving off his bar stool, I figure it's the latter, which suits me fine. I'm not looking for chitchat. I just want a drink, a phone, and a little peace and quiet to figure things out.

I ask for a double scotch, no ice, from the bartender, a bag of bones whose tired eyes are held open only by their wariness of everything. "I used to drop by this place," I say, "when Morty—"

"Morty's dead, heart attack," the barkeep says, his face like stone. "I bought the place from his widow." He looks me over as if he's getting ready to smash me one to the jaw. But all he says is, "This ain't your kinda bar."

I don't like being told I don't belong. And though I learned a long time ago I'm not going to change anyone's mind, nothing is going to change my mind, either. If I can tell cops not to boss me around, I can tell it to this backwater barkeep, too. "Look, bud, I'm here for a drink, not trouble, though if you want it, I can certainly provide it. So just pour me the scotch, and we can both end the night without a black eye."

But he doesn't pour me a drink. He cocks his head, and the next thing I know, two of the guys at the other end of the bar are suddenly on either side of me. One of them is thick and brawny, all bulk and beer belly under a plaid shirt. The other's wiry, all sinew under his unzipped brown lumber jacket and red shirt.

The other two guys at the bar just keep their eyes to themselves, and keep drinking.

The wiry guy says, "You deaf? The man said this ain't your kinda place."

The bulky guy says, "So you're leavin'."

I say, "Even if I buy you boys a drink?" Sometimes a little sugar works, too.

The wiry one says, "I don't drink with pree-verts. So get outta here."

I say, "No."

And that's when the wiry guy gets stupid: he pushes me, slams his finger in my gut, and rams his other hand hard against my shoulder. He shoves so hard, my breath clogs in my throat then bursts out, my hat falls off and tumbles to the floor. He's shoved so hard, he's unleashed the outlaw who takes no guff from the unrighteous.

The wiry guy never saw my jab coming, and it will be a few miserable days until his right eye sees anything at all.

But there's a sudden slam into my lower back from the bulky guy's fist into my kidney, doubling me over. I don't like the pain, but being doubled over is slick cover for my hand slipping under my coat, and when I finally straighten up, my gun's in my outstretched hand. It's tough for me to speak, but I manage. "I'll take that drink now, barkeep. And if you've got a phone back there, put it up on the bar."

The barkeep's face isn't stony anymore. It's pale and pasty as he pours me a rotgut scotch and brings up the bar phone. My two attackers back off, the wiry one with his hand to his eye.

Keeping my gun in my right hand, I pick up the scotch with my left, down it in one pull. It restores my gut, settles my nerves. "Another," I say to the barkeep, who pours another scotch without complaint but with a sullen look. "Now go away," I say, and put a buck on the bar. He moves off. "You, too," I tell the two guys, and they don't argue. No one argues with a gun.

Alone now at my end of the bar, I dial a number. I check my watch while the phone's ringing. Nearly eleven thirty. Maybe he's still up.

A gruff voice comes on the line. "'Lo?"

"Let me talk to Sig."

"He's just gone to bed. Call back tomorra."

"Get him up," I say. "Tell him it's Cantor Gold. Tell him there's another problem in Coney Island."

After a pause while Sig's thug figures which choice is worth his life—to wake the boss or not wake the boss—he bets on the former. "Hang on a minute."

I sip my scotch and light a smoke while I wait for Sig to come on the line. The booze and nicotine keep me steady, blunt the pain in my kidney.

A minute or so later, I hear, "What is so important, Cantor, that you disturb my sleep?" spoken in Sig's slow way that feels likes snakes slithering up my spine.

I say, "Did you send any of your flunkies to poke around in Mickey Day's stuff or his sister's stuff, looking for Mickey's business records?"

"That is no business of yours, Cantor."

"Maybe it is, maybe it isn't, but okay, I'll let that go for now. But here's something I will not let go."

"I warn you, Cantor, it better be important."

"Oh yeah, you bet it is. Did you take over Mickey's outfit and tell two of his thugs to grab Lilah Schwartz Day?"

"That is not important, Cantor."

"Think again, Sig. It's plenty important. Because I think Lilah's the key to Mickey's murder. Not because of anything she might know, but because of who she is. If she disappears, or winds up dead, all the players, all the new real estate money boys vying to divvy up Coney Island, all the crooked cops, and all the Coney operators, will be at each others throats, and not even *you* will be able to control it, Sig."

Sig Loreale didn't rise to be New York's—and the whole country's—number one crime lord by being careless. He weighs everything, examines everything, just like I know he's doing now through his silence. It lasts only a few moments but feels like eternity, until he finally says, "No, I did not take Miss Day. When did she go missing?"

"About fifteen minutes ago. Two thugs snatched her right in front of me."

"I see." That's all he says before he lapses into a rough breathing silence that doesn't end the conversation, just signals me to be quiet while he thinks. He finally says, "You are certainly involved in a mess, Cantor. You would be wise to clean it up. Do you understand?"

You bet I understand.

"And I must say," he goes on, "it seems you keep losing things in Coney Island. First your client's goods—"

"I found the goods, Sig. I made my money."

"Good for you. But now you've lost Miss Day. You seem to keep losing women, Cantor. Good night."

He hangs up.

He's just wounded me worse than the two barflies who attacked me, worse than any cop who's beat me up, and all he had to do was raise the specter of Sophie.

Eddie's loading a gumball machine when I walk into the arcade. It's well past midnight, but the place is busy with plenty of insomniac locals feeding the machines, making the games clang and chime and buzz, keeping the players better company than their empty beds. When Eddie finally sees me, he's even less happy about it than when he saw me earlier. Right now, he looks like he's about to be sick. "What'll it take for you to leave me alone?"

I answer his question with the venerable New York tradition of asking a question right back at him. "You familiar with the boys in Mickey's outfit? Particularly a pointy-faced guy, and a husky guy with a nose like a Christmas lightbulb?"

"Not sayin' I do."

"And you're not saying you don't. Spill it, Eddie."

"You're lookin' to get y'self killed, Cantor," he says, sour as stale beer. "And get me killed, too."

"I'm not looking to get anyone killed. I'm looking to keep Lilah Day from maybe getting killed." He gives me a look a little less sour, but a little more worried. I wonder if he has a soft spot for Lilah, or at least for the good old days Lilah recalls to Eddie's mind, when he was a young player, before he was just an old gofer for the big boys.

"Yeah," I say, "they grabbed her. So I want to know who they are, and where they live."

He doesn't answer me right away, just looks at me, then looks around, nervous, like he's scared of being marked a rat.

"Listen, Eddie, if it's any comfort, you won't be telling tales behind Loreale's back. I just spoke to him. He didn't order the grab on Lilah. Pointy Chin and Bulby Nose aren't working for him, and he couldn't care less what happens to them."

"Yeah, but does he care about Lilah Day?"

"Personally? Probably not. But he cares about the mess she's in the middle of. He wouldn't mind if I cleaned up the mess of Mickey's murder and Lilah's grab. So give me a hand, Eddie. Sig won't mind. I'll even put in a good word to him about you."

The old guy straightens up a little, says, "You'd better," more a plea than a command.

I nod my promise.

He wets his lips, takes another moment or two to get a little more sure of himself. "Yeah. The guy with the pointy face. That'd be Al Berg. And the other guy sounds like Frankie O'Byrne."

"Know where they live?"

"You won't find Miss Day at O'Byrne's place. He's got a room in a flophouse on Kensington. His room's barely big enough for himself and maybe a pet roach. Better off tryin' Berg's joint. He's got a bungalow in the Gut, on Third Street. A real tumbledown place, green with brown shutters. Be careful, Cantor. They're real tough boys. That Berg, he's plenty—"

"Handy with a knife, not bad with a gun. Yeah, I know. Thanks, Eddie."

He answers with a joyless chuckle that rubs against my nerve ends. "Don't thank me yet. I didn't do you any favors. When I buy you a nice coffin, then you can thank me. G'night, Cantor."

Chapter Sixteen

Sig owns most if not all of the cops in the Coney Island precinct, so I'm gambling that maybe a badge boy or two might give me some help cleaning up the mess Sig wants me to clean up, or at least help me find Lilah. I don't make a habit of working with cops. In fact, the number of times I've worked their side of the street has been exactly zero. But as much as I don't trust cops, I trust the current Coney Island players even less; that is, if I could even get a handle on who the hell they are. With Mickey gone, I don't know who's trying to pull the local strings behind Sig's back. Eddie Janko has one story, Mona Carlotti has another, and I wind up talking to myself and bumping into my own reflection over and over again. I might as well be trying to work my way through Coney's funhouse mirrors.

So if I want to find Lilah, I'll need a little insider help. And since I don't know if Lilah's being held by only Pointy Chin Al Berg and Bulby Nose Frankie O'Byrne, or if they've surrounded her with Mickey's reconstituted little army, getting her away from whoever's got her could be tricky, so the more guns backing my play, the better. If I'm lucky, maybe Sig's Coney cops will figure that if it's in Sig's interest, it's in their interest.

The police station over on Eighth Street, built during the Gay Nineties, is as weirdly phantasmagorical as so much else in Coney Island. Its turrets, arches, and fake timbered facade conjure up a fantasy Alpine castle, not a house of billy clubs and guns. But don't let the fairy-tale exterior fool you. Plenty of blood stains its history; its jail cells breed madhouse dreams. When I was a teenager, I endured one of my first police beatings in there, dragged in by a couple of patrol guys who gleefully pointed out that my dungarees and sport shirt buttoned on the wrong side. It seems to be in the nature of cops to beat you up, or drive you crazy, or be driven crazy themselves by all the savagery they see, which may be why they beat people up. Or maybe they're nuts to start with. Maybe it's a job requirement.

Any resemblance to a fairy-tale castle stops inside the station. It's dingy inside, busy and noisy with middle-of-the-night hauls of drunks hollering obscenities or crying for their dead mothers, hookers screaming from their cells for their lawyers or pimps, and bad boys with tattoos who've just knocked over a gas station yelping their innocence. Only the pros like me stay quiet in their handcuffs. Pros get our phone call, call our lawyer, get a little shut-eye until we're sprung, and if all goes well—and that's a big *if*—no one gets hurt, unless, of course, you're someone like me, wearing those wrong clothes. Of all the scars on my face, some are souvenirs of my outlaw life, and some are from cops who've taken issue with my fashion sense.

The plainclothes cop who snares me when I walk in probably looked better in uniform. His suit, an off-the-rack gray number that hasn't been sponged or pressed in weeks, is up-to-date for a date sometime around V-E Day, and neckties haven't been that wide since the Roosevelt administration. After he looks me up and down, gives me that cop sneer, I figure I'll have to talk my way out of my own night in the cells. But all he says is, "You're Cantor Gold, ain't you. Been hearin' about you all damn day. I didn't figure you to be the type to just drop into a police station."

"I never lack for invitations, if you know what I mean."

"Uh-huh. Well, if you're lookin' for a welcome—"

"Nope, just looking for a little help, like any other citizen."

A familiar voice behind me says, "Since when are you a regular citizen?" The guy with the voice comes around: it's Esposito. He's in his shirtsleeves, his tie—a cheap red and blue one but more up-to-date than the other guy's—hangs limply open. He's got a juicy cigar stub between his fat lips. The smoke veiling his chubby face makes his olive complexion look sickly and his steady stare from his brown eyes seem humane.

"What are you doing here, Lieutenant?" I say. "I thought you were a day-shift guy. Shouldn't you be home in bed?"

"I got two murders on my hands, Gold, Mickey Day and that other guy, his tattoo flunky, Gus. Until I clear those up, home will have to wait. Captain pulled me in on this last night. I'm the senior detective, see? And Mickey Day was a big deal killing." He adds with a shrug, "Too bad about Gus. The guy was just in the way, I guess. But what the hell are *you* doing here, Gold?"

"Is there someplace where we can talk?"

He eyes me like I might have head lice under my hat, but finally says, "My office."

One thing that could result in attracting a better class of cops to the ranks is a better class of furniture. Nothing says you're worthless like crappy furnishings supplied by the boss—the boss, in this case, being Joe Taxpayer. Inside Esposito's cramped office, there's a crummy chipped desk, lumpy desk chair, an old-fashioned coat stand with Esposito's coat and hat, and a rickety wooden guest chair. The pale blue walls need painting, and the only thing relieving all that sooty blue is last month's calendar pinup for December 1951, a very buxom blonde severely underdressed for Christmas, her Santa hat notwithstanding. If I didn't find the pinup so tasty, I might say the picture's insulting, treating the dame like a Christmas gift for the taking. But I don't kid myself; if Miss December 1951 came gift wrapped to my door, I wouldn't take her to the returns counter.

I'm pulled back from my arousing daydream by Esposito plopping his chunky bulldog frame into his chair, making the miserable contraption squeak its pain. He plunges his cigar stub into an ashtray, says, "Okay, Gold, whatever's on your mind, it better be good."

"I need your help."

The chair squeaks plenty as Esposito slowly sits up, never taking his eyes off me, his expression like he's just heard the worst joke in the world by the worst baggy-pants comedian. "To do what?" he says. "Maybe you'd like me to help you rob a bank? Or maybe run a bunco job? How about we set up a murder, like we ain't got enough of them around here lately."

"I'm not trying to be funny, Lieutenant, and you shouldn't either. Lilah Day was grabbed off the street, right in front of me, by two guys who mean business when it comes to killing. One of them killed a doorman in Manhattan. Yeah, I know, that's outside your jurisdiction, but not Sig Loreale's. And he'd like the whole mess cleaned up."

"Oh, would he? Well, in that case, I'll jump right on it." He drips enough sarcasm to strip whatever shellac finish remains on his battered desk. I've seen cops resent their paymaster overlords before, but never this bad. And besides, the money lining their pockets tends to take the sting out of their betrayal of their badge. Maybe Esposito's just all clutched up about being stuck out here in the Siberia of police precincts, hauling in drunks and carny hucksters, instead of working one of New York's big-time precincts, putting steel bracelets on big players. He can't spill his resentment on Sig, but I guess he figures he's pretty safe spilling it all over me. "Okay, so who are these two bullies who stole Miss Day from you, Gold?"

"Al Berg and Frankie O'Byrne."

The lieutenant stops playing the fool. What he thought was a bad joke suddenly hits him with the punch line of an even worse one, one that's not funny at all. "Mickey Day's muscle," he says. "Yeah, I can see why Loreale would want this business cleaned up. Mickey was in his way, but—"

"But you and I both know Sig didn't order the hit on Mickey."
He stares at me like he suddenly knows me, suddenly knows I have the goods on him that he's Loreale's man. It takes him a minute, but his stare loosens, gets more comfortable. Maybe he's come around to realize I don't care if he's Loreale's man. When he finally gets back to being his cop self, he says, "Sure, Mickey wasn't worth it. And besides, Loreale's hits are cleaner than that, and Mickey's hit was a sloppy job, taking Gus out like that, blood all over the place." Esposito shakes his head, *tsk*s his disapproval like a connoisseur of finer murders. "You think it was Berg and O'Byrne? You think they turned on Mickey to take over his operation?"

"It's starting to look that way," I say. "And now they've got Lilah. Maybe they figure she'll challenge them for leadership of Mickey's outfit, and now they want her out of the way, too. And you know Loreale. All these loose ends floating around in all that blood aren't good for his new plans for Coney Island."

"Yeah, he wants to clean up his money with real estate." He says those last two words, real estate, like they're the punch line of a dirty joke.

"So what do you say, Lieutenant? You gonna help me find Lilah, get her away from Berg and O'Byrne? It may be just the two of them holding her, or maybe she's surrounded by more of Mickey's thugs, if he has any more. I don't know. I'll go it alone if I have to, but an extra gun would improve the odds."

Esposito sits back in his chair, the contraption's squeak like a shriek of the damned. The minute he takes to eye me up and down while he thinks things over crawls slow as an hour. His thick satchel lips finally move, opening slowly, like he's not altogether convinced that saying whatever it is he's planning on saying is a good idea. "Okay," he finally says, drawing it out, giving himself that extra second to change his mind. "Okay, I'll back you." The chair gives a dying shriek when he gets up and gets his hat and coat from the stand. "I don't like murderers on my beat. And even though I don't like you, Gold—I think your life is disgusting—I get the feeling you don't like murderers, either. Let's go."

"Where's your shadow? Where's Pike?"

"Home in bed, if he's smart. Just because I can't let go of this case doesn't mean he has to."

Seems I found the one decent bone in Esposito's bulldog body.

❖

Eddie pegged Berg's place, all right: a tumbledown green bungalow with brown shutters, the colors muddy in the streetlight. The Dodge Berg drove away with Lilah and O'Byrne is parked at the curb. I mention it to Esposito, who only nods as he walks to the side of the shack, then back to me. I can't see his eyes too well under the brim of his hat, but his thick lips are pursed like leather bags.

"What's wrong, Lieutenant?" I say.

"Something's goin' on. There's a lotta lights on for one thirty in the morning. Looks like a parlor light, maybe a kitchen light, and a back bedroom. We won't have much cover."

"Could you see inside? Could you see where they've got Lilah?"

"Shades are down. Just saw shadows, couldn't make 'em out."

"Then the hell with cover. We'll have to take our chances and just get inside." I head for the stairs to the door.

I'm on the first of the three sagging steps when Esposito tugs me back. "Okay, I'm gonna ask you a stupid question. You got a gun, right? You're not walkin' in there empty handed?"

If he throws me stupid questions, I can't pass up the fun of pulling the guy's leg. "Don't you know, Lieutenant, I'm not the kind who tells?"

"Very funny. Cantor Gold, comedian."

I start up the stairs again, open the screen door, ready to knock, but the bungalow door opens and a gun barrel's in my face. A revolver, long barrel.

The guy holding the gun is silhouetted against the light inside. A little guy: Pointy Chin Al Berg. "Get in the house," he says. I've had more cordial invitations from funeral directors. "You, too, Esposito." Berg's even less polite to him.

Inside the door, with Esposito next to me, Berg maneuvers behind us, his gun at our backs. "Keep walking," he says. "Hands where I can see 'em."

Esposito's face is sweating under his hat. It's not sweat from heat, not in January. It's sweat from anger, his cop's blood boiling at being bested by a lowlife like Al Berg.

Berg marches us through the shabby parlor into an even shabbier greasy yellow kitchen. But the mood in the kitchen is lively, the laughs supplied by three people enjoying a bottle of whiskey at the kitchen table. One of them doesn't surprise me. One of them I didn't expect and didn't think he had the stones to mix it up with this crowd. And the third is one of those horrible surprises that knocks the light out of life from time to time. The no surprise is Bulby Nose Frankie O'Byrne, who seems to be more interested in the whiskey than in the company. The one I'd never expect is Sergeant Pike. Without his hat, his long face looks longer, his big ears even bigger, his dull eyes duller, and his bad haircut of lifeless brown hair makes them all even uglier. And the surprise throwing the shadow across my soul is Lilah, still in her black high-necked sweater and black-and-green plaid skirt, the jazz club outfit even more out of place in this shabby kitchen with this shoddy crowd than it was in Mona's parlor.

Lilah wasn't being kidnapped outside Mona's. She was being rescued. From me.

Esposito doesn't seem surprised by any of it, or if he is, he's hiding it inside a stony coldness veteran cops develop. He just stands there, hands raised, staring at Pike, who ignores him.

Berg says, "Get their guns, Frankie."

Bulby Nose O'Byrne gets up, but Lilah gets up, too, and steps in front of O'Byrne. She says, "You get the lieutenant's gun, Frankie. I'll get Cantor's." Her smile, seductive and cunning, wants to strip me naked. I like the smile; I have second thoughts about the woman. We stare at each other, I match her smile for smile, but there's no seduction in mine, just wised-up chill. She reaches inside my coat, slides her hand inside my suit jacket, and slips my gun out, her fingers as confident and sure as they were last night, when those fingers slid all over my body.

"You killed him, didn't you," I say. "That was quite an act you put on, screaming to set the scene for Eddie and me when we saw Mickey with a knife in his back. You killed your own brother so you could take over his racket, then slit the sleeping Gus's throat just because he was there and could snitch."

Lilah holds my gun the way a kid would hold a favorite toy, though there's nothing childish about the way she's looking at me. She still has that strip-me-naked smile, except there isn't much in the way of warmth behind it. But there's some. Just enough to hook my attention. "You've got it all wrong, Cantor," she says. "I didn't kill Mickey. And I didn't kill Gus. I actually liked Gus, a sweet guy. I feel bad he's gone, but I guess he got in someone's way."

"Yeah, just another citizen who meant nothing."

Her smile dries up. She looks uncomfortable, like I just shoved her into a lumpy chair. But her discomfort doesn't last long, and though she's not exactly smiling again, she's not far from it. With a shrug, she says, "Anyway, whoever put that knife in Mickey's back did me a favor."

"Sure, I guess so."

"I don't think you understand, Cantor," she says with a puffed up defensiveness, but it quickly loses air. "Well, maybe you do, a little. You saw how Mickey spoke to me, how my own brother treated me, like I was nothing more than flesh for his profit. And his pleasure." There's pain in her eyes, in her voice. It's no act. It's real and raw, and it claws at me, begs me to believe she's not a killer.

O'Byrne's back at the table pouring himself another drink, Esposito's gun in his pocket. Berg's joined him, pouring himself a whiskey with one hand while he holds his gun on us with the other. Pike continues to drink silently. I wonder if those big ears of his are taking in everything on the Q.T. I bet Esposito's wondering, too.

Lilah's still near me, still looking at me, her eyes still asking me to believe her.

Esposito breaks the mood. "Listen, girlie," he says to her, "you can try and romance Gold all you like, but she's not the one you have to convince. So why don't you drop the poor little sister routine and talk to me. And you can start by telling me what the hell Sergeant Pike is doing here."

Pike picks up his glass of whiskey, says, "Don't tell him anything, Miss Day." If he's trying to sound forceful, his nasal voice is killing it. But behind those droopy eyelids is the cold stare of a cop who's sold his soul to cheap grifter Mickey Schwartz Day and his pals Berg and O'Byrne. "He'd only blab it to Sig Loreale, and believe me, that's the last person you'd want knowing what goes on here," he says, then he knocks back the whiskey in one gulp, looking not at Lilah, but at Esposito. When he's done with the drink, he puts down the glass and gives Esposito the sort of smile you want to forget you ever saw but never will. His usually dull eyes aren't so dull now. There's a gleam in them, a touch of fever. "You know what I'm gonna do now, Lieutenant?" he says. "You and I are goin' out to the little shed in the back. Al keeps supplies in there, stuff like tools and rope. You and I are gonna walk back there, and then I'll take a nice long rope and tie you up and leave you there, all alone in the dark, and you won't be able to move a muscle."

Esposito says, "Why don't you just kill me?"

"I'll let the rats do it. And oh, yeah, I'll stick my handkerchief in your mouth so no one will hear you scream when the rats chew on your fat flesh."

I gotta hand it to Esposito. He doesn't flinch at Pike's gruesome threat, his stony cop coldness still in control. All he says is, "You never were much of a cop, Pike. So I'm not surprised you're not much of a killer, letting the rats do the work for you."

"You wouldn't know, Lieutenant. That's been your problem all along." He pulls his service revolver from his shoulder rig, shoves the barrel in Esposito's face, laughs, then moves the gun to the lieutenant's ribs. "Now get moving."

Esposito still doesn't flinch, but before he starts walking he's still close enough for me to hear his sudden, sharp breath.

With Pike now behind him, his gun at Esposito's back, the two cops walk out a side door of the kitchen. I don't want to think about anything past that door.

None of this fazes Berg or O'Byrne, or even Lilah, who joins the long list of disappointments in my life.

With Berg's long gun pointed at me, he says, "What do you want I should do with Gold, Miss Day? I can take care of her nice and quiet if you like."

"Maybe later," she says. "Right now I want to talk with her alone." Aiming my own gun at me, but talking to Berg, she says, "You have any rope in the house?"

"Nah, just back in the shed." I swear, he glows a little when he says it. I bet he wishes he was back there now with Pike. Sick bastard.

Lilah ignores Berg's lust for gore and just says to me, "Okay, then take off your tie, Cantor—no, wait. I have a better idea. Keep your gun on her, Al." With a smile so seductive it could melt the North Pole down to a steaming puddle, Lilah raises her hands to my throat, loosens my tie, and slips it off, slowly, so that the silk whispers as it slides under my collar and along my neck.

Yeah, it's the little things that make a pro.

Stepping behind me, she pulls my arms behind my back and uses my tie to tie up my wrists. "Now, let's take a walk, Cantor," she says.

"Where are we going?"

"Not far. Just to your favorite room."

"I didn't know this place had a bar."

Lilah laughs. Berg doesn't. He says, "Don't get cocky, Gold. Just do what the lady says."

"With pleasure."

I hear Lilah behind me. "Start walking. Down the hall, first room on the right. Door's open."

The hall beyond the kitchen has a room on either side of me. Obeying the woman with the gun at my back, I walk into a too-long-lived-in bedroom whose gray walls and old gray chenille bedspread give the room the feel of a perpetually gloomy day.

Just as Lilah closes the door when we're both inside, we hear the side door to the kitchen open and close, and heavy footsteps walk in. It's Pike, coming back from the shed. Lilah looks at me, then looks away. I keep my eyes on her. I want to know how she feels about the horror Pike let loose on Esposito in that shed. But whatever she's feeling, if she's feeling anything at all, she keeps hidden.

She seats herself on the bed, says, "Sit down, Cantor." When I start for the chair at the dressing table, she says, "No, not there, here," and pats the bed.

She's got the gun. I do as I'm told.

The bed's one of those old-fashioned iron jobs with a headboard and footboard like metal fences. I lean my back against the one at the foot. "Now, suppose you tell me what's on your mind, Lilah. You didn't take me back here for some hanky-panky, not with my hands tied up."

She answers that with a naughty smile that crawls up the length of me. "I just want to talk to you, Cantor. I'm worried about you."

"Well, then, I feel better already. Warm all over. I can feel the heat of the boiling oil you're about to throw me into."

"No, you keep getting things wrong. First you think I killed Mickey, and now you think I want to do you harm."

"Lilah. You're pointing my own gun at me, and you've tied my hands behind my back with my own tie. Friendly gestures, they ain't. So yeah, I think you want to do me harm. The only question is, will I enjoy it?"

My little taunt lands somewhere other than her funny bone. She's not laughing. She's not even smiling. She's gone paler than her blond hair. "Why do you want to hurt me, Cantor? We had… we had something special last night, at your place, in your bed. Didn't you feel it? We could have that again, if you want to. I want to." She puts the gun on the bed like she suddenly realizes she has it and wonders how it got into her hand. Then she kicks off her shoes and slides over to my side of the bed. She takes my hat off, then tosses it aside and brings her face to mine, looking at me like I'm a drink she's thirsted for for years. I see myself reflected in her green eyes, my own face staring back at me, imprisoned in the dark centers of her eyes, unable to break free. She kisses me. It's the kiss of dreams, a kiss whose softness lulls with warmth and comfort but hints at dangerous pleasures.

She takes my face in her hands for a moment, then slides her hands down to my coat, opens it, wraps it around her, and presses against me. Kissing me again, her body moves against mine, and mine against hers, a conversation of lust, and tears. She's crying softly, and talking to me through her kiss. "I didn't kill Mickey, I promise. I didn't kill anybody."

I whisper through our kiss, too. "Then what are you doing here with these guys?"

She takes her mouth from mine, looks at me as if maybe I have the secret of life, then lays her head on my chest, quietly weeping. "Okay, I didn't kill my brother, but you're right, Al and Frankie work for me now, and we're all trying to figure out who killed Mickey."

"And Gus."

"Sure, okay, and Gus." She says it like she's grown tired of hearing his name.

I keep pressing. "And Pike? What's he got to do with it?"

"He's been Mickey's man for months," she says. "Esposito belongs to Loreale, but Pike belonged to Mickey."

"And now you."

"Yes. And now me."

"Then you've made your first mistake as Coney's newest rackets boss."

That sits her up. "Mistake? What mistake?"

"Esposito is Sig Loreale's man in the Coney Island precinct, right?"

"Sure. Everyone knows that."

"Well, Sig doesn't like his people picked off behind his back, especially not by small-timers like—well, like the remnants of the Schwartz gang, or their associates. Believe me, Lilah, Sig's not going to let this go."

She does her best to look like she's in charge, worthy of the title of Coney's newest rackets boss. "Well, I guess Pike will just have to take his medicine."

"You mean hand him over to Loreale."

"If I have to."

"Oh, you'll have to. But that won't satisfy Sig. He's not the type to leave the head on a snake."

That shakes her.

"Yeah," I say, pressing the issue, "he'll come after you, too."

"But I didn't tell Pike to—"

"Torture Esposito? You didn't tell him not to, either. Look, you want to be a rackets boss? You've got a lot to learn, kiddo, like how to keep your people in line."

It seems Lilah knows only one way of getting what she wants and needs, and she uses that talent now, placing her head on my shoulder, sliding her hands along my body, slowly, skillfully arousing me, softening me up until she's ready to deliver the punch line. "Then I need you to teach me how to be in charge, Cantor. Will you? Or maybe we can run things out here together! Listen," she says, lifting her head and facing me now, "even Mickey knew Coney is ripe for the pickings. Loreale wants to turn his money respectable, clean it up with real estate and make a fortune. What does he need with Coney's nickel-and-dime rackets anymore? For the right deal, I bet he'd give them up."

Her hands no longer exploring me, no longer distracting me with temptations of the flesh, my head clears. "You may be right," I say. "Sig might be willing to unload his old Coney rackets if the deal is good, but he didn't want to deal with Mickey, and he won't want to deal with you. Sig won't deal with the last of Solly Schwartz's kids if that kid stood by while one of his local guys was murdered. At least not until the rest of this mess is cleaned up."

"Then help me, Cantor, please. I need you. I need your help." She kisses me again, falling back into her tried-and-true skills to get what she wants.

I let her kiss me, because I like it, and because it keeps her attention away from my last hidden fidget with my hands, until the silk finally slips and I'm free, free to grab Lilah's shoulders and pull her off me, free to grab my gun.

She looks surprised enough to faint and annoyed enough to kill me.

"That's the thing about silk," I say. "It's slippery, lousy for knots, except the fancy kind at the collar, the kind I like having a beautiful woman like you slip open."

She grabs my arm as I get up from the bed, her grip as much a lure as a plea. "See?" she says, "I always knew you're smart. Knots can't hold you, but maybe I can. Maybe Coney Island can. We can rule it together. Come on, let's go back into the kitchen and tell those lugs who's boss now. It's you, Cantor. It can be you. Now kiss me."

She gets up from the bed, brings her face to mine, those green eyes offering everything she has to give: her life, her body, her pleasures, her world. And when I kiss her, I see it all. I see us in bed, taking each other until we're limp, and I see us running Coney Island, letting the hucksters do our work for us while we rake in cash from the top…and I wonder if I could give up everything I've become, risking life and limb for people with too much money and too little soul just so they can have pretty pictures on their walls, or have museum wings named for them. I wonder if the hold Coney Island has on me is the truth of my life, if my past and my future are one and the same, and have been staring me in the face all this time.

The kiss ends, and the only reality staring me in the face is Lilah, whose smile is pretty but small, just like her dreams, just like this little corner of Brooklyn, and I know I'll go on risking my life in a world bigger than Coney Island. My dreams are bigger than Lilah's. Like Sig, I need more than just this honky-tonk isle, even if some part of it still lives inside me, and always will. As any Coney local will tell you, you can never get rid of the sand in your shoes. Maybe that's why Sig still can't completely cut himself loose from his Coney rackets. Maybe without that sand in his shoes, his shoes would be too big.

And there's another matter, too, one that makes me stand back from Lilah, hold her at arm's length. "You think I'm going to play around here with you while Esposito's being eaten alive in that shed? Just what kind of a no-good do you think I am? Don't bother answering, Esposito doesn't have time. Just tell me, is there another way outta here besides the front door and that side door in the kitchen?"

Hurt, scared, she shakes her head.

I open the window, say, "If you call for the others, so help me I'll use this," and make a big show of my gun, aiming it at her forehead. "I'll hate it, seeing that lovely face of yours covered in blood, but I'll do it."

"I wouldn't—"

I don't want to hear her desperate promises, so I cut her off. "Better yet, to be on the safe side, you're coming with me."

That puts the color back in her cheek, and a spark in her eyes.

"Put your shoes on," I say.

We slip out the window, Lilah first, then me.

Halfway across the yard to the shed, I realize I left my tie and my hat back in that crummy bedroom. They say if you leave things behind, it means you're coming back. Frankly, I'd rather buy another hat.

It's pitch-black inside the windowless shed. I flick open my lighter. The flame throws my shadow across the room, along a wall hung with tools and rakes. There's no sound except the horrible, scratchy whisper of tiny, scurrying paws.

Lilah, behind me, says, "I think there's a light switch somewhere."

"No, don't turn it on. The boys in the kitchen might see the light seeping under the door and know we're here." I have a bad feeling as I say all this to Lilah, because my own voice is the only voice I hear. There's no painful moan from Esposito, no weak cry for help.

I let my lighter's flame find my way. Three steps along, my foot slides in something slimy, and I nearly trip over a large, soft bundle. The slimy liquid is blood. The bundle is Esposito, half of his neck chewed to the bone, his face chewed completely off.

CHAPTER SEVENTEEN

My car's still parked back on Sixteenth Street, but the black Ford cop cruiser Esposito and I arrived in is parked at the curb in front of Berg's bungalow. I'm tempted to take it, hot-wire it, and get me and Lilah out of the Gut fast. But heisting a cop car is never a good idea, even if I plan to give it back. Cops never believe my good intentions, and all I'd get for my trouble is handcuffs.

So we have no choice but to hoof it, which is the quieter method in any case. Berg, O'Byrne, and Pike don't seem to know we're gone yet—at least, they haven't looked out to the street—so avoiding the noise of an engine is a good move.

"Don't dawdle," I whisper to Lilah, who's in a daze from the horror movie memory of Esposito. "We have to keep moving."

"We…just…left him there," she says.

"What were we supposed to do? Throw him over my shoulder and take him to a funeral parlor? Okay, he didn't deserve to die like that. Nobody does, not even a cop. But look, here's what'll happen. The boys, *your* employees—"

"*Mickey's* employees. They're sons of my father's old gang, so they were loyal to Mickey."

"And now they're loyal to you."

Waving that away, she says, "I don't think they'll be taking any more orders from me after tonight."

"Maybe they will, or maybe they won't. But in the meantime, they'll take Esposito's body to some out-of-the-way spot and bury him where he'll never be found. His precinct will list him as missing, they'll search high and low, never find him, and after a while he'll be listed as presumed dead. And that will be that. One less cop in the world. Now don't dawdle."

"I'm cold," is all she says.

"Here," I say, and give her my coat. She slips into it, letting the good wool keep her warm, wrapping it around her as if it might keep out any more lousy doings this night could throw her way.

"Where are we going?" she says.

"Mona's."

"But it's the middle of the night. She'll be asleep. She's no kid anymore, Cantor. Banging on her door in the middle of the night could give the old woman a heart attack."

"I doubt it. In order to have a heart attack, you have to have a heart. I'm beginning to think Mona's went missing. Or maybe it got buried with her dog."

"That's cruel."

"So's this whole situation," I say, my voice and annoyance rising. "So's what happened to Esposito, and what happened to Mickey. And the way Mickey treated you. And the way Esposito treated Pike, to make the guy hate him so much. And if Sig Loreale jumps in to finally get rid of the whole mess, then cruel will take on a whole new meaning. He'll make what happened to Esposito look like the work of a naughty kindergartener with dull scissors and too many red crayons."

Sig's reputation for bare-knuckled brutality isn't lost on Lilah. It's been part of the Schwartz-Day family lore for years, since Sig muscled in on the Schwartz gang and left Solly bleeding to death on the beach. My saying it only brings it up to date and makes Lilah wrap my coat around her more tightly, more protectively.

She says, "Why are we going to Mona's?"

"Suppose you tell me," I say, keeping up the pressure, letting the edge in my voice slice through my every word. "You said you went there to hide out from whoever searched your house and the tattoo parlor. You said you felt safe at Mona's. And you *were* safe there, Lilah. Because Berg and O'Byrne were keeping watch outside." I'm not crazy about badgering her like this, because despite all, despite her sneaking around with Berg and O'Byrne, her brother was murdered, knifed in the back, and her own life could be on the line, too. But if badgering her is what it takes to crack the truth out of her, then I'll keep it up, no matter how crummy it makes me feel. "The boys weren't there to kidnap you, Lilah. They were there to protect you, and then to whisk you away from me and the threat I represented in getting too close to whatever you and the gang were up to. But you could've gone to Berg's in the first place, and been even safer. Instead you went to Mona's. Why? What's her angle in all this?"

She doesn't answer right away, just keeps walking beside me, but stiffly, like she's walking to a funeral. She finally says, "Maybe I'd better let her tell you."

"Yeah. Maybe you'd better."

Mona's bungalow's dark when we're finally on her doorstep, but that's no surprise. She'll be in bed at two thirty in the morning. It takes several knocks for a light to come on, and for Mona's sleep-graveled, wary, "Who's there?" to come through the door.

Figuring I'm the last person Mona wants on her doorstep again, I squeeze Lilah's arm and motion with my head that she should do the talking.

"It's Lilah. Open up, Mona."

The door opens. Mona stands in the doorway, silhouetted against the parlor light. She doesn't say anything, doesn't move, doesn't let us in. I'm pretty sure it's not Lilah she's worried about, it's me, the bad penny that keeps showing up at her door. With her face in shadow, I can't tell if she's surprised to see me, or just annoyed. Or maybe she's scared.

Still holding Lilah's arm, I don't wait for an invitation, just walk past Mona and bring Lilah inside and into the parlor.

I say, "Sit down on the couch, next to each other. That way I can keep an eye on both of you."

They sit down, grudgingly, Mona's attitude bitter, Lilah's resigned. It's sort of fun watching both women treat what their wearing as if it might protect them from whatever I'm going to throw: Mona wraps her aqua robe tighter; Lilah pulls my coat more securely around her. I understand the age-old cunning relationship between the female of the species and clothing, sometimes dressing for protection, sometimes as lure, and sometimes, like me, to proclaim a life.

Mona says, "I don't understand. Why do you come around here again, Cantor? What do you want from me?"

I sit down in a chair opposite the couch, open my suit jacket, let it slide back just enough to reveal the butt of my gun in my shoulder rig. I have no plans to use it on either of the women, but it makes a dandy crowbar when people try to keep their mouths shut. A little fear goes a long way in prying loose information people don't want to tell you. "Right now, I just want you to listen, Mona. But be a good student and listen hard, because there'll be a little quiz when I'm done."

"Hah, funny," she says, without a trace of laughter in it.

I light a smoke, offer one to both women. Mona says no, Lilah says yes, and as I lean across the coffee table to light it for her, the way she looks up at me begs me to be kind. But there's a lot more going on in those green eyes, too. There's heat, and there's cold, and both reach deep inside me and grab on tight.

When I sit back down, I need a deep drag on my smoke to smother that feeling of connection to Lilah. It's not easy. That her heat rouses my passion doesn't surprise me. It's the chill inside her that worries me, a chill that dares me to fess up to a deep, dark, cold place of my own, the place Sophie used to fill with love and warmth. It worries me that maybe Lilah wants to merge her chill with mine, create a partnership of icy power whose only heat is in our loins. It worries me that I'm tempted to let her.

My criminal life began here in Coney Island, but I don't want it to end here. Lilah's doesn't have to, either.

But I can't go down that road, at least not now. I have to take back possession of my skin and my senses, and behind a cloud of exhaled smoke, I do, and start my spiel. "Last night, Mickey Schwartz Day sent his thugs to steal something from me. Then he sent his beautiful sister to lure me back home to Coney Island. It worked, too, because I followed her skirt all the way to Mickey's tattoo parlor. It seems all I had to do to get my property back was set him up with a meeting with Sig Loreale. Well, I never got the chance to set it up—not that Sig would've met with a gutter operator like Mickey—because the next thing I know, Mickey's dead, knifed in the back. Gus, his ink man, was dead, too, his throat slashed. Nice way to keep the poor schnook from talking."

Mona, her heavy face pinking up, says, "Why you telling us this now? You told me all this last night, when you helped me with my sweet—" She chokes up, wipes an eye with the back of her hand. I'm thinking it's quite a show, but the tear running down her puffy cheek is real enough. "My sweet Miss Theresa," she finally says.

"Yeah. Miss Theresa," I say. "This is where the story gets interesting. Funny, how coincidence brought me here last night—"

Mona snaps, "No. Not coincidence. It was your fate, Cantor. The cards told you so. The cards—"

"Forget about the cards. You make them say what you want them to say, Mona. I remember you in your fortune-teller's stall telling the marks whatever they needed to hear for them to fork over their dough. Only you weren't trying to make me fork over cash. My being here might've been coincidence, the odd result of a little nostalgia I should have been smart enough to resist, but a sharp operator like you saw a way to use me. And I don't mean just helping you bury your poor pooch."

"The cards told me you'd be here. I know it. The cards knew…" Her voice trails off, her face drooping in a trance I don't believe anymore.

Lilah's evidently had enough of Mona's show, too, giving her trance act a sharp elbow and a *tsk*, and says, "Get off it, Mona. Cantor's on to you. At least, mostly on to you."

Mona's trance melts fast as cotton candy on a hot summer tongue, replaced by a huffy, pursed-lip silence.

"Yeah," I say, "mostly. And the mostly part has to do with you setting me up, Mona, not during my first visit, when you thought maybe you'd never see me again, but my second visit, when I came here with Lilah after Mickey's death. I was inside the situation now. You could use that."

She makes a sound somewhere between a hiss and a swallow, something between annoyed and cornered.

I say, "So, now, here's the little quiz, Mona. It's a short quiz, only a few questions. First question: What's your part in Mickey's operation? Aw, c'mon, Mona, don't give me that look, that *I'm just an innocent old lady* look. You gave up your innocence when you read your first palm."

"You were always the smart one," she says. "Smart enough to get yourself a fancy racket and leave us small-time carny folk behind. So what's it to you what I do to make a living? Why should I tell you anything?"

"Because I'm the only one who can untie the knots in this mess and keep Sig Loreale out of it."

It seems every time I mention Sig's name, people go pale, but their mouths open.

Mona's gone pale as a spook-house ghost. It's time for her to open her mouth, time for me to take my shot. "You know a

Sergeant Pike, Mona?" She goes from pale to ashy to a kind of sickly gray and finally to a fear-induced pink. "I guess you do," I say. "Just like you, he was part of Mickey's cut-rate scheme of things. Well, Pike's just killed a cop. Killed Lieutenant Esposito. Yup, crossed that line, the one that brings hellfire from the blue boys and gold shields."

Lilah says, quick and sharp, "But you said Al and Frankie will just bury him where he can't be found, and the precinct cops would eventually stop looking for him!"

"That's true," I say. "That's what will happen. But you were so scared, I left out the part about what the cops will do in the meantime. They'll roust everyone in Coney, every operator, big time and small potatoes. They'll twist arms and fill their lockups until someone points a finger at some patsy who's marked to take the fall. They'll never look at Pike, a brother cop, unless someone tells them to, but no one will tell them to. So," I say, turning to Mona, "that's what you set me up for, isn't it, Mona? To keep the cops from looking where you didn't want them to look."

"You saying *I* killed Mickey and tried to hang you for it? You are *pazzo*, a crazy person, Cantor."

"Don't worry about it, Mona," I say. "You didn't kill anybody. I was here with you, burying Miss Theresa when Mickey took it in the back. But you didn't want the cops, or me, or anyone, looking under your robe, and when coincidence sent me your way, a finagler like you knew an opportunity when you saw one. You found a handy mark in me."

Mona's crinkling eyes and tight lips make it clear she hates every word I'm saying, and probably hates me, too. I'm not a mark now, I'm a threat she can't hide from anymore. She pulls her aqua robe tighter, like a schoolmarm desperate to cover her prim goods.

But I'll keep going until I expose those goods. "You told me just enough to keep me interested," I say, "and keep me curious about the wrong people. So what is it you're not saying, Mona?

And who'd you rather tell it to? Me? The cops? Or worst of all, Sig?"

Mona, an old-line Coney operator who knows how to keep secrets, hangs tight, doesn't give an inch, doesn't say a word. But her sigh is so heavy, the breath she takes so deep, I worry she'll blow up and burst like a balloon.

I need to seep the air out of that balloon. "You know how Esposito died, Mona?"

I hear Lilah's sharp breath. She bends her head and shields her eyes, protecting herself from the remembered horror in that shed.

I keep pressing Mona. "Pike set rats on Esposito, and the rats were hungry." There's a flush rising in Mona's neck, and a tension in her eyes. I don't let up the pressure. "Esposito was Loreale's man in the Coney Island precinct, and Sig doesn't like having his operatives murdered. He'll punish not just the killer, but anyone associated with the killer, anyone in the whole damn outfit. You understand what I'm telling you, Mona? So, if you want me to keep your name out of Sig's ear, you'll do me a little quid pro quo. You answer my questions, I keep Sig's attention elsewhere."

Mona finally looks at me, her baggy eyes full of anger, but also begging for mercy. "You got to promise to keep Loreale away from me."

"I promise."

"Yeah? And with just a snap of your fingers, I should trust you?"

There's only one way to convince her, and that's with the truth. "I may have left Coney Island, but as I'm finding out, Coney never left me. You know the code of the place, Mona, right?" She gives me a nod, a grudging one but with a little satisfaction in it, too, the satisfaction that comes from sharing a language with someone, and the world that language comes from. So I ease up a bit, talk to her more gently. "That code is part of me, Mona, always will be. Coney people make a promise to each other, we keep it, right? Deception is what we give the marks and suckers. So yeah, Mona, you can trust me."

She actually smiles, not a big one, just a small pleasure she finally allows herself to share with me. "So okay," she says, nodding. "I believe you."

"Good. Then tell me what you did for Mickey."

Her sigh this time isn't fearful, just resigned and a little sad, weighted with regret. "When my Vito died, and all those thugs come around demanding a bigger cut off the top, I couldn't handle it no more. I lost the fortune-telling stall and moved into this place. I didn't know what to do with myself. Listen to the radio all day? Watch the television? How many times could I hear the same Hit Parade song, or watch the same commercials on the television over and over again? Lemme tell you, Cantor, I could hear that damn shampoo jingle in my sleep! *Halo everybody, Halo...*"

She sings it like she's trying to spit the soapy words out of her mouth, even wipes her mouth with the back of her hand.

Then she says, "So I went to Mickey, see if he had anything for me to do. I hated the stupid *buffone*, but who else was I gonna ask? Hell, I know how to work a racket with the best of 'em."

"I don't doubt it. But why Mickey? Sig still has the biggest piece of what goes on in Coney. Why didn't you go to him?"

"Mr. Invisible?" she says, eyes wide with as much fear as annoyance. "The only part of Loreale that's still in Coney is his fist. The rest of him is in some fancy place in the city. And anyway, such a big shot, he'd never talk to me. Probably forgot my name."

"Not likely," I say. "Sig didn't become the most powerful guy in town by forgetting anyone's name, or anything they did. I bet he even remembers the guy who sold him his first subway token when he was a kid in knickers. Anyway, Sig has people here in Coney who handle his local business. Why didn't you talk to one of them?"

"You mean like that louse, Eddie Janko? Hah, don't make me laugh. Eddie would just as soon cut your heart out as give you a hand." She gives Lilah a nudge, says, "Tell her, Lilah, tell Cantor what that slime Janko did."

Lilah, who'd retreated into a wound-licking silence, suddenly sits up as if Mona just woke her from the dead and wishes she hadn't. Whatever Mona was talking about, whatever Eddie did, the memory of it shakes Lilah to the core. Her hand trembles as she stubs out her smoke, then runs her fingers through her hair like she's trying to put out a fire of memories inside her head.

She finally says, "About a year ago," her whisper so raw, her words seem to scratch at the air, "Eddie came to the tattoo shop and told Mickey he wanted to buy him out, take over the tattoo front and my action in back. Everyone knew Eddie was one of Loreale's mouthpieces, so Mickey figured Loreale sent him. Eddie said he was moving on Mickey on his own, but with Loreale's okay."

Sure, that sounds like Sig. Having one of his own people in place, Sig could squeeze Mickey out and take over the operation from Eddie later, or get rid of the whole setup when he's good and ready. Then he could either put Eddie out to pasture or decide he's outlived his usefulness. And as always, Sig wins.

Lilah keeps talking. "But Mickey just laughed at him. Told Eddie he was a has-been geezer, a loser backing the wrong horse. Eddie didn't like it. Walked out of the tattoo shop real mad. He came to see me later at the bungalow, when Mickey was out. I'd just finished up with a client—"

"Hold on," I say. "I thought you only did business at the tattoo joint."

She doesn't answer me. She doesn't have to. Her guilty shrug and cat-that-ate-the-canary smirk says it all.

"And none of the johns snitched back to Mickey?" I say.

"Why would they? I gave them a better price. And besides, they figured Mickey would kill them, and maybe me, too, for cheating him out of his profit."

So little sister had her own racket on the side. A dangerous one. A single unsatisfied john might be stupid enough to tattle back to Mickey, and Lilah would've been a goner. But I can't see that happening. I doubt Lilah's left any client unsatisfied.

I say, "All right, let's get back to Eddie. What did he do?"

But it's Mona who speaks up. "He beat the daylights outta her, that's what he did."

Lilah picks it up, tries to sound steady, but barely makes it. "He slapped me around so bad, I was bruised all over. He said I should've squared his deal with Mickey. So he slammed me black-and-blue. Bloodied me, too. I couldn't work for days."

Every bone in my body scrapes against the next one, every nerve in my flesh burns. Of all the violence I accept in my life, violence I've dished out, or received—from thugs, cops, rivals for my business, even from exes who think I've done them wrong and slap me silly—guys beating up women rouses my avenging demon. Eddie never liked me. He's about to like me even less.

But that's later. Right now, there's more immediate business right in front of me. "And you couldn't tell Mickey who battered you," I say to Lilah, "or he'd know about your side business. So what did you tell him?"

She almost laughs, says, "That an unhappy john from the tattoo shop found me," the vague laugh a tiny triumph over the brother who used her like a rag. "Mickey threatened to hurt the guy, even kill him, but I told him he'd never find him. I told him the guy left town, disappeared, he was just a passing john from I don't know where, I didn't even know his name."

Mona says, "So there's your Eddie Janko, Cantor. There's the guy you let into Lilah's life again and into my house last night. When he came by for Lilah this morning, I was scared he'd finally finish her off. Just for spite. And you sent him!"

Mona's accusation cuts to the bone, but I let it go. I have to. If I'm going to be any use to Lilah, or even to Sig, I have to keep to business. "Lilah, when you came back to the tattoo parlor after your walk last night and saw Mickey and Gus dead, was Eddie already there?"

Mona jumps all over it before Lilah can say anything. "You say Eddie killed Mickey? Sure. Sure, he's an animal. He could do it!"

Lilah, shaking her head, says, "But Eddie came in after," putting the kibosh on Mona's hopes to pin all the world's troubles on Eddie Janko. "He said he heard me scream."

"Uh-huh," is all I say, looking at the idea that Eddie might've come and gone earlier, killed Mickey and Gus while Lilah was on the beach, walking off her humiliation by her brother.

But Eddie is Sig's man, and Sig doesn't hire stupid people. Putting a hit on Mickey without Sig's okay would be a stupid move. Eddie might have slipped up when he beat up Lilah, but he knew better than to take things all the way to stupid. And I believe Sig when he told me he didn't order Mickey's murder. Sig knows better than anyone that murders can bring the wrong attention, disrupt the quiet flow of business. So when Sig wants someone gone, it's done with care and planning, everything sewn up tight. And the job's done neat and tidy, not the sloppy scene of carnage I saw at the tattoo shop.

But I'm not ready to take Eddie off my list, because I'm not stupid, either.

I don't linger in what might be a dead end and get back on the main road. "Okay, Mona, it's still quiz time, and you haven't answered my question. What was your part in Mickey's racket?"

"You gotta answer *my* question first, Cantor. You gonna let Eddie get away with throwing his fists on Lilah? That's why she came here last night, y'know. For protection."

"Yeah, from the guy who searched Lilah's bungalow and the tattoo shop," I say, "and I bet that guy was Eddie. He probably wanted to find the goods on Mickey's scams, something to hold over you, Lilah, to pry the business from you."

Lilah, putting it together, lowers her head in her hands.

"Sure," Mona says, with flashing eyes and a nod that sends a wisp of her stringy hair across her cheek. "I wouldn't put it past that slimy little arcade toot. Anyway, that's why the boys were outside watchin' my place. With Mickey gone, they were protecting her from Eddie. You just got in the way, Cantor."

"It seems I've been making a habit of that lately. Look, Mona, let me worry about Eddie. Right now, tell me what I want to know. What did you do for Mickey?"

With a *tsk* and an impatient breath that Mona can't stop from turning into a little smile of professional pride, she says, "Okay, okay. I'll tell you. I was the shillaber for a Look See."

It takes me a second to clue into *shillaber*, a word I haven't heard since my early days in the rackets, when I was learning a thing or two from Mom Sheinbaum, and from Sig. It's an old-fashioned word for decoy. But Mona's an old-fashioned girl. And the Look See racket's been around probably since the first Dutchman hit these shores and had himself a look around an Iroquois wigwam.

Mona says, "Mickey would arrange a setup down the way in Manhattan Beach, where all those new people with a coupla bucks since the war are building fancy houses and buying new cars in all kinds of crazy colors and with lotsa chrome all over 'em. I swear, them cars look like they're all going to a whore's wedding."

Lilah's head comes up from her hands. She doesn't say anything, just looks at Mona like her own mother stabbed her in the back.

But Mona doesn't even notice. Just goes on with her story. "Mickey also got us setups on the other side of Brooklyn, y'know, near the bridge, where people live in fancy old-timey row houses with fancy old-timey furniture."

"Brooklyn Heights?" I say.

"Yeah, that's the place. Anyway, Mickey ran a business supplying entertainment when the money crowd had parties.

He'd set us up to play those places. I was all dolled up in my old gypsy fortune-teller outfit. Big earrings, scarf on my head, noisy bracelets to distract the suckers. Y'know, the whole picture. I was Madame Mona again, just like I used to be in my stall on Jones Walk." A little nostalgia creeps into her story, slowing her down.

"Go on," I say, pulling her into the here and now.

"Sure, yeah," she says, getting back to it. "So two of Mickey's boys would be on the bartending crew. Durin' my show, when the lights were low except over my table, and everyone was payin' attention to me—"

I finish for her, speed things up. "The boys would have themselves a little look-see around the place, see what was worth heisting. But they didn't take the stuff that night. They just reported back to Mickey, told him about the stuff they saw."

Mona picks it up again. "Right. You know your rackets, Cantor."

"Uh-huh. If you lifted stuff the same night, it would be too suspicious. The cops could tie the thefts to that fortune-teller and her bartender friends. So the boys would come back maybe a week later, maybe two, after they'd case the place and know when the family was out. Then they'd pick the locks and get in, and haul the stuff Mickey told 'em to get."

Mona says, "Yeah, but nothin' too fancy. Mickey didn't handle the high-end stuff. Didn't have the clientele for it. He was more or less in the trinkets business, sold his stuff by the bagful to gift shops and cheap jewelry joints, places like that. From what I hear, he had knickknacks brought in from all over the place, even Europe. Seems he had connections over there from his army days durin' the war."

"Yeah, so he told me," I say, my delivery dry as dust.

"Probably bragged about it," Mona says, taking the wrong meaning from my annoyance.

I let it go, don't bother to tell her that with Sig dragging his feet on his promise to me, I'd hoped Mickey might use his overseas connections to help me get a line on the boat that stole Sophie. But I'm not about to share that bruised part of my heart with Mona. I don't know if she'd get all sentimental and cry over it or try to tell its fortune. Either way, it would be baloney. Instead, I just stub out my smoke and say, "Here's the second question in your quiz, Mona. Besides Eddie, you have any idea who might've killed Mickey?"

She shakes her head. Her stringy black hair sways like snakes.

"Lilah, what about you? Did you and the boys come up with any ideas about who might've shivved Mickey?"

"Uh-uh. Pike even wondered if maybe Loreale had Esposito take Mickey out, but Pike would say that, the stupid fool." She says it with more than just dislike for the guy, she says it with revulsion. Can't blame her; Pike's that least attractive of human combinations: brainless and vicious.

So it keeps coming back to Eddie, but it's not a perfect fit.

I feel like I'm looking through a window full of cracks. Light comes through, but the view is broken into pieces, angles going every which way, making what's out there impossible to put together. It's a mixed-up view of Coney Island, its past in the sharp, jagged cracks, its present spread across the angles. I catch glimpses of all the players in the crazy sideshow of Mickey's murder, everyone trying to crawl from one angle to another, trying not to cut themselves on the sharp edges of the past, where everything in this Coney Island spook ride of murder was set in motion. I see Solly Schwartz, his wife and kids strolling on the boardwalk. I see those kids, Mickey and Lilah, all grown up and bitter at their fate, taking up with the likes of Pointy Chin Al Berg and Pulpy Nose Frank O'Byrne. I see Sig Loreale, and Eddie Janko, and me. But I can't smooth out the picture, can't figure the angles, or where any of us belongs on them.

And then one of those angles suddenly sticks out, nearly pokes me in the eye. "Lilah, you came here last night to feel safe, right?"

"Yes, I told you."

"And the boys were outside to protect you."

"Yes, Cantor. You already know that."

"Al Berg was out there."

"Yes," she says, antsy at being questioned without a letup. "What's this about? What are you getting at?"

"What I asked you earlier: Why didn't you just go to Berg's in the first place? You probably would've been safer there than here. But you came here. Why?"

The two women sit stone still on the couch: Mona, like an aqua-wrapped gnome; Lilah, in my black coat, like an angel of death frozen in time.

Getting the truth from these two has been like trying to pull screws from a wall. My patience, stretched as far as it will go, finally snaps. I pull my .38, get up and walk around the coffee table, point it at the women staring up at me from the couch. "I don't give a damn about whatever it is you've got cooked up between you. Make your money any way you want. But I'm going to get to the bottom of Mickey's murder, or die trying. Sig will see to that. So unless you want me to use this, someone better start talking."

Lilah, skittish as a nerve end, says, "You wouldn't shoot us, Cantor."

"Well, I won't kill you. But I can make you bleed unless you tell me what's going on." I make my point by cocking the gun's hammer.

I can't tell if Lilah's really found some courage or just figures she has nothing to lose, but she drops the skittish bit, stands up from the couch, and moves close to me. She lets the front of my coat drop open, lets the barrel of my gun come up against her body. With a hand on her hip and a smoldering look that could set the winter ocean to a boil, she slides her other hand up my gun arm, along my shoulder, and to my neck. Her fingertips know what they're doing. "No, Cantor," she says, "I don't believe you. You won't harm me. You can't."

But I'm not playing. Not this time. I say, "Don't bet on it." Sticking with my boast not to kill her but not shying away from letting the gun do its work, I slide the gun's nose to her shoulder.

The look in her eyes cools a little but doesn't go away as she sits back down on the couch. She's back to being the sultry little vixen that she was in that crummy bedroom in Berg's bungalow, the pro who knows how to rouse heat in my loins. I guess it's the strongest card in her deck, the one she always relies on. Another night, another place, I might even let her play it. But not tonight, not while the Dead Man's Hand is still in the deck.

I say, "Why did you come here, Lilah, instead of going to Berg's?"

It's Mona who answers, suddenly sitting up straight, her jaw out, her mouth tight, her tough attitude finally fracturing. "*I* told her to come here. I told her. I said to come because she owed me money."

One of those angles in the cracked window smooths out a bit, clarifying a tiny corner of the view. Art lover that I am, I like it when things come into focus, when the picture—even the most abstract—clears up. I smile at such moments. I smile now.

"Come on, Lilah," I say. "Let's go."

"Go? Go where?"

"I'll let you know when we get there."

Chapter Eighteen

I drive around, past the shuttered mom-and-pop grocery stores, shoe stores, butcher shops, and delicatessens on Neptune Avenue, past the car repair places, clam and pasta joints, and the train station on Stillwell, past the bumper-car rides, arcades, shooting galleries, and the carousel on Surf Avenue, all boarded up until the sun and the heat and the hordes arrive for the summer. I drive under Coney's streetlights and neon signs that brush Lilah's blond hair and pale skin with the glow of night. The drive lets me think, lets my mind work through a knot that's starting to untie.

Lilah's smart enough to catch on that I'm not taking her anywhere in particular, that this ride isn't a pleasure cruise or a quick trip out of town. It's a ride through the streets, a ride through my mind. She doesn't say anything, doesn't question me, doesn't pump me to start chatter. She's retreated into that easy breathing silence that comes when you know there's nothing you can do about anything for the moment, so you might as well just roll along.

When things are a little clearer inside my head, it's me who finally talks. "How much did Mickey owe Mona? That's why you went over there last night, right? She called you to pay off her cut of her last job for Mickey?"

"Yeah, sure, that's it. And it was two hundred bucks, if you must know. So what?"

"Two hundred? That's it?"

"Well, excuse me, Big Shot Cantor Gold, but that's a lot of cash around here."

Either Mickey was stingy as Scrooge, or his operation was even less than small potatoes. "Mona seemed pretty sure you had the money to give."

"Listen, I'll say it again: So what?"

"Well, it could mean one of two things," I say. "Maybe you had the dough socked away from your little side business, or maybe you figured why bother spending your own when you suddenly had access to Mickey's money. I'm guessing the latter."

Her breathing is a little less easy. There's an edge to it now, a quickness. "Well, why not? He was family, after all. His money would come to me."

"Suddenly you're an heiress? Try again."

"Cantor, honestly," she says with enough sugar behind it to supply the cotton-candy spinners for a lifetime, "I don't know what you're talking about."

"Don't act coy," I say, tired of her giving me the runaround. "You know exactly what I'm talking about. Mickey didn't have a fortune for you to inherit. He had a business. A two-bit operation of knickknacks and selling your flesh." I hurt her. I catch her wince out of the corner of my eye, but getting to the truth can be like surgery without the gas, knife sharp and plenty painful. "But a cash business is a cash business. You know that as well as anybody, Lilah. You fine-tuned your own cash operation right under Mickey's nose. And when you found him dead, you made your move to take over his rackets and get your hands on his cash, such as it was. But it was enough to pay off Mona. Maybe you called the boys from the tattoo shop, told them what's what and won their loyalty, yeah, before you screamed." I don't ease up on her, but I save a smile for this last bit. "After all, you're still Solly Schwartz's kid, and their fathers were loyal to Solly. Or maybe you called from Mona's after I brought you there last night. Either way, you didn't waste any time."

"Look, I don't know what you think I am—"

"I don't know what you are. I don't know if you really are Coney's newest rackets boss, or a scared rabbit in over her head. But as soon as Mona blabbed that you owed her money, it's like the lights came on. I saw the game you tried so hard to play, may still be playing."

"There's no game, Cantor. I promise, there's no game."

"Sure there is, so stop trying to throw me curves. Mona Carlotti's no fool, Lilah. She's been around since your father's day, seen Solly's gangland reign end and Loreale's reign of terror begin, and she's survived it all. She knows who's who and what's what in Coney the minute she sees or hears it, and she realized you're the new who's who. Mona called you for her dough because she figured she was dealing with the new boss. And she was right."

"Until tonight," she says at the end of a sigh. "Look, like I told you, after tonight, after skipping out with you from Al Berg's place, I doubt the boys will be taking any more orders from me. I made a lousy rackets boss, all one day of it."

"Oh, I don't know. You're doing all right."

It's as if the air around her freezes.

I hack my way through the ice. "What did you tell the boys, Lilah, when everyone realized Esposito and I were at Berg's door? Did you tell them that no matter what happens, just stay put? Isn't that why they didn't show up at Mona's just now? We were yakking in there for a good half hour, plenty of time to get there from Berg's bungalow. Mona's would have been first on their list of places to look for us. *If* they'd been looking."

She doesn't answer me, just stays still inside her chamber of ice.

I keep chopping away at it. "Listen, I don't know what your endgame is, but I can pretty much figure your current play. You want to keep an eye on me, see what I've got, and what I'll do with it. But there's a part that you didn't figure. You didn't figure on Pike torturing Esposito."

The frozen air around her finally cracks open. "Pike's a monster. I—I can't control him. I thought I could, but I can't."

"Guys like him are beyond control."

"Yeah, but I can usually—" She buries the rest.

"You can usually what? Control men? Yeah, I bet you can."

"If they're sweet on me, sure. And that lug Pike is as sweet on me as a guy can get. Wants to marry me."

It's funny to imagine Lilah in the kitchen, puttering around like a suburban housewife, dolled up in high heels and an apron over a shirtwaist dress like the fantasy wives in those new television commercials, whipping up steak and potatoes for her big bear Pike to come home to. "Frankly, I don't see you as the kitchen apron type," I say. The idea would make me laugh, except Pike's probably the kind of guy who'd bring his fists to the marriage if he didn't like the way Lilah cooked the steak.

I've turned onto the Bowery, a short stretch of rides and fun houses a block from the boardwalk and beach. They're all dark now, boarded up and empty for the off-season. Only their signs, their colors sliding through my car's headlights, hint at the fantasies inside: the Tunnel of Laffs, Fun in the Dark, The World in Wax. We're passing Pleasureland Arcade when Lilah says, "What type *do* you see me as, Cantor?" There's that sugar again, only now, with her hand on my leg, it's the heated variety, melting all over me like syrup in the sun.

Lilah's temptations are the type I like giving in to, the type which blinds me to everything except my rutting urges. But blindness isn't a good idea when Sig Loreale is watching my every move, and I've got to watch my step, and my driving.

Keeping my hands on the steering wheel, I nod down to Lilah's hand on my leg, say, "That's not a good idea."

"Then maybe here's a better one." I nearly crash into a game stall when Lilah leans over, takes my face in her hands, and kisses me. With my hands still on the wheel, I can't get out from her, so I stop the car.

But I don't stop the kiss.

I don't stop it because it's everything I need in a woman's kiss. It's soft, and warm. It's hungry for me while feeding me, too. It's the taste of life through flesh. Lilah Schwartz Day, whose eyes promise danger, whose short blond hair gives her the look of a Valkyrie riding the wind, is the woman I always take to my bed, but not to my heart, not as long as there's hope that Sophie is alive.

The thought of Sophie breaks the spell Lilah's cast with her kiss. I pull away, but gently.

I'm about to tell her that I can't do what she wants me to do, but she gets in ahead of me, whispers, "I've really loused everything up, Cantor. I need you. I need you to find Mickey's killer."

"That's what I've been trying to do."

"I know, but I need you to find the killer before the boys do."

"Sure, I would, too, but why would it matter?"

"So they don't kill you, too. And they will, unless you find Mickey's killer, and hand him—"

"Or her."

"Her? Who—?" But she doesn't finish. Maybe she's afraid of barking up the wrong tree. Maybe she's afraid I still think she *is* the tree.

I start the car.

"Where are we going?" she says. "Not just driving around again. Please, no more of that."

"No, no more of that," I say, and drive off the Bowery and back toward the root of all the evil that's called me home and ambushed me in Coney Island.

❖

I park in front of the tattoo parlor. Its lights are off; there's no gaudy yellow glow hitting the street, just a darkness as dead as its previous owner and his unfortunate front man.

"You have a key?" I ask Lilah.

"In my handbag. But my handbag's back at Al's place. What's so funny?"

"You must be the only woman alive who leaves without her handbag."

"And you must be the only dagger who leaves without her hat."

We both laugh a little, even enjoy the laugh. A little.

We get out of the car. My lock picks take care of the tattoo shop's locked door problem, and in a few seconds, we're inside.

Lilah says, "Well, you certainly come prepared."

"Always," I say.

Lilah turns on a light, revealing the yellow walls and tattoo sketches still blood spattered, a gaudy art show of murder. I have a hankering to ask Lilah how she could still service yesterday's john in this slaughterhouse, and I wonder about the guy's willingness to be serviced amid so much blood. But I realize they're stupid questions. Lilah would fall back on the *I need to make a living and keep my appointments* line she gave me yesterday; and the guy, well, back there in the bedroom, he wouldn't see the blood. He wouldn't see anything, but he'd feel plenty on the way to his burst of paradise.

I stand behind the chair where I first saw Gus, asleep, when Lilah brought me here for my meeting with Mickey. "The killer was right-handed," I say.

"Yeah? How do you know?"

"The blood. The killer had to come up from behind while Gus dozed, and then cut his throat from left to right. Only a right-handed slice could throw the blood in this direction." I say it with a slicing gesture that makes Lilah wince. "See how the blood's spattered all over the stuff on the table and the wall?"

She doesn't look at the blood, just looks around the room at nothing in particular. "Well, that gets us absolutely nowhere," she says. "Just about everybody in the world is right-handed."

"Even you."

"Yeah, even—hah, nice try. How many times do I have to tell you? I didn't kill anybody. Why don't you believe me?"

"Who says I don't believe you?"

She wrinkles her nose and gives me a shrug, which even under my coat comes across as sharp and petulant. I almost think she'll stamp her feet. "Oh, you're impossible! What are we doing here, anyway?"

"I need to have a look around, see if there's anything I missed. Maybe the killer got sloppy and left a trace somewhere."

"Don't you think the cops would've found it? They went over this joint with a fine-tooth comb."

"Sure, but it wasn't *my* comb."

There's nothing around Gus's chair, or anywhere else in the tattoo room, that gives up the identity of the killer: no bloody fingerprint, no out-of-place cigarette or cigar butt, no mustard-smeared napkin from Nathan's hot dog joint nearby. And if any of those things had been here, the cops would've taken them. I'm looking for things the cops wouldn't see, things that remind me that even killers are human beings, and human beings touch things or take things or have a look at things. So I look to see if maybe there's an odd empty space on Gus's table, like maybe the killer treated themselves to a favorite color ink. Maybe one of the drawings is askew on the wall. Maybe the killer's nuts for Rita Hayworth and had a closer look after slicing Gus's throat.

But there's nothing that rings my bell, nothing to help me figure who sliced Gus and Mickey. The killing itself was sloppy, but the killer knew enough to leave the scene clean.

Lilah follows me into the back room, the one tricked out like a cheap living room, where I met with Mickey. His body's gone, but his bloodstain is soaked into the coffee table. "Maybe you should wait outside," I tell Lilah.

"No, I'm all right. What are you looking for?"

"You tell me. You know this place inside out. Anything look off to you?"

She walks around the crummy room, examining the chipped walls and ratty furniture like she's thinking of buying the place, looking for any flaws to give her an edge on price. "Hard to tell," she finally says. "Don't forget, someone searched in here, so everything's a little off." Opening my coat like she's planning to stay awhile, she says, "I could use a drink. How about you?"

"Scotch, neat," I say, and prepare myself for the same lousy scotch Mickey gave me.

"Sure," she says, "I know." Lilah walks out of the room, presumably into the kitchen. I stay in the living room, look around for myself. Like Lilah, I examine the chipped walls and tatty furniture. By the time Lilah comes back with two glasses of scotch, nothing in the room's jumped out at me. It's just as crummy as the last time I was here, maybe even crummier, and sadder with that bloodstain, a reminder that Mickey was knifed in the back. I didn't like the guy, he was a louse to his sister, a creep who belonged in the gutter, but his killer was worse. His killer was a coward.

The scotch bites my throat, but shakes my thoughts back on track. "Listen, I hate to do this, Lilah, I hate to send you back to last night, when you found Mickey dead, but I need you to remember it. I need you to remember what you saw and did when you walked in from the beach. Tell me everything down to the last detail."

She sits down where her brother sat when we talked last night, on the couch opposite the chair I sat in, and where I sit down now. Sipping her scotch, she looks around, at first earnestly, then almost dreamily as she gets up from the couch and walks behind me to the doorway from the tattoo area.

I turn and watch her in the doorway. She's looking at Gus's chair, and taking a deep swallow of the scotch. Stiffening from the whiskey's bite, she says, "I came in the front door, and the first thing I saw was Gus. That's when I screamed." She turns back around to the living room. "Then I ran in here. I don't know why. I was scared. I wanted my brother, wanted his—his protection. But then I saw him. I saw him dead. I screamed again."

"Do you remember Eddie coming in?"

She shakes her head.

"Do you remember me coming in?"

She shakes her head again. "I was in a daze. But I remember you talking to me, asking me what I saw, and I remember telling you that I found Mickey and Gus dead. And then you took me to Mona's."

"And that's where you called the boys, told them you were taking over?"

She gives me a nod, the wobbly kind, when you know there's no use lying, before she walks back to the couch and sits down as if her bones are dissolving. "I'm tired, Cantor. I'm so tired."

"We've had quite a night. And it's after four in the morning," I say, checking my watch.

"It'll be dawn soon," she says. "Dawn on Coney is something special, especially on the beach." Her eyes closed, she seems to find a moment of peace in her imagining. When she opens her eyes again and looks at me, I even see a small light of joy in her, a joy she's eager to share. "You used to live around here. You remember how beautiful dawn is? The light on the water touches everything. Makes everything clearer, brighter. Coney's colors really sparkle."

"Sure. I remember."

"How come you left, Cantor?"

It's a line I don't expect. But I give her the only answer I can. I give her the truth. "I needed a bigger world."

"Hmm, yes, I'm sure you did. Your world must be wonderful."

"It has its charms."

"And I bet they're all beautiful." Her smile, sly but gentle, makes it clear she's not talking about pretty scenery, but the pretty women she imagines I escort through that scenery.

So I smile back.

"Is there someone special?" she says.

It's another line I don't expect.

It's not a question I want to answer, but before I come up with a dodge, she says, "Do you take her dancing? Take her to the Green Door Club? Or maybe the Copacabana, or El Morocco? I read about those places in the gossip columns in the paper, about all the society people and Broadway stars who go there. Everyone in gowns and minks, or tuxedos. I bet you look wonderful in a tuxedo."

"Lilah, let's stick to—"

"Is your special someone rich, too? Or just beautiful? I could see you with someone rich. I'd love to meet a rich woman."

That's the third line I don't expect, and the way it comes at me I can't stop myself from taking a swing at it. "I thought you like to control men."

She gives that a snicker that grows into a rollicking laugh but with a bitter undertone. "Control, sure! That's easy. It's how I earn my living. But I can't love them. Don't want to, either. I thought you knew."

"I figured you danced with whoever asked."

"Hell, no. That's why Mickey sent me to, um"—her smile actually has a little light humor behind it now—"lure you out here. He knew your reputation, but he knew my tastes. He figured the combination would work." She puts her glass of scotch down on the coffee table, not even noticing she's placed it right in the middle of Mickey's bloodstain. Sitting up, looking straight at me with a curiosity freighted with a need neither of us knows what to do with, she says, "Does that change your mind about me, Cantor?"

I don't know how to answer that. I don't know what to say to this puzzling woman in her high-style, jazz-club getup who finds refuge like a needy child inside my coat. I can't answer her because I don't know what the answer is. And I don't want to know what the answer is. So I say nothing and bank on my silence to stub the question out.

She looks straight at me a minute longer, then leans back against the couch, not so much in defeat as in resignation. "If not me, then who, Cantor?"

I'm not going to talk to her about Sophie. I'm not going to tell this woman, who's touched the darkest part of me, that no matter how deeply her eyes search me, no matter what they find and waken in me, no one can make me feel the way Sophie made me feel. I won't tell her that loving Sophie, being in her arms, was like having all the world's mysteries revealed to me, until she became a mystery herself, a mystery which eats me alive in my dreams every night. "No one," I say. "There's no one special."

She picks up her scotch again, takes a swallow, then says, "You're lying."

"There's no one special, Lilah. Now get off it."

"Then what's that I see in your eyes? There's love there."

"That's enough, Lilah. Let's get back to business."

"No, wait," she says, staring at me. "There's pain. What happened, Cantor? She dump you for another dagger? Or maybe married some guy? Yeah, that can hurt like hell."

"None of this is going to help me find Mickey's killer, Lilah."

"I'm worried about you, Cantor. So you're in pain. So what. So's everybody. What do you do? Sit and drink every night at the Green Door Club, maybe pick up some dame who'll soothe your misery for a few hours while you hope time stands still? Is that why you picked me up?"

That snaps me. "I thought it was you who picked *me* up," comes out of me like spitting nails at a target.

I didn't mean to terrify her, but the wide-eyed look on her face says that I did. Until I realize it's not me she's looking at, not me who's terrified her.

I turn around and see Pike through the door, striding through the tattoo parlor toward us in the back room.

CHAPTER NINETEEN

Pike's so love struck by Lilah, he even takes off his hat, which makes his bad haircut stick straight up, making his long face look like a turnip topped by old, dry leaves. "Are you okay, Miss Day? This pree-vert try anything funny?"

"I'm all right," she says, doing a reasonably good job of keeping her terror of the guy out of her voice. "What are you doing here? Why aren't you with Al and Frankie?"

"Those other guys were okay with letting you go and do whatever you want, but not me. I had to find you. Make sure you're okay. And those guys got other things to do, anyway." His silly nasal voice makes it sound as if the boys are off doing childish things in a dirty playpen.

I've never felt a chill as cold as the one crawling through my flesh right now. I'm sure those other things involve taking Esposito's chewed remains to some godforsaken spot to bury him deep, or maybe out in the ocean, with bricks tied to what frayed entrails are left of him.

Lilah's gone gray as ashes, but manages, "Listen—it's Tom, isn't it? Your given name's Tom?" She plays it smart, talks to him as sweetly as anyone can talk to somebody who's just tortured another human being to death.

"Yeah. It's Tom." He sounds like a shy schoolboy. His big ears even turn red. "I didn't think you knew my full name."

"Well, what kind of—of boss would I be if I didn't know who's working for me?" The woman wasn't lying when she said she's good at handling men. Little by little, she's even getting the upper hand with Pike, a guy she thought she couldn't control.

Considering Pike hates my guts, I certainly couldn't do any better, so I keep out of Lilah's way. I'm not sure exactly what she's trying to win for us—time? information?—but whatever it is, I let her play her hand.

"So, listen, Tom," she says, "we're fine here. I got Cantor away from the boys because—well, never mind why. And now she's just helping me look through some of Mickey's things. Decide what I'd like to keep, y'know? Cantor's old Coney, like me and Mickey. She'll know which things to remember my brother by."

Pike fingers his fedora like he's trying hard not to tear it in two. "I don't know why you'd want to remember him at all, Miss Day, the way he treated you." He says it with the sadness of a three-hankie movie, but there's a trace of a snarl under it, a tiny, strangled snarl that rides on a boyish smile that scares the hell out of me.

Just like the way the lights went on when Mona blurted about being owed money, the clouds part when Pike speaks. There's still a lot of mist, things aren't altogether clear, but I think I see a glimmer of sunlight, a glimmer of truth.

But until that glimmer becomes more than just a weak ray in a bleak sky, I can't make a move to do anything about it. I can't handle it on my own or take it to a higher-up, to Coney's absentee landlord, Sig, because if I'm wrong, Sig's fist will come down on my head. He may not even let me keep my head.

Meantime, Lilah stays on Pike, keeping her mood sweet as candy apples. "I appreciate your concern, Tom. I always have. But Mickey was still family. You know how it is. So you don't have to hang around. It's late, go home and get some sleep. I'll see you later."

"I'd rather stay, if you don't mind, Miss Day. I don't trust this pree-vert to be alone with you. I've heard what her kind does."

I almost laugh. I'm sure whatever he's heard were fantasies from the wrong side of the bed. On the other hand, maybe not. He's a cop, and cops have been throwing my kind in jail for a long time. Maybe some desperate sister spilled our secrets, gave him an earful in exchange for not beating her up.

"I'll be fine," Lilah says, a little sterner this time, the would-be rackets boss making things clear to an underling. "Go on home."

Pike's heavy sigh has plenty of hurt, and a stab of anger.

That stab signals that it's time for me to take a chance. Maybe I can get Pike's angry stab to finally part those clouds all the way.

I get up from the chair, make my way over to Lilah, just in case my play goes bad and I have to get her out of here fast. But I talk to Pike. "It was you, wasn't it. You killed Mickey. And Gus, too, so he wouldn't talk. Slitting Gus's throat was a killer's move, and you're a killer, Pike. The guy wouldn't have anything to talk about. He was asleep. He'd have found Mickey already dead, and you gone."

Pike might be a vicious killer, but he's still a cop. A dirty cop, sure, but dirty or not, like most cops, he'd rather gag on what he's feeling than expose it. So he doesn't flinch at my accusation, just says, "You tell a good story, Gold."

Lilah says, "Cantor, what are you talking about? Pike was Mickey's man in the Coney Island precinct. He kept an eye on Loreale's people for us, people like Esposito. Mickey was Pike's meal ticket. Why would he kill him?"

Maybe the lady can control men, but she doesn't have a clue about love. "Don't you know?" I say. "He wanted to be a hero. A real Romeo hero. He hated the way Mickey treated you. He told you so himself a few minutes ago. He was going to save you from all that. Wasn't that the idea, Pike?"

The other thing cops hate, even more than having their emotions pried loose, is being humiliated, and I've just humiliated him, which wasn't the smartest thing to do. A humiliated cop is as dangerous as a cornered rat. And if Pike's torture of Esposito, his slitting the sleeping Gus's throat, and sneaky stabbing of Mickey in the back are anything to go by, Pike is a dangerous guy, even without the power of his badge and the firearm that comes with it.

So if I want to get out of here alive, and get Lilah out, too—I don't think Pike's the type who'll take being a spurned lover with just a shuffle and a gee whiz—then I need to soothe his hurt. It won't be easy. He hates me, but whether he likes it or not, there's something we share, something about him I get. It's that thing that's snared everyone in all of history who's ever been crazy in love. If I play it right, it just might smooth him out enough for me and Lilah to slide out of here. "I don't blame you, Pike," I say.

Lilah blurts, "What? But it was murder! He murdered my brother!"

"Try to see it his way, Lilah. He was protecting his woman, the woman he loves. I'd do the same thing." What I don't say, though, is that I wouldn't want to be sneaky about it. I don't say it because what I'd want and what I'd do might be two different things. If I ever find the flesh slavers who took Sophie, I don't think I'll give a second thought to putting a bullet in their heads in their sleep and then tearing them limb from limb.

But Pike evidently doesn't want to share a lovers' fantasy with me. He simply puts his hat back on. He's not leaving, he's freeing up his hands, getting ready to pull his gun. But my hands are already free, and my gun comes out before his hand even gets inside his coat.

He only smiles. It's a foul, toothy smile, the sort that scared you as a kid, made you pull your blankets over your head as protection against the grinning monsters lurking in the corners of your bedroom.

"Are you gonna be stupid enough to kill a cop, Gold?"

"No more stupid than you," I say.

"You mean Esposito? *I* never laid a hand on the guy. And they'll never find him anyway."

I give him a grin that's icy cold in my mouth, but refreshing to my mood. "Yeah, but they'll find you, Pike, dead, here in Mickey's joint, a place you have no business being at—What is it now? Nearly five o'clock in the morning? And as far as the other cops in the precinct are concerned, I was never here. Isn't that right, Lilah?"

"Yes, that's right. You were with me, at my house." Smart girl. Catches on fast.

I say, "So the Law will look elsewhere for your killer, Pike. And Sig Loreale will tell them exactly where to look. He probably has several people in mind he'd like to get out of his way."

Lilah, with a sudden flash of worry, says, "But Loreale had no interest in Mickey's death. That's what you said."

"He had no interest in killing him," I say. "He knew it would make noise, which it did, and noise is bad for Sig's business. But Sig knows an opportunity when he sees one, and with Mickey dead anyway, and him in the clear of any part in it, he has the opportunity to get rid of the last of Solly Schwartz's loyalists."

Lilah's face goes pale. "Al Berg, and Frankie O'Byrne, and me." She says the names like she's reciting a roster of the dead.

"No. Not you," I say. "Mickey's business is destroyed, and very soon his henchmen will be gone. Berg and O'Byrne and our cop friend here don't know it, but they're on their last breath. I don't give them more than twenty-four hours, if they're lucky. But you're no threat to Sig anymore, Lilah. Sig doesn't kill for pleasure. He only kills for business, or revenge." The color comes back into Lilah's cheeks.

I'm not finished with Pike. "So, Sergeant, here's the deal I'm offering you. I don't kill you now, I let you live—"

"But leave me to take my chances against Loreale? Some deal."

"You could always pack your bags and leave town. The subway is just up the street. You could be at Pennsylvania Station in an hour, take that trip out west maybe you've always dreamed about. But that's up to you. Meantime, I'd love to say it's been nice chatting with you, but I save my lies for better occasions. Come on, Lilah. Let's get out of here."

"You're letting him live? He killed my brother!"

"Then you kill him. Here, take my gun."

But she shrinks back from that.

"Murder's not so easy, is it," I say.

My gun stays on Pike as Lilah takes my arm like it's a lifeline and we walk around the coffee table to the door. But Pike blocks our way, doesn't budge. "You're gonna have to shoot me, Gold. You got the stomach for it?"

"Don't tempt me."

Lilah's grip on my arm tightens, a brittle grip of fear. "Please, Tom, just let us go. If you care for me at all, you'll just let us go."

His big ears, like cranes holding up his hat, grow red again. And there's a look in his narrowing eyes I don't like, a hardness that seems to devour their usual dullness. "And let you walk out with this—this pree-vert?" he says. "Or are you a sicko, too, Miss Day?"

I say, "Watch your mouth, Pike. Or maybe you've forgotten I have a gun pointed at your belly?"

"I haven't forgotten," he says, and pulls a move I hadn't counted on, a gutsy move that leaves me gasping when his fist rams into my stomach.

Doubled over, my breath out of me, I manage a raspy, "Run, Lilah!" Her grip slides from my arm. From the corner of my eye, I see her make a run for the door.

But Pike's more covetous than smart. He chases after her, shouts, "Get back here! I'm talking to you! Get back here!" and makes a grab for her. But he's left me to catch my breath, and left me with my gun.

I get back upright and run after him in one motion. He's got his arm around Lilah's waist while she struggles like a fish on a hook. I'd shoot, but she's wiggling so hard, she's shaking Pike, too, and I'm afraid I'd hit her in the bedlam. So I use the butt of the .38 as a club, crack him a good one on the back of his skull.

He lets Lilah loose with a bellow of anger and pain.

I grab Lilah's arm, pull her out the door.

CHAPTER TWENTY

Pike's outside, nearly on us, before I can open the door of my car. So I grab Lilah's hand, shout, "Come on!" and run toward the boardwalk. I don't take us up the stairs, but run underneath instead. In the predawn darkness, we'll be shadows in the sandy murk, not easy for Pike to spot us.

Lilah's behind me, crying, running, grasping my hand as I pull her along. I hear Pike roar, "Get back here, you tramp!" and, "You're dead, Gold! Dead!"

I pull her harder, run us faster, though it's tough going with two of us in the sand, one of us in high heels. I'm tempted to run us all the way past Coney to Brighton Beach, lose us in the streets and alleys of that residential neighborhood, but I'm afraid Pike will catch up to us before we get there. But another idea presents itself, a better idea: let Coney's own thrills and chills hide us.

I pull us off at Jones Walk, run under the girders of the giant Wonder Wheel, a steel-and-air confection tall as a skyscraper, famous for its double set of cars, some stationary, while others slide along rails to the center and back to the edge again as the wheel turns. I open the door of a stationary car at the wheel's far edge. "Get in and get down as far as you can under a bench," I tell Lilah, keeping my voice low. I follow her in, close the door, and crouch on the floor, each of us hidden as much as we can under the car's two wooden benches. Only the upper half of the car is steel mesh. The car's solid lower half can help hide us.

I can see just enough of Lilah's face in the near-dawn gloom to know she's tense and terrified, her face rigid, like she's holding her breath. I'm holding my breath, too, while my hand's inside my jacket, holding my gun.

I know Pike's looking around. I hear his footsteps, stopping, starting, back and forth near the Wonder Wheel and away from it. But not far away from it. And then he's back again.

I haven't taken or exhaled a breath since I heard Pike's first steps near the wheel. I doubt Lilah has either, though I can still just barely see her face, even in the first weak purple-gray light of dawn. But what little I see of her is stiff and pale, as if death has already staked its claim and is just waiting to make it official.

My heart's beating so loud I'm surprised it's not echoing through Coney's streets, bouncing off the steel ribs of its thrill rides. But maybe it is, maybe Pike hears it, which may be why he's almost near our hiding place.

Lilah's even more terrified than she was barely a minute ago. Her eyes are wide now, glassy in the thin dawn light, staring at me, staring at nothing. And she's not stiff anymore, she's trembling, her hands and body shaking, not a lot, but just enough to betray us: the car squeaks on its axle, gently sways, leading Pike to our door.

I hear the click of his gun. Then the door's pulled open. "Get out!" That nasal yell eats into my flesh right down to my bones.

Lilah's too scared to move, which is perfect, keeps her out of my way when I crawl out from under my bench. With my hand still inside my coat, I start to get out of the car, then pull my gun and lunge at Pike, slamming him across the face with the barrel of my .38. My move surprises him, the hard steel hurts him, and he lets out a grunt more animal than human. But my move doesn't stop him, and I'm barely away before he makes a grab for me. He misses, tries for another grab, but I roll away on the ground. I'm still rolling when Pike shoots and misses, the bullet striking the ground, sending bits of concrete in my face. Lilah screams, distracting Pike's attention from me to her. He runs back to the car, shouting, "I was loyal, damn you, Miss Day! I won't let you choose that pree-vert!"

When I get up from the ground, I'm too far away to make a grab for Pike, get him away from Lilah, but I'm near a contraption that will get Lilah away from *him*: I slam my hand down on the operator's button, and the giant wheel starts turning, the car with Lilah rising up and away from Pike. He'll have to wait until the wheel makes a full turn in order to catch her, but the huge wheel turns slow, the better to give the summer customers a sky-high view of Coney Island and all across Brooklyn, the towers of Manhattan, like Oz, in the shimmering distance.

Plenty of time for me to deal with Pike.

But Pike's not a patient man, and his anger is making him crazy to boot, crazy enough to grab a steel girder and start climbing the wheel!

I can't let him reach Lilah, can't take the chance that he'll either shoot her or grab her, forcing her out of the car and into a miserable lover's leap. I aim and take a shot, but the wheel's taking Pike farther upward, and my shot does no better than ricochet off one of the wheel's steel ribs. Pike's hat flies off, floats in the wind.

I have to get closer to the action. I have to climb the wheel, too.

So I grab on, remind myself that I've swung from ships on a rope ladder high over New York Harbor. The Wonder Wheel, my childhood friend, couldn't be scarier than that.

The wind grows stronger, louder, the higher the wheel takes me, the higher I climb. It's tough to hang on, but I figure it's tough for Pike to hang on, too. But a crazed person is often a strangely strong person. Pike's crazed; I'm not. I grip each girder with every ounce of strength I've got.

"Cantor!" It's Lilah. I look up, see her frantic in the car as Pike grabs the door. She's holding it closed from inside, screaming. She's no match for his strength. It won't be long until he rips the door open.

Unless I get there first. But I'm too far away to reach her in time. I try another shot at Pike, but the shot goes astray when I take my gun hand off the wheel, and nearly lose my grip on the steel girder.

I'll never get to Pike or Lilah by just climbing.

But maybe—again—Coney's thrills and chills, the excitement of my childhood, can save the day.

I climb a few feet more, press against the wind that wants to kill me as sure as Pike does, and make my way to one of the sliding cars, yank the door open and climb inside just as the car slides toward the center axle of the wheel as it turns. I can hear Lilah screaming, her screams more desperate as she uses all of her strength to keep Pike from ripping open her door. I lean out of my car. It swings and slides back and forth as the wheel turns, taking me higher but keeping me wobbly, the sky, the sea, and the Earth swaying above, below, and around me in a dizzying whirl. But I'm closer to Pike than I was, maybe close enough. I aim and fire.

The wildly swaying car sends my aim off, and the bullet hits only a girder, but the girder's in front of Pike's face. The smashing bullet must've sent sparks into his eyes, blinding him, disorienting him, and he falls from the wheel, flailing in the wind, until he smashes to the ground.

Lilah's calmed down by the time I get her back to her bungalow, make us both a cup of coffee and spike it with some rye I found in the kitchen. I sit her down at the kitchen table, seat myself near her at the end. She's wiped her mascara-streaked tears from her face, but her eyes are still red, her hand still trembling as she takes a sip of coffee and then puts her cup down on the table.

"What'll they do to me, Cantor?" she says, her voice shaky. "The cops, I mean. Someone must've found Pike's body by now."

"Nothing will happen to you," I say. "No one's around the Wonder Wheel or any of the rides at dawn this time of year. No one saw us or what went on or they would've called the cops, or even called Sig, who might've sent Eddie or any of the badges on Sig's payroll to see what was up. But no one showed up, no one saw you, no one can put you there, so nothing will happen to you. And since Pike was Mickey's guy, Sig has no interest in finding out why he died and who made it happen. He'll make sure the whole business is buried. No cops, no questions. It's just one less Schwartz-Day ally for him to take care of." I take a hefty gulp of the coffee, let the caffeine wake me up for the long drive home while the whiskey puts my nerve ends back in place after the thrill ride on the Wonder Wheel. Lighting a smoke, and offering one to Lilah, I say, "You're free to do whatever you want, Lilah. But whatever you decide, I'd forget about doing it with Berg and O'Byrne. They're dead men any minute. Sig will see to that."

She takes a long pull on her smoke as I light it, her hands cupping mine, the flame bright in her green eyes. Through a haze of exhaled smoke that curls around her face like lace curtains, she says, "And you're sure Loreale won't come after me?"

"He has no reason to," I say. "Like I told you, he doesn't kill for pleasure, only business. Couple of loose canons like Berg and O'Byrne, they're bad for Sig's business. But unless you're standing in his way, unless you're in the way of some business deal, he'll ignore you. So don't stand in his way," I add with a shrug. "Sooner or later, he'll want your real estate. Sell it to him."

That sits her up. She looks at me like I've just told a dirty joke. A slit of a smile slides across her mouth, with a bitter laugh escaping through that knife-slice smile. "He won't just take it? Like he took everything from my father?"

"Get rid of that grudge, Lilah," I say. "It didn't do Mickey any good, and it won't do you any good, either. Look, times have changed. Sig knows that muscle is the last thing on the menu now, not the first, like in the old gangland days. Sig stays at the top of the heap because he uses brains first, fists last."

"How can you be so sure? A leopard can't change its spots, they say."

"You're right. Sig hasn't changed, but the rackets have, and Sig's smart enough to play the modern game. His transactions have to be legit now, with bills of sale and all the other paperwork that will keep his other rackets out of sight and keep him out of the tax man's eye. So Sig won't muscle you unless you hold out on him. And if he muscles you, he'll do it so carefully, so quietly, you won't know you're dead until you're in your coffin."

She buys it just enough to lean back in her chair, relax again. Her bitter smile disappears, turns into a pert smile that hints at something up her sleeve. "What if I sold him this shack and the tattoo parlor now?"

"You could try," I say, "but he might not want them now. He'll want things on his schedule, not yours. But maybe you'll get lucky. Maybe he'll say yes, and you'll have a few bucks in your purse. What will you do with it? Leave Coney? Start over somewhere else?"

"That depends."

"Yeah? On what?"

"Not on what. On who. It depends on you, Cantor." She's got her cigarette between the fingers of one hand, while the fingers of her other hand stroke my cheek as she leans in close to me. "So many scars," she whispers. "So much life. Let me taste some of that life, Cantor." And then she kisses me.

Being kissed by Lilah Schwartz Day is like having darkness and light spread through you at the same time, chilling you and heating you at the same time, until your body can't tell the difference between pleasure and pain, and you want more. I want more.

And then she takes the kiss away, because the only way she'll give me more is on her own terms. Still leaning close to me, she says, "I want to know your life, Cantor. I want to know that life in the bigger world."

"Then live it," I say. "But not with me. And not through me."

It wasn't quite a slap in the face, but it stings her enough to make her sit back from me.

"You have to find your own way in that bigger world, Lilah. Everyone does." I stub out my smoke, lean in to her and kiss her cheek before I get up from the table. "You know where I live, and my number's in the book. I'll show you around that world, Lilah, but I can't live it for you, or with you."

She doesn't look at me again, just sits at the table smoking, as I leave the kitchen and walk out the front door.

I've got one last bit of business before I leave Coney Island.

I pull over at a corner of Neptune Avenue, get out of my car, walk into a phone booth, page through the book until I find the number, then drop my dime in the slot and dial.

The number rings six, seven, eight, nine times before a gruff sleep-interrupted voice says, "Yeah?"

"Wake up, Eddie. And listen carefully."

"Who's this?

"Cantor Gold," I say.

"Cantor? What the hell you doin', callin' a person at this hour? What time is it, anyway?"

"It's almost seven o'clock in the morning and I'm calling to threaten you, Eddie. Yeah, you heard me, not warn you, threaten you. If you ever lay a hand on Lilah again, if you even go near her, you're a dead man. I'll kill you. Or maybe Sig might send someone to kill you. He doesn't like his operatives getting out of line, beating up anyone without his say-so. And beating up women is way out of line, Eddie. Sig might even let me be the one to kill you. You don't want to die, do you, Eddie?"

He doesn't speak, just breathes shallow, raspy breaths that come through the phone more pathetically than any pleading.

"Good-bye, Eddie."

❖

The Belt Parkway leads me out of Coney Island, a modern highway taking me away from old memories, away from the history that caught up with me. The highway takes me past all the new housing ex-GIs and their wives are grabbing up since the war, modest two-family brick jobs along Shore Road with a nice view of New York Bay and Staten Island. For a little money down, and a little cash on loan from the US government, a fella and his sweetheart can cut their ties to their cramped, immigrant ancestral past and replace it with a shiny American future of backyards, barbecue grills, and television sets with shows full of blond children.

It's a dream I can't share, even if I wanted to, because as I drive toward the towers of Manhattan looming ahead in the morning sun, the wild neon razzmatazz, the sleight-of-hand, the thrills and chills of Coney Island aren't entirely behind me. They are all inside me, whether I want them there or not. I always figured I wanted to be rid of them, now I'm not so sure. I brought them with me a long time ago. They'll always be with me.

I turn on the radio, and have to laugh: Patti Page, a pretty blonde whose short-haired look is a little like Lilah's, is singing, "Back in Your Own Backyard."

Chapter Twenty-one

When I wake up, it's almost ten in the morning. But it's another morning. I've slept nearly twenty-four hours.

I had all the best intentions when I got back to my apartment from Coney: call Judson at the office, catch up on what's going on with any clients; call Rosie, make things right with her. Things have to be right with Rosie.

But my good intentions, like my exhausted mind and body, collapsed with me into my bed. I was asleep in seconds, a sleep so deep and thick it had no room for dreams.

And now it's the next day. I put up a pot of coffee, let it perc while I take a long, hot shower, as hot as I can stand it, let the needles of water soak through remnants of Coney Island still taking up space in my mind: Mona Carlotti's duplicity, Eddie Janko's cruelty, Lilah's sadness. That last bit lingers. Lilah wanted me to take her sadness away. I couldn't. I didn't even try.

I can live with that.

The coffee, and spiffing up in fresh duds—dove-gray suit, a crisp white shirt, blue and buttery yellow striped tie, yellow pocket square—help bring me back into the here and now, back to the life I made and risk everything to keep.

Even a glance out the window fortifies me. From my roost on the tenth floor, I can see people walking along the street in quick New York rhythm, bundled up in overcoats, men holding on to their hats in a wind. The roofs of cabs, some bright red, some green, some yellow, and the silver painted roofs of buses, all catch sunlight, sending up a colorful gleam. All together, the cabs, the buses, the people are like some great abstract painting, but better, because its parts keep moving and the picture never stays the same.

Through the windows of the apartment house across the street, I watch folks having their coffee, or doing some dusting, vacuuming the carpet, reading the paper, or catching the trials and tribulations of the poor souls in all those new soap operas on television. New York is living its life, enjoying all its new money since the end of the war, all the new gadgets that come with it, all its new hopes and dreams. The smart guys say that New York's—and America's—best days are just ahead, that this second half of the twentieth century will see wonders the likes of which the world has never seen before. Could be, I guess, but so far, all they've given us are televisions and washing machines, soap operas and the soap to wash our troubles away, the American Dream powered by the gadgetry of schlock.

I'm about to grab a coat from the closet, looking forward to a second cup of coffee, a bagel and lox breakfast, and homey conversation with Doris down at Pete's luncheonette, when the buzzer sounds at my apartment door.

There's that pounding of my heart again, the way it always does when there's a buzz at my door. It pounds with the hope and prayer that when I open the door, I'll see Sophie, Sophie finding her way home.

It's Mom Sheinbaum.

My heart slows down, slinks back into my chest, my bones again my heart's protective cage until the next knock at my door.

Mom's dressed like she's going to the opera, her short, hefty body wrapped in a mink coat even though it's only a little past ten thirty in the morning.

"What's the matter," she says, "you don't answer your phone? All day long I called you yesterday. Okay, so maybe you're not around during the daytime, but what about night? You don't come home to sleep? Wait, maybe this I don't want to know." This speech accompanies her through the door, and she's now in my living room, unwrapping from the mink. She's no longer dressed for the opera, but in a blue cotton dress and sensible shoes. The dress fits her like a belted tent; the shoes barely contain her pudgy feet. But the dress and the shoes don't matter. Only the mink matters. Mom uses it to announce herself on the street, an *I'm as good as any of you* attitude that she wields against a world which might have preferred her tribe stayed in the shtetl.

I guess it wasn't only dreams which found no room in my sleep. Evidently no sound got through to me either, not even the phone.

"Here," Mom says, handing me the mink, "hang this up. And be careful. Those are good pelts. Delicate."

"And good morning to you, too." I hang up the precious coat, then say, "What's going on? You rarely venture away from the Lower East Side. The only time I remember you and me together above Fourteenth Street was when I was a little kid and you ferried me to the Metropolitan Museum. But that was a lifetime ago, so what's so important that you traipse all the way to Midtown to see me?"

"And it wasn't easy, I tell you. You try getting a cab in my neighborhood this time of day."

"You could take the subway."

She looks at me like I'm an idiot from Stupidville as she sits down in one of my living room chairs, her handbag in her lap, the chair's red upholstery surrounding her like a cape that's too small. "You think I schlepped across an ocean with nothing but the rags on my back, worked hard all my life, built a good business in America, in this golden land of opportunity, just so I could take a dirty subway?"

"You've robbed this golden land blind," I say with a low laugh. "I don't think it owes you a steady stream of taxicabs."

"Huh. A lot you know."

"I know where the subways go," I say, and sit down in an opposite chair. "Look, what do you want? You didn't drop in for a social call."

Her smile, imperious, sly, speaks of her place in the hierarchy of New York's underworld: the Empress of Crime, with the goods on everyone from the gutter all the way up to the crooks in the penthouses. She may not have the power of a Sig Loreale, but even he won't cross her. He could get away with it, but he'd lose the respect of everyone on our dark side of the Law. Even the light side. "You keep any money here?" she says.

The safe in my bedroom holds extra supplies of the requirements of my life: spare guns, ammunition, a knife or two, extra lock picks, and plenty of cash. But all I say to Mom is, "Some. Why?"

"Whatever you got, you'll need it." There's a gleam in her little button eyes.

"I always need it. Want some coffee?" I say.

"No thanks. Let's get down to business. I am not happy with you, Cantor."

"That's nothing new. You haven't been happy with me in years."

If I didn't know better, I'd say I've wounded her, judging by the puzzled look on her face. But I do know better. Mom made her feelings for me very clear the night her daughter died; she didn't want her precious girl anywhere near that deviant outlaw in a suit, me.

I say, "So why aren't you happy with me this time?"

She folds her arms across her ample chest, changes her mind, uncrosses them, and leans forward in her chair, gripping the armrests with her chubby, ringed fingers. "You cheated me out of my ten thousand dollars, Cantor."

"Is that so? And just how do you figure that?"

"A man came to see me yesterday," she says, leaning back again, owning her place in the chair with the confidence of someone who assumes they may even have helped pay for it. "A man in a uniform, a chauffeur's uniform. This man, a servant no less, a pisher, a nobody, says to me that my services are no longer needed, but his employer thanks me for my time. And then this—this pisher hands me a check for a measly thousand dollars. And you know who signed that check, Cantor? Your society missy, Miranda van Zell."

"Easiest grand you ever made, Mom."

"You think so? You think I'd take *nishtik* money like that? And a check yet? A piece of paper? And all the time, I was tapping my sources all over the place for information about that pixie—"

"Pyxis." I'm actually enjoying this. It's a rare moment to see Mom Sheinbaum sidelined by the very people she's been catering to for decades. She's bought their diamonds, sold their diamonds, even stolen their diamonds then sold them back to their pretty necks. She had the goods on them, their secrets, their scandals, and I guess she figured they'd dance to her tune. What she didn't understand, despite the mink whose pelts could compete with anything on Fifth and Park Avenues, is that the rich and powerful have their own instruments and their own tunes. Hell, they own the orchestra. They do business with Mom Sheinbaum, but they'll never hear the music she makes. They don't hear my song, either, but I never figured they did. I just take their dough, and go dance to the tunes at the Green Door Club.

Mom says, "Pyxis, shmixis," waving the pesky word away. "Or whatever you call it. And *then* I see in last night's paper that this Mrs. van Zell is having a wing named after her at the museum, and there was a picture of her with that pixie."

"Pyxis."

"So I figure you must've found the damn thing without me. Where was it?"

"In a bathhouse in Coney Island."

I haven't seen Mom laugh, really and heartily laugh, in a long time. Our warped friendship, if you can call it that, made me forget how much she enjoys laughing, and she's enjoying the hell out of it now. Every wrinkle in her face wriggles, every pound of her fleshy body shakes, the blue dress rippling like a stormy sea. "That must've been something for you, Cantor, schlepping back to Coney Island!"

"Yeah, lucky me."

Her laughter winds down, she wipes her face with her hand. "Well, your luck cost me ten thousand dollars."

"Come on, Mom," I say, with an easygoing shrug, "you know as well as I do, you win some, you lose some."

"Sure, but it depends who you win or lose with." The humor's gone. The tough Empress of the Underworld is back in business. "I know you since you still had baby fat, and this is how you treat me? After everything I taught you? Listen, mommaleh, it wasn't nice, going behind my back like that. What? You couldn't pick up a phone and tell me you found your—your whatchamacallit? I was scratching a lot of backs to get information for you, but who knew I was wasting my time?"

I hate to admit it, but she has a point. I probably should've told her I'd found my Dancing Goddesses. But there are a lot of things in life I should have done. And I bet there's a lot Mom should have done, too, like not make me believe, when I was a kid, that she gave a damn about me.

But spilled milk is spilled milk, and the best I can do is mop up this latest spill from under our feet. "All right," I say, "it was crummy. My apologies. When another deal comes my way, I'll make it up to you."

The little gleam is back in her tiny dark eyes. A smile spreads from one flabby cheek to the other. There's a lot of pleasure in that smile. There's plenty of greed in it, sure, but something else, too, some secret Mom's enjoying.

"You know," she says, "someone's been stringing you along."

"Yeah? Well, it wouldn't be the first time. Who's the latest guilty party?"

"Sig."

His name drops like a sandbag thudding to the floor. There's only one issue between me and Sig that could qualify as stringing me along.

A million questions rise inside me, get bottlenecked in my throat. I can't even speak, can barely breathe.

Mom, sensing my ordeal, says, "Don't you know him by now, Cantor? Whatever he does, he always has his reasons. Maybe he just wants to keep you in line. Maybe he thinks you'll get too independent if you get what you want. Who knows how that murderous momzer thinks."

I finally manage, "How do you know he's been holding out?" more a desperate grunt than a question.

Mom says, "Of course I know," as if I've committed the sin of doubt. "So all right, maybe I didn't really know, but I suspected plenty. Sig is always so proud of his contacts—all over the world, he says—so he should've had your information a long time ago. So I figured something wasn't quite kosher. Well, let me tell you something else, mommaleh, I had contacts when the high and mighty Mr. Loreale still had Coney Island sand in his underwear."

Now it's me who leans forward. I grip the arms of my chair until my fingers hurt. My throat's gotten so tight, it even hurts to speak. "Where—? How long have you—?"

"You think I held out on you, too? I wouldn't do such a thing. Didn't I train you right? Okay, maybe I didn't teach you so good, since you didn't tell me you'd found your tchotchke."

"Damn you! *Where. Is. She?*"

I've annoyed the empress, pressed Her Majesty too hard. With a glare that has the force of a strong hand pushing me back into my chair, back into my place, she says, "Don't get all upset. I only found out last night. After I saw that business in the paper about that van Zell woman and the museum, I needed a way to get my money from you. So I ask around. I make calls. I got friends all over the place, Cantor. More places even than you, or that clever kid you've got working for you—"

"Judson."

"Yeah, Judson. What kinda name is that for a person? It sounds like a telephone exchange. Anyhow, it will do you good to remember that I got deep connections. Got 'em on the docks, in City Hall, in little huts across the ocean, everywhere. Sig says he couldn't find things out for you in all this time? Hah! It took me maybe three, four hours to get the goods on that boat you've been looking for. Yeah, I know where your girl is, your Sophie de Whatsis. But it'll cost you."

I feel my lips part, my teeth bare, but there's a howling in my ears, a storm of rage and need, and I barely hear myself growl, "How much?"

"Don't ask stupid questions. I want my ten thousand."

Time seems to slow to a crawl as I get up from the chair, walk out of the living room and into my bedroom. The three and a half years since Sophie was stolen feel like a fast blink compared to the sludge of time and space I'm trying to walk through now. When did my bedroom get so far away? When did the Picasso hiding my wall safe get so distant and small?

But time picks up speed again as I turn the dial of the safe, my fingers suddenly so alert and sensitive I could swear they feel the dust motes in the air.

Next to the guns and the ammo in the safe, under the spare lock picks, is a stack of cash. I count out the thick wad of bills—just making it to ten grand with little to spare—with the speed and precision of a bank teller making change.

Mom's putting a handkerchief back into her handbag as I walk into the living room. Seeing the cash, she gives me a hungry smile, extends her hand, and when I give her the money, she palms it and puts it into her handbag in one flowing movement, then snaps the bag shut.

"Where is she?" I say. It comes out as a whisper, or maybe a shout. I don't know. I can't even feel my throat, my tongue, or any part of me. "Where is Sophie?"

Mom's smile isn't greedy now. It's triumphant, sure in the knowledge she's about to secure my loyalty for the rest of our lives. She says, "Pack a white linen suit. You're going to the tropics."

About the Author

Ann Aptaker's debut novel, *Criminal Gold* was a 2014 Goldie Award finalist. Her second book, *Tarnished Gold*, was a 2015 Lambda Literary Award and Goldie Award winner. Both books have earned excellent reviews from *Curve* magazine, Crimepieces, Rainbow Reads, and other print and Internet venues. Her Cantor Gold crime series celebrates her favorite themes: dangerous women, crime and mystery fiction, and New York City history. Like her protagonist, Cantor Gold, Ann resides in her beloved hometown, New York, where she is an adjunct professor of art and art history at New York Institute of Technology.

Facebook: Ann Aptaker, Author

Books Available from Bold Strokes Books

A Quiet Death by Cari Hunter. When the body of a young Pakistani girl is found out on the moors, the investigation leaves Detective Sanne Jensen facing an ordeal she may not survive. (978-1-62639-815-3)

Buried Heart by Laydin Michaels. When Drew Chambliss meets Cicely Jones, her buried past finds its way to the surface—will they survive its discovery or will their chance at love turn to dust? (978-1-62639-801-6)

Escape: Exodus Book Three by Gun Brooke. Aboard the Exodus ship *Pathfinder*, President Thea Tylio still holds Caya Lindemay, a clairvoyant changer, in protective custody, which has devastating consequences endangering their relationship and the entire Exodus mission. (978-1-62639-635-7)

Genuine Gold by Ann Aptaker. New York, 1952. Outlaw Cantor Gold is thrown back into her honky-tonk Coney Island past, where crime and passion simmer in a neon glare. (978-1-62639-730-9)

Into Thin Air by Jeannie Levig. When her girlfriend disappears, Hannah Lewis discovers her world isn't as orderly as she thought it was. (978-1-62639-722-4)

Night Voice by CF Frizzell. When talk show host Sable finally acknowledges her risqué radio relationship with a mysterious caller, she welcomes a *real* relationship with local tradeswoman Riley Burke. (978-1-62639-813-9)

Raging at the Stars by Lesley Davis. When the unbelievable theories start revealing themselves as truths, can you trust in the ones who have conspired against you from the start? (978-1-62639-720-0)

She Wolf by Sheri Lewis Wohl. When the hunter becomes the hunted, more than love might be lost. (978-1-62639-741-5)

Smothered and Covered by Missouri Vaun. The last person Nash Wiley expects to bump into over a two a.m. breakfast at Waffle House is her college crush, decked out in a curve-hugging law enforcement uniform. (978-1-62639-704-0)

The Butterfly Whisperer by Lisa Moreau. Reunited after ten years, can Jordan and Sophie heal the past and rediscover love or will differing desires keep them apart? (978-1-62639-791-0)

The Devil's Due by Ali Vali. Cain and Emma Casey are awaiting the birth of their third child, but as always in Cain's world, there are new and old enemies to face in post Katrina-ravaged New Orleans. (978-1-62639-591-6)

Widows of the Sun-Moon by Barbara Ann Wright. With immortality now out of their grasp, the gods of Calamity fight amongst themselves, egged on by the mad goddess they thought they'd left behind. (978-1-62639-777-4)

18 Months by Samantha Boyette. Alissa Reeves has only had two girlfriends and they've both gone missing. Now it's up to her to find out why. (978-1-62639-804-7)

Arrested Hearts by Holly Stratimore. A reckless cop with a secret death wish and a health nut who is afraid to die might be a perfect combination for love. (978-1-62639-809-2)

Capturing Jessica by Jane Hardee. Hyperrealist sculptor Michael tries desperately to conceal the love she holds for best friend, Jess, unaware Jess's feelings for her are changing. (978-1-62639-836-8)

Counting to Zero by AJ Quinn. NSA agent Emma Thorpe and computer hacker Paxton James must learn to trust each other as they work to stop a threat clock that's rapidly counting down to zero. (978-1-62639-783-5)

Courageous Love by KC Richardson. Two women fight a devastating disease, and their own demons, while trying to fall in love. (978-1-62639-797-2)

One More Reason to Leave Orlando by Missouri Vaun. Nash Wiley thought a threesome sounded exotic and exciting, but as it turns out the reality of sleeping with two women at the same time is just really complicated. (978-1-62639-703-3E)

Pathogen by Jessica L. Webb. Can Dr. Kate Morrison navigate a deadly virus and the threat of bioterrorism, as well as her new relationship with Sergeant Andy Wyles and her own troubled past? (978-1-62639-833-7)

Rainbow Gap by Lee Lynch. Jaudon Vickers and Berry Garland, polar opposites, dream and love in this tale of lesbian lives set in Central Florida against the tapestry of societal change and the Vietnam War. (978-1-62639-799-6)

Steel and Promise by Alexa Black. Lady Nivrai's cruel desires and modified body make most of the galaxy fear her, but courtesan Cailyn Derys soon discovers the real monsters are the ones without the claws. (978-1-62639-805-4)

Swelter by D. Jackson Leigh. Teal Giovanni's mistake shines an unwanted spotlight on a small Texas ranch where August Reese is secluded until she can testify against a powerful drug kingpin. (978-1-62639-795-8)

Without Justice by Carsen Taite. Cade Kelly and Emily Sinclair must battle each other in the pursuit of justice, but can they fight their undeniable attraction outside the walls of the courtroom? (978-1-62639-560-2)

21 Questions by Mason Dixon. To find love, start by asking the right questions. (978-1-62639-724-8)

A Palette for Love by Charlotte Greene. When newly minted Ph.D. Chloé Devereaux returns to New Orleans, she doesn't expect her new job, and her powerful employer—Amelia Winters—to be so appealing. (978-1-62639-758-3)

By the Dark of Her Eyes by Cameron MacElvee. When Brenna Taylor inherits a decrepit property haunted by tormented ghosts, Alejandra Santana must not only restore Brenna's house and property but also save her soul. (978-1-62639-834-4)

Cash Braddock by Ashley Bartlett. Cash Braddock just wants to hang with her cat, fall in love, and deal drugs. What's the problem with that? (978-1-62639-706-4)

Death by Cocktail Straw by Missouri Vaun. She just wanted to meet girls, but an outing at the local lesbian bar goes comically off the rails, landing Nash Wiley and her best pal in the ER. (978-1-62639-702-6)

Gravity by Juliann Rich. How can Ellie Engebretsen, Olympic ski jumping hopeful with her eye on the gold, soar through the air when all she feels like doing is falling hard for Kate Moreau, her greatest competitor and the girl of her dreams? (978-1-62639-483-4)

Lone Ranger by VK Powell. Reporter Emma Ferguson stirs up a thirty-year-old mystery that threatens Park Ranger Carter West's family and jeopardizes any hope for a relationship between the two women. (978-1-62639-767-5)

Love on Call by Radclyffe. Ex-Army medic Glenn Archer and recent LA transplant Mariana Mateo fight their mutual desire in the face of past losses as they work together in the Rivers Community Hospital ER. (978-1-62639-843-6)

Never Enough by Robyn Nyx. Can two women put aside their pasts to find love before it's too late? (978-1-62639-629-6)

Two Souls by Kathleen Knowles. Can love blossom in the wake of tragedy? (978-1-62639-641-8)